BEAUTIFUL TEARS

by

C. P. MANDARA

Published by **Chimera Books**
ISBN 9781780804019

The healthy man does not torture others - generally it is the tortured who turn into torturers.
Carl Jung

Chapter 1 - Harper

I kicked his tombstone and then screamed. It should have been a relief. I was twenty-five years old and free of the crushing weight that had been strangling me for the past five years. Now I could start afresh, get a job, and reclaim my independence. Maybe I could find myself along the way. I'd been lost for so long, I wasn't sure I would be able to piece myself back together - but I was going to give it a damn good try. Kicking the slab of mottled grey granite once more, I sank down upon the wet grass and sobbed my heart out. The tears weren't for my late husband. They were for what might have been, or what should have been if lady luck had seen fit to smile upon me. I swear I was born under a star of ill-fated misery. Some days I wanted to drown in self-pity, but I knew first-hand where that would get me - absolutely nowhere. It was more important than ever that I stand on my own two feet now, else I was going to drown in the crap surrounding me. When one chapter ends, another begins. Never had a truer statement been said. Unfortunately, I feared this chapter might be worse than the last.

Brandt was going to be released from prison in one week's time. I had seven days to hightail it out of London before all hell let loose, and there was no way I was waiting around for that. To be fair, I deserved his hatred and he deserved his revenge, but I was too much of a coward to stick around and wait for him to come to me. I was tired of being a victim. If Brandt wanted to waste his time and energy trying to find me that was his prerogative, but I wasn't going to make it easy for him. I wanted my happy ever after, and once upon a time Brandt might have been that, but he certainly wasn't now. He would be after my blood, and more than that, he'd want to spill it. Five years ago I put him behind bars and didn't even watch as the judge served him up a ten-year sentence. Good behaviour had meant he'd only served half of that, but five years was a long time to rot in hell. I should know.

Rubbing furiously at my tears, I dashed them away with two hands in an attempt to put the past behind me. Who was I kidding anyway? Brandt had never looked twice at me. That happy ever after had only been in my head. Rich kids don't look twice at poor trash, and that's all I had ever been; something to ignore or sweep under the carpet. He'd already been lined up with a bride back then, and she'd come from old money, too. Money marries money, or was that nobility marries money? Who the hell cared? It was just another reason he'd hate me. I wondered if Helena Foster-Lyle was still waiting for him. Think of something else, I told myself sternly.

The walk back to my apartment in Beckton was swift. You didn't hang around in London. You walked everywhere with purpose and didn't look behind you. I'd learned through experience never to carry a handbag, and the clothes I wore were drab and unremarkable. It was almost as if I was trying to blend into the scenery. Having spent so many years trying hard not to be noticed, disappearing into the English countryside should be a snap. Beckton and I had something in common, though. Once upon a time it had been a toxic spoil heap, but then Princess Diana came along and opened an artificial ski slope complete with a posh Swiss-style bar at its base. That was several years ago. Now it was rather bleak and derelict, which pretty much echoed the sentiment of my life at the moment. I needed my fairy godmother to come along and sprinkle a generous helping of fairy dust around. She'd need a skip load of the stuff to put right the mess I'd made of my life.

Walking briskly up the ten flights of stairs to my one bedroom flat, I frowned when I saw the lift was out of order yet again. It didn't matter on my account. I had heart failure just thinking about getting stuck in one, but I knew my neighbour, Mrs Omerod, would barely be able to cope with the ridiculous hike. She was a month shy of her eightieth birthday, and her cane went everywhere she did. Mrs Omerod had been sweet to me these past few months. I had a feeling she'd known what I was going through, especially when she told me if I ever needed a place to stay, I could come and live with her. She'd almost made me cry with that offer of kindness - if only life was that simple. Sniffing, I'd taken her hand and thanked her profusely, but assured her that everything was fine. Everything was always fine. I knew the script well.

The last two flights of stairs were always the killer for me. My heart would beat double-quick time and I'd start panting, but the fear that was usually there at the prospect of coming home had been absent these past few months. A new dread had settled in my stomach, and it loomed closer and closer.

Think of something else. Anything else.

I wasn't on the top floor of this dingy block of flats by choice. If I'd had my way I'd be down at the bottom, but those rentals didn't come cheap. The sorry fact of the matter was that I didn't have enough money to afford to stay in this hellhole, and I was going to be evicted in two weeks time if I didn't pay my rent. There was no money left to settle my bill, so I was packing my bags. The reasons were twofold. I was going to start a new life as someone else and hopefully bring a bit of good luck my way, and I was going to hide from Brandt. Did that make me a coward? Absolutely, but I'd deal with my troubled conscience later.

Opening my front door I found three letters on the threadbare rug. One was another eviction notice, so I threw it straight in the bin. The second was a flyer for cavity wall insulation, so that went in the same place. The third was handwritten and filled me with terror. Swallowing tightly, I wondered if I should put it straight in the bin with the rest. My fingers wavered over the stained white plastic swing bin, unsure of what to do. Whatever was in that letter wasn't going to good news. I had no family to speak of, and whatever friends I had in the past had learnt not to bother contacting me. There was only one person this could be from, and that meant that nothing inside it was going to

3

be pleasant. *Throw it in the bin. He just wants to scare you.* My hand dithered for a moment longer, but as much as I wanted to let that letter slip from my fingers, my conscience demanded that I read it. I owed him that much.

Opening the letter with trembling fingers I found nothing more than a slip of white paper inside. It was barely four inches by two. It didn't need to be any bigger, though. There was only one short sentence written on it. In bold black marker, the words *I'm coming* stared back at me. The piece of paper dropped from my fingers and drifted featherlike to the floor. I had to blink several times to stop the tears from resurfacing. I'd always known this was going to happen. It wasn't as if this was a surprise.

Get a grip and start packing, woman.

There was no point taking the note to the police. I already knew that Brandt hadn't posted this while on the inside, and with my criminal record the cops would probably laugh in my face. I doubted the writing was even his own. He just wanted to scare me. My heart bubbled up into my throat as I fought for air. 'You can escape this life,' I whispered to myself. 'You can reinvent yourself and forget all about Brandt. He'll lose interest if he can't find you.' The words were hollow, and I didn't believe them for a second.

Walking numbly towards my bedroom I pulled out my flimsy holdall and began packing my meagre belongings. At least I would travel light. A couple of pairs of jeans went inside, with a few T-shirts and sweatshirts that had seen better days. A hairbrush, toothbrush, and some soap followed them. The only shoes I had were the sneakers on my feet. My packing was done. One less thing to worry about, huh?

Heading back to the kitchen I took the kettle over to the sink, filled it up and slammed the switch down. I needed a cup of tea and a few minutes to decide where to go. My finances were limited. Wherever I went it wouldn't be far. I just had to hope it would be far enough.

Chapter 2 - Brandt

Laying back on my hard plastic mattress which was barely two inches thick, I thought about all the things I was going to do when I got out of this hole. A mere seven days separated me from purgatory and the outside world. Five years in prison might have been a relatively short spell when I began comparing my woes with the other inmates, but it seemed like an eternity in hell to me.

If I'd committed the crime I'd been sent down for - well, that might have been different. But being imprisoned for something you hadn't actually done was a total mind fuck. For the first year my rage had been almost uncontrollable. The only thing that held me in check was the thought that I'd be inside even longer if I unleashed myself upon some of the bastards inside here. Wait, that wasn't strictly true. When I'd first ended up in here I was a one hundred and twenty-pound weakling who didn't pose much of a threat to anyone bar myself. Five years and a heck of a lot of gym work later, I was a solid wall of muscle and sinew. With any luck my huge bulk was going to scare the fuck out of Harper in a few days' time.

Harper Wilkinson was the cause of most of my anger. That lying, filthy piece of trash had got off scot-free, while I took the rap for her crime. How in hell the woman could live with herself was beyond me, but as soon as I was out I was going to even up the score - my way. She'd taken five years from me, and I was going to steal five years from her; making her pay in every way imaginable.

I'd always had an itch for the girl that I couldn't scratch. Back when we'd been at college she'd always had some guy hanging off her arm and drooling over her tits, so I'd kept my distance. Don't get me wrong - I looked - but knew better than to touch. Some of the bastards she hung around with were mean fuckers and I wasn't stupid enough to give them a reason to hurt me. Harper and I had been friends though, or so I'd thought. When she'd popped round to my dorm one day and asked if I'd help move a couch for her I'd happily agreed. The next thing I knew I was having ten years of my life chopped off. I still had no idea why. Had it been a game to her? Had it been a dare to get the little rich kid into a whole shitload of trouble? I was about to find out. I was going to find her, follow her, fuck her, and fucking forget her - but not until those five years were up. Her ass was mine, and I was going to put that delectable little package to good use. After a week of her crawling around on her knees and sucking my cock I might feel a bit better. After a month of paddling her sorry ass and handcuffing her arms and legs to my bed I might sleep a little better too. We'd see. But she'd get what was coming to her, and she'd pay in tears and blood. I had.

I wondered if she'd look the same as I remembered. Five years is a long time. I should know. Would she be the same little firecracker I remembered? Bright chestnut curls, sassy red lips, and long lithe limbs came to mind. My mother would have had a fit if I'd brought her home. White trash, she'd have called her. Still, I didn't have to worry about my mother any more. She'd already disowned me, along with my father. Oh, they hadn't said it outright, and nor had they cut me off, but they made it very apparent they wanted nothing more to do with me. When I got out I was to stand on my own two feet somewhere very far away and be careful not to put a foot out of line. If I did the money would disappear. Fuck the money. I didn't need it, and I didn't need them. Whatever I used when I got out of this joint, I would pay back and deliver to their doorstep. Being the black sheep of the family did come with some benefits though. I wouldn't be expected to marry the stuck-up heiress my mother had planned for me. My criminal record would see to that. Considering the woman looked like the back end of a bus, Harper had done me a favour in that regard. But I still wasn't about to forgive her any time soon.

And there was another bonus to getting my hands on Harper. I've always had a dark streak in me half a mile wide. I've tried to curb it, for the sake of my parents, but I'm as kinky as fuck in the bedroom, and I'm damned if I'm going to live my life with some vanilla socialite before I've acted out nearly every one of my sordid fantasies. Harper had all of them to look forward to too, and let me tell you my mind is a twisted place. The woman had better fucking brace herself.

They weren't my only plans though. After I cut myself off from my parents I'd need to find a decent job and start building my own empire. I had ambition and lots of it. I didn't want anyone's help to get where I was going, and I intended to make it on my own. Victory would be mine and revenge, well, that was going to be sweet, in a dark, twisted and tortured kind of way.

My thoughts turned in a different direction. Now, how did I go about finding Harper? Liam would have delivered my little note by now, so I was sure she would run. But she couldn't run anywhere that I wouldn't find her. I wanted her to know that she could run to the ends of the earth and never escape my crushing grip. I needed to see the light slip from her eyes as she realised she'd never be free of me unless I chose to let her go. Most of all, though, I sought to destroy her. She would feel every humiliation I'd been forced to endure, and any more that I could think up. I wanted her to know how it felt to be imprisoned, helpless and at the whim of another. Putting a single foot wrong in prison could mean the difference between life and death. While I didn't intend to kill her she didn't have to know that. She'd toyed with my life, and now it was my turn to repay the favour. I hoped she enjoyed the experience just as much as I did. The woman was in for quite a ride.

Before I could get lost in my thoughts the door to my cell unlocked. I knew without looking that the time would be exactly five-fifteen and that most of the other inmates wouldn't be stirring for a little while yet. I liked to get myself down the chow hall as early as possible, avoiding as many nasties as I could. The plain oatmeal they served wasn't worth getting excited about, but it was a fuel my body needed if I wanted to work out in the gym later. Just seven more days of oatmeal, milk, broth, and bread; I could already taste my freedom in the shape of a McDonald's hamburger. There were so many things I had missed. Bacon, decent cheese, steak, chocolate cookies, and lemon meringue pie were the tip of the iceberg. We were served roughly the same food over and over again each week. Having your freedom taken away was depressing, but having every little item of your life dictated to you was soul destroying.

It struck me as somewhat ironic that I entered prison utterly innocent of any wrongdoing, and yet as soon as I got out I immediately intended to commit a crime. Life worked in mysterious ways. Revenge was the only thing I lived for. Well, that and the need to get out of here as soon as possible and preferably in one piece. I'd had my dark days, that was for sure.

Walking quickly down the concrete corridor, I wondered how long it would take Harper to obey my every word. Would she fight me or would she immediately become my little lapdog to abuse and torment? I hoped it would be the former. If she played by the rules from the beginning I'd almost be disappointed, but if she came biting, kicking and screaming, well I had ways of dealing with that. Time would tell.

Picking up my plastic breakfast tray I waited in line for the slop to fall with a smile on my face. It was a first.

Chapter 3 - Harper

I had one hundred and seventy-two pounds to my name and an old debit card that was already well into its overdraft limit. That was it. That was the sum total of what my life was worth at the moment - if you didn't count the rent arrears, of course. Where was I going to go with that? I didn't have a clue. All I knew was that I wasn't going to be able to go very far. Even a cheap bed and breakfast would be twenty pounds a night, so I was going to have to hope I found a job pretty quickly. I suspected I'd still have to spend a few nights sleeping rough unless I was very lucky. The thought scared me. Hell, right now everything scared me.

Hitchhiking was going to be my next disaster. Yes, it was a stupid idea, but seriously, what choice did I have? I could hitchhike and let fate have some fun with me, or I could wait to be evicted and greet Brandt with a cheery smile and open arms. I shuddered. There was no money and food was more important; it was a risk I had to take.

I'm coming. What did that even mean? I'm coming to kill you? I'm coming to slap you about a bit? Pain I could deal with, but I didn't want to die just yet. Struggling up the street, dragging my holdall with its one busted wheel, I didn't dwell on the thought. I just needed to concentrate on staying alive.

It was a twenty-minute walk down to the A1020, where I thought I stood as good a chance as any of hitching a ride. I didn't care where I was going, as long as it was at least an hour or two's drive away. One part of me wondered whether I should wait and just let Brandt take me. Could my life get any worse than it was already? Brandt was a reasonable guy, right? Uh yeah, he might have been before I put him in prison for a crime he didn't commit. There was a good chance he was all kinds of fucked up now. So, running and hiding was the way forward. I had no idea how long I would be able to stay under the radar, but I intended to give it my best shot. While I owed Brandt a rather large apology, I didn't owe him my body or my life. He'd want at least one of them, maybe both.

At least the weather was being nice to me. Although it was April it wasn't too cold, and it wasn't raining. It rains ninety-nine percent of the time here in England, so maybe someone was looking out for me after all. Yeah right. Sticking my thumb out into the oncoming traffic with a resigned air of defeat I prayed that all of London's axe murderers were taking the day off. It was a grim thought.

Less than half an hour later I was in the heated cab of an articulated lorry that read *Norbert Dentressangle* on the side. The truck was a bold shade of red, and if I'd been Chinese it would have been a lucky omen. My fingers were still crossed on that score. The driver was friendly enough, and when he asked me where I was headed I just said 'Up north'.

"Will Nottingham do?" I nodded and clambered into the passenger seat.

Anywhere would do, and it was far enough away from London to give Brandt a run for his money. That was all that mattered.

The driver pulled back on to the road and turned the radio on, and whatever they were playing was upbeat and cheerful. Another good omen, perhaps?

"Did you want a sausage roll, love?" He reached into the glove compartment and pulled out a greasy white paper bag. It had evidently held more than one in the past, but for some reason this little fellow had been left all alone, just like me. The warm, meaty smell the bag gave off made my stomach rumble warningly, reminding me that I hadn't had breakfast. I silently told it to be quiet and demanded that it go back to sleep. I was limiting myself to one meal a day until I managed to get back on my feet.

"That's very kind of you, but I can't pay you I'm afraid. I'm absolutely broke." I smiled at his kindness. At least he seemed a world away from the axe murderer or psychopath I'd been expecting. This was good.

"I kind of figured that out as you're hitchhiking, lady. I don't need any money, so have the sausage roll. You look half-starved." He winked at me.

What could I do? It would be rude to refuse such a kind offer, and he was right, I was hungry. Reaching for the paper bag tentatively I gave him a timid smile, thinking this was more than I could have hoped for. Perhaps my luck was turning after all.

"Thank you," I whispered. "That's very sweet of you."

"Not at all. Sometimes it's just nice to have some company up here. It gets lonely on the road."

I accepted his gift graciously and savoured every bite of my treat. It had been an age since I'd tasted meat, and the flavour nearly exploded on my taste buds. Soft, flaky pastry crumbled under my tongue, and juicy sausage meat made my mouth water. I could feel tears welling up at his simple act of kindness. I blinked them away. If I started I'd never stop. Repaying his generosity in the only way I could, I started talking.

It didn't take me long to learn that his name was Leonard Shanks and he'd been a lorry driver for the past twenty years. He had a wife, two children, a couple of dogs and an unsociable cat. So unsociable in fact, that it lived mostly at his neighbours. This was down to the very posh cat food his elderly neighbour served up. Food was obviously where the heart was - unless you were me. Then you couldn't afford to think about food. On the plus side, I had a size six figure that most women would kill for. Scrap that. I bordered on anorexic. Still, as soon as I got a job I'd feed myself properly. Some fruit and vegetables would make a nice change.

"Well, that's enough about me, love. Now it's your turn. I want to hear your story." He turned to me expectantly and gestured with his hand that I should begin my tale of woe.

That was the last thing I was about to do because I couldn't risk Brandt finding any clues to my whereabouts. I felt terrible lying to Len, namely because he was such a nice guy, but there wasn't any other option if I didn't want to spend the rest of my life looking over my shoulder.

"Oh, I'm not very exciting," I said. "My name is Sandra Leeson, and I've been living in London for the past six months. Unfortunately I've just lost my job, and finding another hasn't been easy, so I'm going to stay with some relatives up north. I'll pop in on a few friends in Nottingham and then make my way up to Glasgow." Lying was a dangerous game. Once you uttered a lie you had to remember it, else be caught out at your own game. If you told lots of lies and heaped them all on top of one another, it became an almost impossible task of trying to keep up with them. The trick was to stay vague and base your lies on something you could remember. I'd just have to hope that Len didn't ask too many questions.

When I'd been silent for a minute or two he said, "So what kind of job are you looking for?"

Now there was a question. I was looking for anything that paid, preferably cash in hand, although that would be unlikely. I wasn't qualified to do an awful lot, but you didn't need too many skills for waiting tables, bar work or cleaning.

"I was in insurance," I lied again, "so I'll see if I can find anything along the same lines." It was the most boring job I could think of, and Len was hardly likely to remember a waif like me in a few days' time. He'd be back with his wife and kids in Grantham, having a whale of a time walking his dogs.

"I think I know a guy in insurance," Len said thoughtfully. "Maybe I could pass your name along to him."

And therein lay the problem with lying. There were too many sticky situations that you could land in. My heart did a couple of beats quick time, but thankfully this one was easily dealt with.

"Ah, that's very kind of you, but I'm looking to catch up with my family first, and I'll take it from there. I could do with a few weeks holiday if I'm honest.

"Couldn't we all?" said Len, laughing, and thankfully that was the end of that. Pretending to be asleep for the next hour and a half limited any further lies, and I only came to when the centre of Nottingham loomed into view.

Len offered to drop me off wherever I wanted, but as I had no prior knowledge of the city I had no idea where I wanted to go. The train station? The town hall? In the end I opted for the Victoria Centre, having seen the sign as we drove past. I told him I wanted to do a little shopping before dropping in on my family.

Pulling the truck to a halt a few hundred yards away he nodded at me, but his expression was sad. Len had seen through me. I wasn't even half as good at lying as I thought I was.

"Take care of yourself, Sandra. Try to eat something, okay?" He nodded at me.

I promised him I would and thanked him profusely for his generosity again. I hoped someone above saw fit to grant him everything he wanted in this life and then some. Nice people were a rarity in the modern world.

When he pulled away I watched the bright red beacon zoom into the distance and sighed. Nottingham was cold, grey and wet. My brief stint of good luck seemed to have evaporated.

Chapter 4 - Brandt

I had it all planned out. Harper's abduction, her five years of penance, and what it might take to break the woman down into something she wouldn't even recognise. I'd learned a lot on the inside. Dark, nasty stuff that no one should ever need to use. There was so much darkness inside me now. I wondered if I'd ever be the same again. Harper had taken something from me the day she put me in jail; something I would never get back. There was now a little sliver of my soul that had been blackened and charred, and once gone it would never return. She was to blame, and she would become my obsession until I felt the debt had been repaid in full.

Prison had given me the contacts to secure everything I would need in order to kidnap someone. There were faceless people amongst my midst who could get drugs, untraceable vehicles, weapons, and so much more. All they wanted was cash, and I still had lots of that at my disposal. It wasn't a question of 'if' I got my hands on Harper Wilkinson, it was a question of 'when'.

There'd been so much time to think in prison that I'd planned every little detail of her abduction. How I would take her, where I would take her, what I would feed her, what I would do to her, and how I would ultimately break her. She'd taken something from me, and I intended to take something from her. It was going to hurt, and I would enjoy her pain. Each day I planned to reduce her to tears; beautiful, shimmering, messy tears. And when she thought she'd got the measure of me I'd change the game plan, and we'd begin again. She was going to be my little mouse, and I was going to be a goddam lion.

Wiping beads of sweat from my forehead I finished my set of bench presses and slammed the weights back in their holder. This evening my mood was dark, but in a few days' time it wouldn't be. *Hang in there, Brandt. She's waiting for you on the outside.*

Chapter 5 - Harper

My first day in Nottingham found me soaked through to the bone, with two new blisters for friends. Scouring the streets for work I found the local jobcentre, but it had little to offer me. In a newsagents I skimmed through all the local papers, and made a note of anything that might be interesting. Getting dirty looks from the cashier as it became apparent I wasn't about to buy one, I quietly snuck out of the shop.

Trailing around the city I looked at flyers, signs, and ads in windows. After a day's worth of toil I had two interviews on the spot and another two scheduled for later in the week. What I should have been doing was looking for somewhere to stay.

Thankfully, with the help of my cell phone, it didn't prove too much of a problem. The cheapest place to stay in town was the Igloo backpackers hostel. It was roughly twelve pounds a night, which meant I could afford to stay for a few days, as long as I didn't eat. I smiled grimly. Still, I wasn't on the streets. The downside was that I probably wouldn't get any sleep, as I'd be sharing a room with five others. But it was a small price to pay for a roof over my head. I'd just have to hope and pray that I managed to get a job tomorrow.

It took me a whole week to finally land a job, and by the end of it I was going crazy with worry. Thankfully I was now employed waiting tables at a pizza restaurant, but my paycheque wouldn't arrive for two weeks. If I took into account the meagre food my stomach had insisted I buy, and the pair of shoes I'd had to purchase for the job, that meant I'd be on the streets for at least a couple of nights until I got paid. My hands shook at the thought. Perhaps I could scrape together enough money in tips to buy those extra nights? At least I wouldn't need to buy food now. The restaurant provided me with one meal per shift, and there were plenty of scraps to be had if I wasn't fussy where they came from. I wasn't. I was too hungry.

The work was exhausting, but at least it kept my mind occupied. I didn't want to think about Brandt. He'd be out by now. When he didn't find me in London, I hoped he'd give up the search. He'd have people he wanted to catch up with, and things he needed to do.

Scribbling down the order for a children's party of ten while dodging the breadsticks thrown at me, I marched back to the kitchen. I hated thinking about Brandt. Desire spiralled thick and strong, making my body tighten involuntarily. Once upon a time I'd had the biggest crush on him. My then-to-be future husband had known it. I'd go doe-eyed whenever he was in the vicinity and nearly lose the power of speech. Whenever he said something to me I'd blush and fiddle with my hair. I wonder if he'd known how I felt about him? Probably. Brandt wasn't stupid.

Stop thinking about him.

Passing my order form of pizzas and chicken nuggets across to the chef, I thought back to that scrawled note. *I'm coming.* What would I do to someone if they'd falsely imprisoned me for five years? Would I forget about it? Not bloody likely. Neither would Brandt.

"Order for table number forty." One of the chef's voices rang out loud and clear across the kitchen, startling me into movement. *Stop daydreaming.* If I weren't careful I'd lose my job at this rate. Keeping my mind blank of anything but pizza proved to be a challenge for the rest of my shift, but one I was determined to overcome.

The first three days of my new job earned me exactly six pounds and seventy-three pence in tips. It wasn't enough for an extra night in my hostel. As much as I loathed the thought, I was going to have to try and use my debit card because the alternative was damn right scary - sleeping rough.

Don't think that I accepted this fate without a fight. I'd already asked if I could borrow fifty pounds to tide me through until payday, but the manageress of the pizza chain laughed in my face. She also added that if I wanted a loan I'd need to look a little further up the high street. Asking the other employees to lend me money was also met with deaf ears, and I was shut down almost instantly. I'd barely known them a couple of days, we weren't friends, and I could disappear at any time. Was I nuts? They clearly thought so.

Desperation was getting me nowhere fast, and I guessed I'd just have to hope there was some money on my card or accept my fate. He might be able to trace the card, but what other options do I have? Stealing from someone didn't even enter my head. Believe it or not I'm a good person, and I believe in Karma. If I went around stealing from people, somewhere along the line there'd be payback. I was in enough trouble as it was on that score.

It was with a trembling hand that I offered my debit card to the receptionist that evening, hoping upon hope there was enough cash for another four nights, or even another three. I might be able to afford another night if I hoarded my tips up for the next few days.

When the receptionist looked in confusion at the receipt that spilled forward I knew I was in trouble.

"Sorry, Miss. It says the transaction isn't authorised. Do you have another card I can use?" She looked at me helpfully and I wanted to smack the smile off her face, although technically I knew it wasn't her fault.

"Could you try three days?" The receptionist nodded and popped the card in once again. My foot tapped anxiously upon the wooden floor. Someone, somewhere needed to give me a break. I was tired, exhausted, and nearing a nervous breakdown.

The woman shook her head apologetically once more and handed the card back to me. "Did you want to call someone who can wire you some funds? You can use this telephone if you like?" She waved the phone at me like a lifeline, but I had no use for it because there was no one to call.

"Could you try two days, and then one?" I looked at her pleadingly. Anything was better than nothing. The fewer days I had to sleep rough, the better.

She nodded and hummed to fill the awkward silence as my card went through the machine again, emitting an angry squeak before she tried one last time. I wanted the floor to open up, suck me deep inside, and then kill me quietly.

"Oh, it's gone through this time. You're good for one more night." She smiled at me and returned my card, pretending nothing awkward had happened. Yeah, right.

"Thank you, I'll hand the key back in tomorrow," I whispered, as I slowly trudged up the stairs to my dorm.

Fortunately there was no one there when I entered the room. If there had been they'd have had the lovely view of me clutching my stomach before covering my mouth with both hands as the few scraps of pizza I'd eaten for dinner decided they needed to escape my body with impressive velocity. Rushing off to the shared bathroom I slammed the latch on the door and leant over the toilet. My stomach still wasn't used to food and the rebellion it caused inside me wasn't pretty. As the last of the silent heaves left me I wiped several sweaty strands of hair from my forehead. It was the stress of the last few days catching up with me. *You need to calm down.* Tell me something I didn't already know. The trouble was: how did you calm down knowing you were about to be thrown out onto the streets? And if that wasn't bad enough, I had a potential madman on my tail. I'd be lucky if I didn't have a coronary before the week was through.

Chapter 6 - Brandt

Freedom was intoxicating. The smell of it gave me a high so intense it was almost better than morphine. Almost.

Settling down into the Audi A8, I inhaled deeply. I wanted to savour my first taste of life on the outside. What hit me first was the clean fragrance of the pine air freshener, swiftly followed by the subtle scent of leather. The soft, contoured seat that greeted my backside was heaven, and I sank into it gratefully. Comfort was not something they dwelled on in prison.

"Good to see you're still alive." Liam had his Raybans slung over his eyes, and he handed me a pair.

"It was touch and go for a while. There were a few guys in there that didn't like me very much, but we eventually had a chat about that."

"I bet you did. You're fucking huge, man. That the reason you bulked up?" Liam had already pulled away from the prison parking lot and was trying his best to slingshot me towards the motorway. Trying to relax, I settled back into my seat and breathed deeply. The trouble was, I was wired. Adrenaline-laced blood, thick and viscous, flowed through my veins.

"It was one of them." The other reason was to scare the living daylights out of Harper Wilkinson. I wanted her to take one look at me and know she'd lost before the games had even begun.

"So, what you wanna do now, Man? It's your first night out. This needs to be big." Liam turned to me expectantly.

Holding up the dark aviator shades I'd been given, I put them on. I didn't particularly want to extinguish the sunlight; prison had been grey enough as it was, but I didn't want Liam to see my eyes or read my expression. He knew me too well.

"Christ, Liam. I've been gone for five years. What is big these days? You tell me. I do know one thing, though. I need a burger. Then we can go wherever you like." Shoving alcohol down my neck was the last thing I wanted to do. It would dampen the rage burning a bright fire in my gut. I didn't want anything to dull my focus, but Liam had been a good friend and I owed him this. Besides, he'd be suspicious as hell if I didn't do it, and that was the last thing I needed. Tomorrow I would make my excuses and take some time out. I'd tell him I needed to see my family and get back on my own two feet. He'd expect that. Liam wasn't aware that my family had disowned me, nor was he aware that I was innocent of my crime. Infuriatingly, I now appeared to be Liam's hero because I'd done time. He had a lot to learn on that score, and it wasn't the kind of holiday he'd want to experience anytime soon, but hopefully he'd stay on the straight and narrow. As to my plans, I intended to veer so far off the yellow brick road that my path would have more kinks than the Swiss Alps. He didn't have to know that, though. *Where are you, Harper? I'm coming.*

When Liam stopped to fuel up I got my McDonalds. Two Big Mac's with cheese and a side order of fries. I also got a quarter pounder for Liam. If he didn't eat something before we started drinking he'd be worthless company in less than an hour, and I needed someone to speak to. Hell, I'd be happy just listening to the sound of his voice. Shortly he was going to prattle on about his latest conquests and how many girls he'd managed to get naked, which was fine by me. The more he talked the less I had to, and quite frankly, I didn't have anything interesting to say. Well, nothing that he could hear, anyway.

"Right, I figure we'll start off in Leicester Square and take it from there. Don't worry, mate, I have girls planned for the end of the evening." Chewing a mouthful of burger he turned to wink at me.

Girls. I didn't want girls. I had no desire to enter a strip club and watch some blonde bimbo grind against me. I wanted what was mine. What was owed to me. What I damn well fucking deserved after taking the rap for her these last five years. There was only one woman in my thoughts, and I wouldn't be happy until I had her screaming beneath me - in pain. I'd show her what five years of blue balls looked like. There must be a female term for that, surely? I'd have to Google it.

"Oh, and I got you a new cell phone." He tossed a brand new iPhone 8 in my direction, complete with black leather case, and a ball and chain key ring.

I raised an eyebrow at him and smiled dryly. Accepting the gift, because to refuse it would seem rude, I put it in my pocket. I wouldn't be using it for long, though. No one would be tracing my whereabouts for the next few months. I'd need to get Harper trained into some form of obedience before then. When she became too scared to put a foot wrong, that would be my signal to re-enter society. How long would it take? That was anybody's guess, but with the methods I would employ, hopefully not too long. It all depended on how much fight she had in her. Time would tell.

Getting my old cell phone out of my pocket, I re-read the message I'd been given earlier.

She's not at her previous known location. Will contact you as soon as I have more information.

I smiled darkly. The sender was *SS* which was amusing enough, and the guy was a private investigator. Not a legal one, I might add. You certainly wouldn't find him in the Yellow Pages, let's put it that way. Basically, I'd paid a lot of money for someone to hack into Harper's life and let me know as soon as she appeared on the map. A few guys on the inside had assured me of their success rate, so all I had to do was sit back and relax - if I had the faintest clue of how to do that. Five years of prison had taught me to be on my guard at all times. I wouldn't forget the lesson in a hurry. I'd been tipped off with his contact details in prison and had managed to acquire his services, for a hefty price. But I didn't care about money. I just wanted results and fast. He promised me that was exactly what I'd get.

Lying back against the headrest, I breathed deeply.

I'm coming, Harper.

Our first port of call was Harrods. I couldn't go out clubbing in the jeans I was wearing, and I had an itch to wear a suit. After spending so many years in a drab prison onesie I had decided I was never wearing casual clothes ever again. I was also banning the colour orange from my wardrobe. The fewer reminders I had of my time in hell, the better.

The sales assistant put her heart and soul into helping me find the perfect ensemble, quite literally. She spent an hour showering me with Armani, Versace, Boss and Ralph Lauren. When I walked to the till with four different suits and two pairs of dress shoes she discreetly handed me her business card and winked at me. In another lifetime I might have taken her up on the offer, but not today. I wouldn't be dating until I'd put my demons to rest.

After Liam had grumbled good-naturedly about my wasting valuable drinking time, we then set about putting the world to rights. Pubs, glitzy wine bars, cellars, and rooftop gardens - we tried them all. I drank beer, wine, cocktails, and mixed them all with abandon, until Liam was drunk enough not to notice that I didn't drink, or that when I did it was a glass of water.

"Tell me you're not drinking water, Brandt?" When Liam finally did notice he was happily slurring away to himself.

"Fuck no. There's a slice of lime in this beauty," I said, pretending to slur myself, before necking it all back. The ice clinked around happily, oblivious to my lie. "Thought I'd try a gin and tonic. I'll be back to beer in a moment." As I'd already had two pints of apple juice, I sincerely hoped not. With any luck Liam would pass out shortly. Whenever I'd bought a round he'd been drinking doubles, and we'd been doing this for the better part of six hours. His eyes were all over the place, and he could barely keep his head up straight.

"Should we... should we head down to..." Liam had to think for a long moment. "Secrets. It's Secrets, right? We need to get you... get you... girls." Liam's head slumped across the table.

Thank fuck. His company had been utterly exhausting. I'd been used to spending a lot of time on my own inside, and being around this many people all of a sudden had my insides clenching unpleasantly. I needed to get out of there and he'd just given me the perfect excuse.

Using his phone, it didn't take me long to call up a taxi firm and get us a ride home. I practically had to drag him most of the way out, which might have been a problem once upon a time, but these days I was a big guy. The problem would be bribing the taxi driver to take us. No one wanted a drunk ass in their car that might wake up and redecorate the upholstery. The bastard had better not throw up over my new suit, either. I was just coming to terms with being clean. I wanted things to stay that way for a while.

We got home around midnight. It had taken fifty quid to get the taxi driver to move, but it was worth it to escape the stench of central London. I was staying at Liam's flat in Chelsea for the time being, but it wouldn't be long before I was out of there. All I needed to do was find Harper.

Slinging Liam over my shoulders like a sack of potatoes, I carted him into his room and threw him on the bed. Removing his shoes, I then dumped a duvet over him and considered my duty as a friend completed.

This wasn't the first time I'd tucked him up, and I daresay it wouldn't be the last. His appetite for alcohol was rather impressive, and women - well that's another story. I didn't see him getting married anytime soon, though. Making my way down to the kitchen I quickly poured two pints of water down my neck before I sauntered into the lounge. My fingers hovered briefly over my cell as I debated something. I had an itch to call Harper. It was doubtful she still had the same number, but I wanted to hear her voice. That way I could imagine how she'd sound when I'd make her scream or cry for mercy in a few days' time. *Be patient, Brandt.* My fingers curled into a fist, but I unfurled them one by one. There was no way I could call her. That could be traced. My search would begin tomorrow.

Sauntering over to the black leather couch, I was pleased to see a brand new MacBook Pro. I'd wired Liam the money a few weeks ago, and he'd agreed to purchase one for me. It was going to be invaluable in my quest for Harper Wilkinson. Immediately opening the box, I got to grips with the charging cable and began setting the machine up.

An hour later, I had the email I'd been waiting for.

I have a hit. She's in Nottingham. I'm sending you her last known whereabouts via GPS coordinates.

The email was from SS. The guy was better than I thought. A half-smile ghosted my face. Harper Wilkinson was mine. Settling down on the sofa, I began making all the arrangements I would need in order to cage my little bird. Drugs, rope, cuffs, groceries, sex toys, duct tape... there were so many things I needed to buy before I could corner her. The good news was I figured I could get everything I needed within the space of a few hours first thing tomorrow morning and then I could pick my rental up. It was nothing special - just a plain white Ford Transit van. While it was unremarkable and pretty dull to drive, it was excellent for carting strays around in the back, due to the fact it had no windows. It wasn't from a standard rental agency, nor was it registered in my name, so I wouldn't have to worry about it being traced any time soon. I'd find another car more to my liking when we reached our final destination.

From the moment the gavel had crashed down, marking me as a criminal, I began to plot my revenge. Five years had given me more than enough time to think and plan. Every conceivable detail had been indelibly printed in my head. It felt utterly incredible to finally be able to put my plan into action. Harper would get what was coming to her and then some. By the time I finished with her she'd wish she had spent the last five years in jail. Prison was going to be a fucking summer camp compared to what I had in mind for her.

16

I'm coming for you, Harper.

Sprawling out lengthwise on the sofa I tried to make myself relax, but my overzealous heartrate was having none of it. The alcohol in my blood didn't help matters, even though I hadn't drunk as much as Liam. Still, there'd soon be plenty of time for sleeping. Right now it just felt good to be alive... and free.

Chapter 7 - Harper

I hadn't stopped looking over my shoulder. Everywhere I went I expected him to suddenly jump out at me. It was stupid. He wouldn't be in Nottingham. He'd be looking for me in London, so I was safe up here for at least a few weeks, maybe even a month. Then I would move on. I figured he'd get bored of the search after six months or so, and that would be that. Hell, I might not even be interesting enough for him to bother with now he'd been released. He'd be catching up with his parents and friends, chatting up girls, and probably drinking himself silly. Breathe. I was probably worrying over nothing, and I needed to calm down. I hadn't been able to eat in two days, and now I had food readily available it was a crime to waste it.

For some reason I'd been particularly jumpy today, although there was probably a good reason for that. Today my cash had run out. Unless my tips this evening were amazing, tonight was the night I would be sleeping rough.

I had no idea where I was going to go. My little holdall with all my worldly possessions was sat in the staffroom, forlorn and miserable - just like me. We had nowhere to go, no money to speak of, and to make matters worse it was raining cats and dogs. It appeared my life had switched back to its usual bad luck streak.

Balancing three enormous plates of pizza upon my left arm, with another bowl of pasta on my right, I waltzed back into the restaurant. My stomach swam with nausea. It might not be as bad as I feared. There were a couple of women's shelters in Nottingham. Maybe they'd have space for me for a couple of nights. That was all I would need, and then payday would hit. If not I intended to wear every item of clothing I had in my holdall and then lock myself in a public toilet somewhere. It wouldn't be warm, and it wouldn't be pleasant, but I might just about get through the night unscathed, if I was lucky, which I wasn't.

The pizzas were gratefully received before I was then barraged with another dozen drinks orders. My memory was shot. Reaching for my pad and pen I scribbled away as fast as I could. Walking smartly back to the bar, I looked at my watch. Today was one of those rare days when I was going to wish my shift would never end, but my watch said differently. I had less than an hour to go. Less than an hour before my life reached its lowest ebb ever and I was officially homeless.

I wanted to cry, but I also wanted to keep my job. I could bawl the streets down later. Now I just had to focus on getting through the rest of my shift without having a complete meltdown. Losing this job was not an option.

When I came out of the bar with my tray of drinks I had the strangest feeling. The skin on the back of my neck prickled and goosebumps erupted everywhere around my body. Looking around madly, trying to find the source of my discomfiture, all I could see were happy customers busily stuffing themselves full of food. Trying again, my gaze reached further - past the glass frontage of Mamma Pollinos, and out on to the streets. It wasn't an easy task as it was dark outside, but I just about managed to make out a strange man's legs walking into the distance around several other milling bodies. My heart sped up.

Put a lid on it, Harper. Seriously. People have better things to do than stalk you.

Scanning the outside of the restaurant several times over until I almost went cross-eyed, I satisfied myself that no one was out there waiting to snatch me. I was going nuts. If I wasn't careful I would probably have a mental breakdown in the next few days. All I wanted right now was to cuddle up somewhere warm and safe. But this evening, even that would be denied to me. Was this punishment for what I'd done to Brandt? Was this Karma coming back to haunt me?

I almost flung the drinks at my customers because my hands were shaking so badly, but thankfully the end of my shift came and went with no further disturbances. Taking my time, I got changed and dressed for warmth. No amount of clothes would be able to prepare me for a night on the streets, but the more I wore the better. I might scrape together a few minutes of sleep here and there, and that was going to be very important if I hoped to do a full shift tomorrow. At least I could get here an hour or two early. Hell, I'd even start early if it meant I got to stand somewhere warm. So what if the staff gave me dirty looks? No one was speaking to me after I'd asked them for money, so I didn't have a lot to lose.

When I'd wasted as much time as I possibly could, I gathered my holdall and slipped out the back door, but not before swinging my head around left and right to make sure no one was there. I'd been spooked earlier and I couldn't shake the feeling someone was watching me. Even though I knew Brandt had been released from prison only yesterday and that it was far too soon for him to be anywhere close, the irrational fear didn't leave me. Walking as fast as my feet could carry me towards the first shelter on my list, with my holdall trailing noisily behind me, I began to look over my shoulder every fifty metres until I nearly gave myself whiplash. If I kept up with this kind of paranoia I'd be seeing bogeymen pop out all over the place before long.

Were the streets of Nottingham kind? I had no idea, but I hoped I didn't have to find out. Thankfully it didn't take me long to reach the first shelter. By accident, I came across a volunteer worker as I was trying to figure out where to go, and she told me that I needed to ring the helpline if I wanted a place. The shelter gave priority to those suffering from domestic abuse or with children. Space was very tight, and it looked likely that they would be full today, but I could always check back tomorrow if that were the case. Handing me over a freephone number she asked if I needed to borrow a telephone, but I shook my head numbly. No. Then I burst into tears.

The volunteer sat me down in a small office, gave me a couple of tissues and brought me a cup of tea. She wasn't unsympathetic, but I could see that I was a low priority when compared to others. I understood exactly what she was saying, and a wry smile played around my face. There was no room for self-pity in my life. I needed to snap out of it. Thanking her for kindness, I took the leaflets she offered me and headed back out into the night.

Refusing to let myself cry again, I walked onward with a wooden gait, one slow step after another. Part of me wanted to give up, find my toilet cubicle and settle down for the night. Hell, I probably wouldn't even get away with that. It would be just my luck for a cleaner to find me and call the police. What do I do now? Looking down with blurry eyes at the leaflet I had been given, I tried to make out the telephone number for the next shelter. I saw no point walking there, just to be turned away again, so I might as well give them a call. Slowly tapping the digits into my phone, my mind whispered over and over, *please have space, please have space.*

It didn't help me. When my call was answered, and I explained my situation, I was told nearly the same thing as before. They were full, and I wasn't a priority. Come back tomorrow. My voice was almost a whisper as I said, "Goodnight." What did I do now?

Wandering around for an hour or two, I finally found a tattered old wooden bench and sat on it. How had my life come to this? One moment I'd been eighteen and in charge of my entire destiny, and in the next it had all come crumbling down around my ears. Bad decisions? Yes. Bad luck? Of course. And then there was being in the wrong place at the wrong time, and being too afraid to stand up for myself. What did that make me? Hopeless. That's what it made me. Utterly hopeless and worthless. I didn't want to spend another day in my shoes. All I did was clutch at scraps, run around, and look over my shoulder. Physically and mentally exhausted, I gave up any pretence of coping. Lying down on the bench I pulled my hood up, pulled an arm over my face and sobbed my heart out.

I have no idea how long I laid there. It could have been an hour, it could have been three, but as soon as I saw those two deep sapphire eyes looming above me I knew my luck had finally disappeared for good.

Chapter 8 - Harper

I didn't scream. In hindsight I should have, but at the time I was too petrified. The ability to make any noise was quickly snatched away as he covered my mouth tightly with his hand. With his other he forced me upright, before yanking my left hand sharply behind my back and drawing it up to my neck, immediately bringing tears to my eyes. Yelling against his hand for him to stop, all that came out was a muffled bleat before his snarling eyes and cruel lips began to devour me.

"Keep quiet, or I'll break your arm." His voice was a whisper, but it rang out loud enough in my ears. Putting even more pressure on my arm to reinforce his threat, I had to bite down on my cries. The pain was crippling.

"Good girl. Now listen carefully." To make sure I got the message he yanked my arm further up my back making me gasp in agony. "You are going to walk with me to that white van over there and get in the back. You will not make a sound. The reason I know you will not make a sound is because if you do, you're going to lose the use of your arm. Nod if you understand me."

I nodded. His voice dripped with lethal venom and sent splinters of ice down my spine. This wasn't the Brandt I remembered. Where once upon a time there had been humour, light and laughter, now there was a black void. If something was alive in there, it was only just barely.

The monster marched me across the road so fast my head spun. My feet couldn't keep up with him, and they collided with each other, causing me to cry out as they slipped from under me. It was touch and go for a moment as to whether my body would hit the tarmac, but suddenly I was yanked brutally upright and the pressure he held against my wrist increased, nearly cutting off my blood supply. He could easily snap me in two. Although he wore a shirt I could see the power lurking in his arms, and how the corded muscle flexed against the material when he moved. Just do what he said, that would have been the sensible option, but since when had I ever been sensible?

"I need my case." Turning around I pulled against him to go back for my tattered old bag. It held all my worldly belongings and damned if I was going to leave it on the streets of Nottingham. All I had was inside that case, and I wasn't going anywhere without it. But as I spun around to retrieve it I met an immovable brick wall. He had a hand underneath my shoulder and one on top of it before I could blink, and then a crushing weight was applied and my knees buckled. Landing heavily on the tarmac I would have screamed, but for the hand slapped over my face. Unless I was much mistaken the bastard had just dislocated my shoulder. The pain was excruciating. For a few seconds I saw nothing but stars. Even breathing hurt.

Brandt loomed over me, his gaze so intense it felt like he was penetrating my skin. "I don't think you understood me the first time. We play by my rules. Do as you're fucking told. When you've learnt to be a good girl I'll consider putting that arm back where it belongs. For now, consider it a present from the guy you put away for the last five years for your fucking crime." Every word was bitten out directly in my eardrum, and I could feel his saliva spattering me. I couldn't think, couldn't focus, and couldn't do anything bar sob pitifully.

Yanking me upright, he caught me in his arms and made short work of getting us in the back of the van. Once inside he wasted no time in slapping a length of duct tape over my mouth, before pulling my hands behind me to tape those together as well. I did scream then, but the duct tape barely heard. Just to make sure I wasn't going anywhere he did my legs as well. Then without a word he climbed out and slammed the door, leaving me in a suffocating net of dizzying blackness.

When the van rumbled to life seconds later I knew with a sinking feeling that no one was coming to rescue me. For starters, I had no family to speak of, and no regular friends I kept in touch with. No one at the hostel would miss me as I'd checked out, and the restaurant staff would barely blink an eye if I didn't turn up for shift tomorrow. The only people that might come hunting for me were... I didn't want to think about that right now. I had enough problems on my plate.

Knowing without a shadow of a doubt that I wouldn't like our end destination, I wondered what the chances were of me somehow managing to undo the door at the back. I knew the van was moving, but if I could wait until we reached some traffic lights or slow-moving traffic, then maybe I could risk jumping. It was an almost suicidal thought. What if there was a car behind that didn't see me and ran me over? What if I broke half a dozen bones tumbling onto the tarmac? What if I somehow managed to get myself mangled in the truck on the way out? Yeah, and what if I stayed to see what Brandt had in store for me? This was payback, and it wasn't going to be pretty. If he was prepared to dislocate my arm and kidnap me, what else was he prepared to do? And to think I'd been worried about an axe murder on the motorway. Screwing my eyes up tight I tried to fight the tears that were headed my way, but they were as unstoppable as a monsoon. There was a tidal wave of emotion that had been crammed up tight inside me these last few days, and it looked like Brandt had managed to put a crack in my shell a mile wide. My shoulder screamed at me to do something, anything to alleviate the pain, but I was trussed up too tightly. Any movement at all had me screaming my head off, and the number of potholes we went over in Nottingham were too numerous to count. The bastard was probably doing it on purpose.

It felt like an age before the tears dried up. I had no idea whether they'd dried up on their own or whether I was too worn out to cry. It had to be one or the other. Then it was another twenty minutes before I could breathe through my nose and focus worth a damn. I couldn't believe how easy it had been for him to take me. Of course, he'd traced that card. But how? It should have been the stuff of movies. In real life there was data protection and bells, hoops, and whistles to go through to get even the most ridiculous bits of information. Then it dawned on me. Prison. Hackers. Darknet. Hell, he could get anything he wanted in there with the money he had at his disposal. All he'd done was lie in wait, waiting for a call. Then he'd followed me or had someone follow me. Next thing, I'm sleeping on a park bench in a deserted part of town just asking to be snatched. What was I? A fucking moron? I didn't want to answer that question.

Struggling upright, I somehow managed to get myself into a sitting position. The pain screaming through my shoulder and upper arm was impossible to ignore, and while I wanted to curl up into a little ball and die quietly, I knew that getting out of this van was my only chance at avoiding something too terrible to contemplate.

The first thing I needed to do was get my hands free of the tape circling them. If I intended to fall out of the back of the van, at the very least I needed the use of my hands. Was there something rough I could use to cut them? Or even something sharp I could use to try and put a hole in the tape and tear it? I'd have stood half a chance if he'd bound my hands in front of me, but behind me was a whole different ballgame. Brandt knew what he was doing. He'd wrapped several layers of tape around me, so just stretching it against my wrists wasn't going to cut it. Wriggling about on my knees I searched around the van for a loose screw or a hook, anything I could use that had a point or an edge I could saw across.

Scouring the inside of the van from top to bottom, I lost count of the times I fell over. Every time I did I wanted to scream in pain but didn't dare, just in case Brandt heard me and came to investigate. When I'd finally explored the contents of the van from top to bottom the best I could come up with was a screw slightly proud of its fitting. Sitting with my back to it, I began trying to work the screw loose with my fingers. It didn't want to cooperate, but three broken nails and several blisters later I'd managed to expose it by a couple of turns. It was enough. Now all I had to do was sit and saw at the rough edges as if my life depended on it. It wasn't as easy as it sounded and took forever. By the time I'd managed to make a small tear I had black spots dancing in front of my eyes. If I wasn't careful I was going to faint. The emotional wear and tear of the last few days coupled with the lack of food in my stomach was taking its toll. But by sheer force of will I managed to keep myself focused while I fought through the pain. It helped that I'd had practise. I laughed wryly. This was not the time to go there. I'd put that behind me, but if I wasn't careful I'd have something new and horrible to look forward to, in a fucked up twisted kind of way.

It took about an hour to form a tear that was less than half an inch long. It was enough. Now I just had to put mind over matter and tear the tape in two. Ordinarily, with two functional hands, this would have been difficult enough given my size and frame. Brandt would have managed it in two seconds with his bulging muscles. I couldn't help but wonder how many years it had taken him to explode into his new bodybuilder physique. Two, four, or the whole five? If he'd been attractive back in college he was now downright gorgeous, if you could ignore the soulless blue eyes and cruel tint of his features. There wouldn't be too many women that could resist Brandt Browning now, and I already knew I wasn't going to be one of them. I needed to get out of here. Brandt would destroy me all too easily, and I wouldn't be able to pick the pieces up again. There was only so much the average human being can cope with, and I'd already had more than my fair share.

Closing my eyes tightly together I prepared myself for what I was about to do. I knew it would hurt. It would hurt so badly that I might not be able to control my screams, so I needed to be ready to grab the door handle immediately. With that in mind, I positioned myself in front of it. The plan was to snap the tape in two with one hard lunge and then grab. The trouble being, of course, that I only had one workable hand and shoulder. Still, this was my only shot, and what was a little bit of pain to me these days? Hell, this taster would be an aphrodisiac, nothing more. Time to get to it.

Counting back from three I braced myself for the worst. I knew my right wrist would have to do all the work, and that my left would go berserk. There was no other option though. It was do or die.

Three. Two. One. I pulled with everything I had and then some. The sound of tearing tape could be heard, and then my arms swung wildly around. One of them I managed to get back under control, the other I could do nothing with. The pain had reached such a state that nausea had taken over and all I wanted to do was spill my guts, but I was made of sterner stuff. Reaching for the door handle I pulled.

Chapter 9 - Harper

The handle didn't budge. Moving the thing rapidly back and forth I nearly wept with frustration. All the pain and agony I'd just gone through for the past hour or two was for nothing. Brandt had locked it and I was going nowhere. Sitting there absolutely numb, I slowly began to peel the tape off my legs. What did I do now? What else could I do? Looking around, searching desperately for ideas, I came to the conclusion that he had me trapped and there was only one thing I could do. Wait.

After that there was no reasoning with me. I went nuts. With my right hand I began hammering on the door as loud as I could, lashing out with my feet. There was little chance that anyone would hear me when we were moving, but I didn't care. Any chance was better than no chance. Brandt was going to annihilate me, and I needed to escape. Being in the same vicinity as him for any length of time was enough of a strain on my nervous system, and I couldn't deal with this new development in my life. Would not deal with it. I needed to get out. The claustrophobia was killing me. It felt like the walls were crashing in on me, wanting to squeeze every drop of air from my body. Lying there sobbing, flailing, kicking and wailing like a madwoman, I gave in to fear. Letting it consume me, I remained that way for some time until the van jerked to a fierce stop. The door was pulled back sharply, letting a flood of daylight in and startling me into a sitting position.

"Well, well, well. What do we have here?" Brandt jumped into the van and slammed the door behind him. He looked murderously angry, and I immediately shuffled as far back as I could.

Squatting down beside me he looked me over, and seemed quite content with what he saw. His hand came towards my cheek and I flinched, expecting him to hit me, but he didn't. When his touch came it was surprisingly gentle. A single knuckle slid up my face, collecting my tears. His finger didn't stop until it reached the corner of my eye, and my heart beat double time wondering what he would do next. Pulling away from me he lifted his hand and sucked his glistening finger into his mouth.

"Oh, Harper, don't look so shocked," he whispered. "You knew this was coming." His quiet, controlled voice turned my insides to liquid. "I'm going to be dining upon your tears for the next five years, so you'd better get used to crying. I've never seen anything quite so beautiful."

"What do you want with me?" My voice wobbled uncontrollably and sounded all wrong, my sinuses thick with mucus and my throat raw with crying.

He tilted his head, considering my question and folded his hands across his chest. "Everything," he finally said. "I want everything and more. You'll find out soon enough." He held his hand out to me and upon his palm rested two white pills. "Take them."

"What are they?" I tried to scoot further back, but I was already against the side of the van.

"Question time is over. Swallow them." He glared at me and waited.

"And if I don't?" Hell, there could be anything in those pills. There was no way I was going anywhere near them. The man was certifiably insane.

"Then I'll fuck you right here, right now, on the floor of the van in every single hole you possess, and when I'm finished you'll wish you took the damn pills. I'm happy with either option. You choose." He looked at me as if I was something unpleasant on the end of his shoe, but there was a flicker of desire behind those sapphire irises, and I had no doubt he meant exactly what he said.

"Are you going to kill me?" The words wobbled around in my mouth as I tried to get them out. If I was already pale due to my shoulder, my face had now gone as white as a freshly bleached sheet.

He slowly smiled at me in answer, which freaked me out even more. Then he got down on his knees, and his hand touched my sweater. I shivered at that small contact and felt a flood of warmth shoot to my core. My body was a traitor. How could I be so scared of someone and aroused at the same time? This was madness. I was going to make it so easy for him to destroy me. Hell, I was virtually giving him the green light to come and do his worst.

"Where would be the fun in that?" His velvet voice snapped me out of my misery for a moment as my face whipped up to stare at him. "Killing you would be far too easy and nowhere near the punishment I endured for your lies. There's no way you're getting off that easily. Oh no. You're going to be my bitch for the next five years, Harper Wilkinson. Not a day more, not a day less. You will learn to do everything I say, or face the consequences. Some days you'll wish for death, other days you'll wish for mercy, and when I'm finished with you, you'll know roughly what I went through, and it wasn't pretty. So you'd better brace yourself."

He almost spat the last sentence at me and I cowered away from him, but his smile grew even wider.

"So are you taking the pills, Harper? Or am I going to start having some fun with you?" He slowly pulled up my sweater, his warm hand a stark contrast to my frozen skin. His fingertips were soft as they roamed upwards and my body prickled with electricity. There was nothing I could do about it. The effect this man had on me had always been powerful, and now it was downright dangerous. Clamping my teeth on the gasp that wanted to burst out of my mouth, I held myself as still as I could. It was as if I wanted to turn to stone; anything to get his fingers off me.

The pills hovered in front of my eyes in his other hand, and I was tempted to grab them and throw them down my neck. Would this end there? What was in those pills? What would they do to me? As his hand reached higher, towards my bra, I blurted out the question I needed to ask.

"Are they sleeping pills?" If they were going to make me sleep, then I was all for it. Anything that would shut this monstrous nightmare out of my head for a few hours or more had my vote of approval. Call me a coward, but the last couple of years had been downright miserable.

His eyes sparked fire as his condescending gaze devoured me. "I'm not going to tell you that, Harper. It's a leap of faith. You can take them, or you can leave them, but my hands won't stop until you do what I want." His fingers swiftly moved around my back, and I heard the ping of my bra being released. The action jolted me forward into escape mode, but he pushed me back against the van door.

"You're going nowhere, sweetheart. So lay back and enjoy the ride. His free hand closed over the pills in a fist, and he put them back in his pocket. I immediately panicked, wondering if that option had now vanished. Since I already knew he didn't plan to kill me, why didn't I just take the things? Because I didn't know what they were going to do to me. He'd already made it more than clear that he wanted to cause me pain, and hell only knew what was in those little tablets.

When his fingers brushed the underside of my breast I jumped against him. There was no controlling my body's reaction. When his fingers caressed me and moved upwards, underneath my bra, towards my already engorged nipples, I pressed myself so hard against the back of the van I thought I might go through it.

"No, no, no," I whispered, but my body told another story. When his fingers closed around one, the gasp that came out of my mouth was unavoidable, and my face turned bright red while burning shame coursed through my body. Oh, he was going to love this.

"The chemistry is still there, isn't it, Harper? And even though you want to hate me as much as I hate you, you can't control your body's response. You want me, Harper. You always have. The good news is you're now about to get me - but it's not going to be the stuff of fairy tales or romance. It's going to be rough, and it's going to hurt, but if you're okay with that we might as well get started."

His fingers pulled my nipple outward, like an elastic band. I sobbed out loud. When his other hand reached between my thighs and began rubbing my sex I choked out a mewling whimper of misery. This couldn't be happening. My skin crawled with apprehension even as it burst into flames. I don't think my body knew what it wanted, but when his fingers began to unzip my jeans I went into panic mode.

Pushing against him with my right arm, as hard as I could, I sobbed, "Stop! I'll take the pills. Gimme the damn pills." For a moment I didn't think he'd heard me as his fingers slipped inside the waistband of my jeans. I held my breath, trying to stifle the tremors ripping through my body. There was the softest caress of his

25

fingers along the top of my cotton panties, and then he lifted the material, making way for his hand to slip down inside.

"Please stop," I begged. I didn't care what was in the pills now. I just wanted his hands off me. If his fingers went much lower he would know exactly what he did to me, even when I was terrified, and I couldn't take any more humiliation. All I wanted to do was curl up into a protective ball and shut the world out.

With my second plea his fingers stilled. When he pulled his face up to meet mine I saw arousal there, and the control it had taken for his body to remain still. I also saw seething hatred. It danced in his eyes like acid; caustic, spitting and burning. Watching as he took a slow breath in and out, I saw his fingers move towards his pocket to search for the pills he had buried in there.

"Open." His command was curt, but I obeyed instantly. I didn't want to give him the chance of changing his mind.

Placing them on my tongue, he watched carefully as I swallowed, eyeing me suspiciously.

"Open again." I did as he asked. I knew he was checking to make sure I'd obeyed.

"Lie on your back." His tone was menacing. His anger seemed to have grown, and I didn't know why.

"You... you said you wouldn't... if I took the pills," I stammered shakily.

"And you believed me?" he said, watching me intently. "More fool you."

"I'm sorry I lied," I whispered. "I didn't want to put you..."

"You have no idea what the word sorry means," he said, "but you will. You're going to learn exactly what sorry means over the next five years, Harper. Right down to the tiniest detail. You think I scare you now? You haven't seen anything yet. Right now, however, I want you on your back for a different reason. I'm going to set your arm straight. So do as you're told and shut up unless you want to lose the use of your left arm."

I didn't. I also wanted the pain to go away. Would that happen if it was set back correctly? I had no idea. Lying down on the cold hard floor I braced myself for something nasty. I had a feeling Brandt was going to enjoy this as much as I dreaded it.

Sitting beside me he pulled my arm away from my body at a ninety-degree angle. He then took hold of my wrist and with a booted foot against the side of my chest, pulled firmly against my arm until I wanted to cry out in agony. Then just as I thought I'd be swallowed up in excruciating pain it suddenly clicked back into place. Brandt then laid the arm carefully across my chest.

"We're done here. The doors are centrally locked, and we're on the motorway, so no amount of banging, thumping or yelling is going to attract any attention, but if you want to wear yourself out that way be my guest. If I were you, I'd get some sleep. You're going to need it because I have big plans for you when we get to where we're going."

With that he pulled the door open and hopped out, slamming it quickly behind him. Before I could blink we were moving again.

I didn't know whether to laugh hysterically or cry. I was finally going to get what I'd spent a good ten years dreaming about - Brandt. It probably wasn't going to be the romantic Cinderella story I'd imagined, but beggars can't be choosers, right? There was a good chance I'd get my hands on him, and once upon a time that would have made me a very happy girl. The trouble was that now he only looked upon me with contempt, as something to hurt and torment, and that could only end badly.

Laying my head back against the wheel well and cradling my injured arm against my chest, I wondered whether I should start praying. It had never worked for me before, but I could really use some divine intervention right now.

It didn't take me long to figure out that Brandt had given me a sedative. Against all the odds, and in the middle of a noisy motorway on a hard floor, I felt my eyes dragging downwards. Thank God. There was no more pain, and for a short while at least, my worries were no more.

Chapter 10 - Brandt

It was with shaking fingers that I retook the wheel of the van. My control had been sorely tested in the back, and it was with considerable shock that I realised I still desired Harper Wilkinson with a ferocity that scared me. When she'd said stop the first time, I hadn't been able to control myself. All I saw was soft skin, liquid heat, and trembling bones. The desire to bury myself in her had hit me upside the head with surprising force, and the burn was still blazing away in my gut, reminding me that I would have to be very careful around her.

Rubbing my eyes tiredly, and trying to concentrate on the road ahead, I blasted the radio up high. It didn't serve as much of a distraction. All I could see was her face. I don't think I've ever wanted to fuck someone so badly in my life.

The pills I'd given Harper were nothing more than a mild sedative and birth control, which was another reason I was so annoyed at myself. I couldn't go anywhere near her for at least the first seven days, so I needed to get used to the pull between us. It wouldn't control me. I was made of sterner stuff.

Leaving her alone in the back of the van sobbing her eyes out and writhing in pain should have made me feel better, and it should have given my revenge some shape and form. But I had nothing but a bad taste in the back of my throat, although I had no idea why. That woman deserved everything she had been given from me and so much more. I'd gone through hell for her, and it wasn't something I would forget easily.

Focusing once more on the road, I tried to slow my breathing down and get my pulse rate under control. There was still a long drive ahead of us, and I didn't need any distractions. The last thing I wanted was to get caught speeding and have a copper on my tail. All I needed to do was keep it together for a little while longer until we reached our destination. Then I could relax. Then my little pet would be behind lock and key, and I'd be free to plot and plan her demise. Once again I would rule my domain, and the feeling would be incredible, especially after having been told what to do for so long.

I felt guilty about her shoulder blade. My conscience nagged at me after performing the first of many different trials I intended to put Harper through. If I was determined to go through with this, I needed to toughen up. I might have thought I was tough after what those bastards had done to me in the clink, but Harper Wilkinson had always been a thorn in my side. There was an instinctive urge to protect her, which was what had probably got me in this mess in the first place. Why couldn't I have seen sense and kept my distance?

It didn't help that she was as beautiful as ever. She had somehow morphed from the adolescent I remembered into a woman. Bright, bouncy chestnut curls framed her face, and I wanted to bury my hands deep into those locks, pull on them a little, and tug her face to mine. At the moment she looked so thin she might break, but I'd sort that out soon enough. I had no idea why she wanted to starve herself silly. What was wrong with girls today and their obsession with a stick thin figure? Guys wanted some curves and a little something to grab on to. Well, I did anyway. I'd make sure she ate on my watch, or there would be consequences.

My mind jumped about as the van made short work of eating up miles of motorway. I began to think about the seven days of trials I had lined up for her. It would be an unpleasant indoctrination into my world, but it would help her see what I'd gone through for her. I figured she owed me that much.

The dislocated arm had happened before I'd planned for it, but it seemed a perfect way to get her immediate cooperation when she'd gone bananas over that stupid old case she'd left behind. After I'd shut her away in the van I picked it up and put it in the passenger well, but only because I didn't want to leave any evidence of our presence. When I looked inside it there was barely anything of value, so I had no idea what all the fuss had been about. Maybe I'd ask her one day if I ever decided she was worth speaking to.

All in all, I should be feeling pretty good about the first phase's outcome. Harper had been captured far easier than I'd thought possible, and I had my hands on her at least a week earlier than expected. Even the first day's trial had already been completed ahead of schedule. I was on a roll.

Taking a trip down memory lane, I remembered my first day in prison all too well. There was endless waiting as I was transferred from the prison van to a holding room, and then to another holding room. Then the humiliation of having all my personal effects taken away, before being strip-searched and given a bright orange jumpsuit, had been a good indication of what was to come. I remembered the sinking feeling as I received my bundle of blankets, plastic cup, spork and plate, and the utter desperation as the bars locked shut on my small cell for the first time.

If that wasn't bad enough, it didn't take me long to find I had company. My cellmate was a big Portuguese guy who didn't speak a word of English. I had to figure everything out by myself on day one, which ended particularly badly when I accidentally trod on a photo frame of the man's wife and daughter. In prison possessions are extremely important. What you came in with was basically all you had, and my accidental blunder was the last straw for this guy. He just went nuts. Although he tried his best to break my arm, in the end he only managed to dislocate my shoulder. But it was a whole night's worth of agony before the prison doctor could be called the next day. Harper had gotten off lightly in the first trial. I'd only left her to suffer for a few hours. She also had the added benefit of having a room to herself when we got to my new house. I was going easy on the girl, believe it or not. Things were going to get a lot worse before they got better.

Chapter 11 - Harper

I had no idea how long I'd been asleep, but when I awoke the van's engine had stopped and we weren't moving. The radio blared from the inside of the cab, so I wondered if we'd stopped to refuel. Immediately kicking and hammering against the side of the van I tried to create as much noise as I could. It wasn't enough. I was already weak from malnourishment, and my bruised and aching arm had really taken its toll on my energy levels. In less than thirty seconds we lurched into movement again, and I fell flat on the floor, gasping for breath. Tears threatened, but I held them back. I needed to be stronger than this.

It was probably time to face reality; Brandt wanted to steal five years of my life. But where were we going? Logic decreed that it would be somewhere remote and desolate. The Yorkshire Moors perhaps, or somewhere in the wilds of Wales? Five years was a long time to keep tabs on someone, though. Eventually he would slip up, and that would allow me a chance to run. Nowhere in the UK was that remote, surely?

What would he do with me? He'd shown no remorse about dislocating my arm. If he could do that without batting an eyelid, then I didn't want to think about what he had in store for me. I was under no illusions that I would be able to cope mentally, although physically - well that was something else. My body would do whatever he asked of it. It always had. The constant battle to stay sane would be trying to resist him. Would he starve me? Would he torture me? Would he do all that and more? My mind went crazy with the many and numerous variants. The most important question was that if there was no escape, could I cope with Brandt's kind of torture for five years? I guess I'd find out soon enough. The thought was a sobering one.

The journey seemed endless. The throbbing in my arm might have dulled, but my anxiety continued to grow with each passing mile. Either we were a long way from home, or Brandt was driving around in circles. He didn't strike me as a man who would mess about. I think he'd planned what he wanted to do with me down to the last tiny detail. If only I'd known how long I'd fallen asleep for, then I could give myself some kind of estimation as to where we were. All I knew for sure was that we were probably heading up north, which kind of fell in with my previous thoughts. It would be remote, unpopulated, and in the middle of nowhere. He would leave little to chance because that was the kind of person he was. Prison had just made him harder - and darker. I hated what I saw in his eyes now. They reflected some of what was in mine, and that scared me. If he'd gone through even half the pain I suspected, then he'd want to lash out, and I didn't particularly want to be his punch bag. If he intended to make me wish I had never been born, I'd look for a way out. I wasn't as strong as I had been. All my edges were ripped and torn, and one pull in the wrong direction would unravel me. There was only so much one person could be expected to endure.

When we finally crunched upon the gravel stones of a driveway apprehension was almost more than I could bear. When the sound of the engine cut and I heard his feet marching towards the back of the van, I felt the oxygen in my body dive down to my ankles. I couldn't do this.

"Get out." The van door swung wide open and he stood there, still pristine in his white shirt, looking as if he'd just finished a day at the office. For a moment I wanted to wring his neck. My jeans were soaked in urine, as he hadn't thought to let me out on the journey, and I stank to high heaven. If there'd been a knife available with which to kill him, I wouldn't have hesitated.

"Don't even think of running. We're at least ten miles from the nearest road and a good forty from the nearest village. With your arm in that state you won't make it down the drive."

"Says who?" I challenged.

A sarcastic half-smile played upon his lips. "Says me. I'd catch you in a heartbeat, and then I'd make you pay."

"You're going to make me pay anyway," I pointed out.

"Not in that way. Not unless you force my hand, that is." There was no mistaking the lie in his eyes. I'd felt his desire earlier; seen it, touched it, almost tasted it. It was only a matter of time.

"You're a terrible liar," I spat, and then slammed my feet into his knees, knocking him sideways before jumping out of the van and belting back down the driveway we'd just travelled up. It didn't take him long to find his feet, but by then I already had a decent head start, and if there was something I was good at, it was running.

Brandt came thundering behind me and I knew after a few seconds there was no way I would win this race. The driveway had to be a mile or two long, and lined with rows of Scots Pine trees. Through the rapidly dimming light I could see that a river surrounded the estate to the right and a wall of stone to the left. The grey, craggy, majestic mountains nearly blotted out the sky, sucking all the light into them and leaving behind an air of morose, dark misery. This was going to be my new home. Searching rapidly from left to right I couldn't see any signs of life for miles. He'd meant what he said. I was trapped.

When he caught me he yanked at the collar of my sweater, nearly strangling me. Grabbing my injured arm he jerked it behind my back until I screamed.

"Stop it! I'll do what you say! I'll do anything you want," I screeched numbly. I went limp in his hold, hoping he'd take that as my acquiescence.

Spinning me around he began marching us back towards the house. He didn't say a word as we trudged over the slippery gravel, but his glower told me all I needed to know. I was in trouble. There would be a consequence for my disobedience. I knew that look all too well.

Stemming the tears that seemed to be forever present, I lifted my head to take a good look at the house that appeared to get bigger with every step we took. As my eyes worked to focus through the unshed tears I managed to make out a Victorian country house, painted in a shade of ivory and surrounded by a jungle of mature trees. Large bay windows jutted out on the ground floor, and chimneys erupted from the roof. I estimated there must have been somewhere between seven and ten bedrooms inside. A tennis court was situated just to one side and behind the house, along with a walled garden and some outbuildings that looked derelict. It took me a while to get over the sheer scale of the place. I had never seen anything so grand before. But it was hard to take pleasure in the impressive history and beauty of the house, as I knew it was about to become my prison for the foreseeable future.

Brandt didn't stop propelling me forward until we were in the porchway of the house, and then we paused only long enough to stuff a key in the door and turn the lock. Jerking me I tumbled onto a Victorian tiled hallway, which had been painstakingly restored to its former glory. The walls around us featured period wood panelling and damask wallpaper in several hues of red. The ceilings had beautifully moulded cornices styled in leaf patterns. Having studied interior design at college, this kind of property would have normally excited me beyond belief, but that was not the case now. Now I was scared out of my mind and wondering what would happen next.

My whistle-stop tour of the house found an incredible sitting room complete with red velvet chesterfield sofas and a grand piano. The dining room had a dressed table to seat ten and a massive teardrop-shaped chandelier. The only room that looked out of place was the incongruous modern kitchen decked out in slate tiles, with cupboards and an island in smooth oak wood. It featured a range oven, an old Victorian clock and another chandelier, this time crafted from what I guessed were deer antlers.

We began to ascend a twisting staircase, surrounded by iron balustrades and a smooth oak handrail. He practically dragged me up it, making me gasp for breath until we reached the top. He, on the other hand, didn't even break into a sweat. Then he bundled me along, and the fact that this entire floor seemed to be filled with bedrooms didn't escape me. I was filled with dread at what was almost sure to come next. Stopping at the end of the landing he pushed me into a room on the right and slammed the door behind us.

"What are you going to do to me?" I knew the question was pointless, because he wanted to toy with me, not chat, but I had to fill the monstrous silence with something. There was no response, nor did I expect any.

My frantic eyes flitted around the bedroom, quickly taking in the four-poster bed, the gold silk ottoman resting at its base, and two arched windows that were covered in gold frills. There was a fireplace, which wasn't often used judging by the large jug of dried hydrangea at its base, and a huge mahogany mirror hung above the mantel. Just as I'd feared, it was a bedroom, and nothing good was going to happen here.

"Strip." His face was hard, mean, and cruel. His eyes sparked with a fury the devil himself would have been proud of, and his fists rested heavily on his hips. This was a stance of power, and I knew where we were headed. My body began to shake as the full weight of what had happened crashed down on me. I'd been abducted. No one knew where I was and there wasn't anybody coming to my rescue. Starting from now, I was at the mercy of Brandt Browning, and he didn't look very merciful from where I was standing.

"Don't make me repeat myself." His voice was a deadly whisper, and the last time I disobeyed it I'd ended up with a dislocated shoulder. It still throbbed from its earlier mistreatment, and I didn't think it would be wise to antagonise him further, but the thought of stripping in front of him was hideous.

"I c-can't... do this," I stammered. Rooted to the spot I held my left arm in protective custody, just in case he thought about yanking it.

"Oh, you can and you will. For each refusal you'll earn yourself ten swats with the paddle, and if you reach thirty I'll come over there and tear them off myself, and I don't think you'll like that much." He gave me another brutal smile filled with malice before he raised his eyebrows at me in challenge.

"P-paddle?" It was a stupid comment, and I didn't want him to explain, but it was the only delaying tactic I could think of. I couldn't be naked in front of him. My cheeks would burn, and my body would go into meltdown. The last thing I wanted to do was let my body practically beg to be taken. There was only so much humiliation I could deal with.

"That's ten spanks. Care to make it twenty?" He sauntered over to an antique mahogany dresser and pulled open the top drawer. Pulling out a long, thick piece of wood with a tapered handle, he caressed its smooth surface with his hand.

"You can't do that!" I exclaimed, horrified. Although I already knew he could do absolutely anything he liked. It was now dark outside, I had no idea where we were, and there was no chance of running for help. He had me trapped, and he knew it. Obey or face the consequences. My face heated at the thought, and it wasn't the only thing that grew hot, fear be damned.

"Twenty spanks, and I think you'll find I can." He swished the paddle in the air experimentally, and the sound made my knees wobble. In a panic my fingers gripped the hem of my sweater and began to pull it over my head. It was almost a mind-over-matter move because as much as I didn't want to do this, I didn't think my backside would be able to take many more. Already knowing Brandt wouldn't go easy on me, I'd already taken on more than I could probably withstand. As my trembling fingers reached to undo the button on my jeans his eyes glued to my body and my core temperature chose that moment to rocket up ninety degrees. Fear and desire warred for supremacy inside me, and I wasn't sure which one would win.

"Are you familiar with BDSM?" He tilted his head as he watched me slide my tight jeans down my body, wriggling each leg to get out of them.

"I'm familiar with it," I said grimly. My knowledge ran a little deeper than

32

that, but I wasn't about to tell him so.

"Good. That will make things slightly easier." He tapped the paddle against his palm, as if eager to begin. I gritted my teeth, swallowed tightly, and stood there in my grey panties and a bra that was still hanging off me from earlier. Once upon a time the ensemble might have been white, but no longer. If he found the picture I made unappealing, so much the better.

"Strip naked." He eyed me coldly, and his penetrating stare went right through me. I couldn't do this. I had to do this. Staring at him blankly, I stood frozen to the spot. My indecision cost me.

"That's thirty spanks." He moved towards me menacingly, trying to make good on his earlier threat to remove my clothes if I refused, but I was too quick for him. Sliding the straps of my bra down my shoulders, I let it fall to the floor and then frantically wiggled out of my panties. I couldn't have his hands on me. If he wanted to see me naked so badly, then he could have an eyeful. Resisting the urge to cover my nakedness with my hands, I glared at him defiantly.

"There will be no clothes for you in this house after I've burned those rags. You will spend the next five years exactly as you are now." His stare was back, and I felt myself cowering under the intensity of it. "Now bend over the ottoman, legs shoulder width apart, arms straight in front of you."

"And if I refuse?" This was more bluster than anything else, but I wanted to know what the evil bastard would do if I decided not to cooperate.

"What happened earlier when you defied me? You want me to do the right arm? Then you can have a matching pair." He raised his eyebrows at me in challenge.

"You wouldn't," I whispered, backing away from him.

"Try me." The eyes that saw through me said he would do exactly that and more.

"Aren't you even going to let me explain?" My voice wobbled on the last word, and my eyes blurred again with tears.

"You think you can explain away my ten-year prison sentence?" He gave me daggers and then began advancing towards me. "I think not." Grabbing a fistful of my hair he marched me towards the ottoman, before placing so much pressure against my shoulder blades that I yelled out loud before my knees buckled. My left arm throbbed again in earnest. "Do as you're told. When I give a command you obey immediately. Failure to do so will result in a punishment. Do you understand me?" Each word was precise, succinct, and extremely unpleasant as he punctuated them directly into my ear.

"Yes," I bleated. "Yes." The pressure on my shoulder subsided. His hands moved to my back, pressing my body into the folds of silk beneath me. They felt like they were burning a hole through my skin. I wanted to jerk each time he touched me, but somehow I managed to control the reaction.

"Why would I believe the words of a liar, anyway? What could you possibly tell me that could take away the pain I've endured these last few years? My family has disowned me. I now have a criminal record that will make getting a decent job almost impossible, and you've ruined my marriage prospects. If that

33

were all that you'd done, then maybe I could forgive you. But your actions reached far wider than that."

His fingers delicately traced a path down my back. He explored my skin slowly, pressing firmly against each nodule of my spine, and I had never felt so fragile.

"Some of your time here, Harper, will be spent going through similar things that I experienced while in prison." Both his hands then caressed me from my shoulder blades all the way down to my waist, and I couldn't help a soft whimper of defeat.

"You're about to discover what happened to me, while I was locked away in a little cage for you. They're the things I can't forgive you for. You have a lot to look forward to, my little liar." His hands continued to caress my body, up and down, until my bones melted and my heartbeat ran ragged in my chest. I waited for the first strike of the paddle, my body burning with heat, but he seemed in no hurry to deliver it.

"Do you want to the know the first thing that happened to me?" The toxicity of his voice scared me. What had happened to the Brandt I knew five years ago; where had he gone?

When I didn't answer he merely chuckled to himself. "No problem, Little Thief. I'll show you."

The sound of something snapping jolted me into awareness, and my head turned sideways to find the fingers of Brandt's right hand covered in a white plastic glove. Twisting my head back around, I buried it in the soft white duvet in front of me. I couldn't watch this.

"You know what I'm about to do, huh? Well, I hope you enjoy the experience as much as I did." There was another snap as the second glove was donned. He then left me for a moment, and I heard the sound of a drawer being opened again. Sorely tempted to sprint from the room, shoot out the front door and keep on running, the only reason I stood my ground was because I knew he would be right on my tail and that he would catch me.

When he came back he placed a bottle of lube in front of my face, just in case I hadn't already guessed what was coming. I scrunched my eyes tightly closed. If this was a nightmare, it was by far the worst I'd ever had.

"You don't get to enter prison unless you've had a body cavity search. You'd be surprised what you can hide inside the human body." I shuddered. I wished this were a nightmare. If it was, I stood a reasonable chance of waking up one day.

"I'm not hiding anything, Brandt. You know damn well there's nothing inside me," I said through gritted teeth.

"That's what I said to the officer who was doing my search, but do you think he took any notice?" Brandt ran a gloved hand slowly up my inner thigh, using his index finger to stroke the smooth flesh he found there. My clit pulsed between my legs. I would have given anything in the world to stop the reaction, but there it was. It couldn't be controlled.

"Which hole would you like me to start with?" His fingers crept higher up my

34

thigh, but I wisely kept silent. I wouldn't have been able to utter a word in any case. When his hand reached the juncture between my thighs and brushed up against me I squawked and bucked upright. He'd been expecting the move and held me down.

"Shall I tell you which hole they searched first?" His lips, so close to my neck, sent electrical current shooting through my brain. My circuits were fried with panic, fear, desire, and arousal. The combination was toxic. Suddenly all hands left my body, and I gratefully sucked in a mouthful of air. He then appeared by my head with a small pen torch. "My mouth. So that's where we'll begin."

Chapter 12 - Harper

"Open wide." I didn't bother fighting him. It would be pointless. He must have weighed at least twice what I did, probably more. If he wanted to force my jaw open wide I had no doubt he could, and I didn't need any more injuries to add to my already numerous woes. So I opened my mouth, and I closed my eyes, trying to erase both Brandt and the world around me.

"Oh no. You're not taking the coward's way out. If I could face my ordeal with open eyes you can face yours the same damn way." When I didn't immediately comply with his demands he barked, "Look at me, Harper! Tell me you feel some remorse for what you did." My eyes forced themselves open and promptly drowned.

Brandt had always been beautiful. Before, it had been in a kind of polished way. His short dark hair had always been immaculate, his clothes were always designer, and his eyes sparkled with humour. He was even more beautiful now but in a completely different way. Now he had an air of darkness around him. There were sharp, spiky edges to his hair, his body was rippling with muscles, and the edge of a stark black tattoo peeked through the collar of his white shirt. Trying to speak around Brandt had always been difficult, but when he was this close to me it was almost impossible. The throb of desire running through me left me mute, and the hum of electricity fried all my neural circuits.

"No remorse, huh? Let's see if a few days in Glemham Hall doesn't cure that attitude." His eyes flashed with something unnameable as his fingers pried my lips open wider. Shoving the torch in front of me, he flicked it from left to right and then up and down. "Raise your tongue." I did as he ordered and there was another flash of the torch.

"Well, that's hole number one. Have a guess where I'm going next?" Moving behind me, his hands were back on my body. Just the lightest of touches, but they seared me. My hands formed claws in the duvet to try and control my body's reaction to his touch, but it was utterly useless. Heat licked me from every angle, reminding me how little control I had around this man. Once upon a time I would have followed him like a little lap dog, given half a chance, and now? Now I was his little lap dog. The thought was terrifying.

"Is the attraction still there, Harper? Will I need this lube in front of me or will your pussy be beautifully wet, begging for my fingers to explore its depths?"

The gloved fingers moved back between my legs, and it was all I could do not to groan out loud. "Hmm, let me see." One by one his fingers trailed up my thigh in slow, lazy steps, and I wasn't sure if I wanted to slam my legs shut or open them wider. As his fingers reached higher the decision was taken from me, because I couldn't move a muscle. My body lay poised in wait, wondering whether he would be rough or gentle, and almost uncaring as to which.

Sliding a beautifully long finger smoothly inside me, he chuckled. "Ah, so the attraction is still there. You can deny it all you like, but your body can't lie. Poor Harper. How does it feel to be imprisoned in this house, alongside a monster whose body you can't resist?" He began thrusting the single finger back and forth inside me until I had to bite the duvet to stop from groaning.

"You'd be such an easy lay, Harper. All I'd have to do is flip you over and make you beg for my cock." His other hand reached for my cheek, drawing circular spirals around it. I wanted to rock back into his fingers and pant in heat, but somehow I kept it together.

"Be a good girl, Harper, and you might even have a reasonably pleasant time under my roof. If I could manage five years with good behaviour, there's every chance that you might be able to do the same, given the right encouragement." One finger became two and the maelstrom going on inside me was exquisite. Five years ago this would have been my ultimate fantasy, but now it was a hideous caricature. Brandt wanted to exploit me, crush me, and punish me - and he wouldn't stop until there was nothing left.

Two fingers became three, and my body begged to be able to move. All I wanted to do was give in to the sensations flooding me and embrace them, but I knew better. I would fight Brandt every step of the way until he gave me my freedom back.

"Taste yourself." A gloved finger positioned itself in front of my mouth, covered in glistening fluid. I shook my head. No.

"Have it your way. I'll get out the paddle then." Lingering for a moment longer, waiting to see if I'd backtrack, he finally removed his finger. His face then disappeared from view for a moment, before the big paddle was retrieved and paraded in front of my eyes.

"You know this will hurt, right?" He tugged on a lock of my hair as if to make sure I was paying attention.

Yes. I knew it would hurt, but damned if I was going to give him the satisfaction of hearing it from my lips.

Rubbing his hand over the twin globes of my ass, as if appreciating their beauty, he squeezed one before moving backward. Gritting my teeth I waited for the first strike to land. When it did the contact made my eyes pop wide, and the resulting sting swept through my body in a torrent of hormones and adrenaline. Another one followed smartly in its wake, then another, and another. I barely had time to catch my breath before another one crashed into my bottom. Left cheek, right cheek, left, right, always perfectly aimed at the exact same spot they'd struck last.

"That's ten. Are you ready to taste yourself now, or should I continue?"

My ass was on fire. The blistering heat prickled in dizzying waves, but that wasn't the worst of it. Don't ask me why - I have always been wired like this - but sexual-style pain makes me go wild. It was the last thing Brandt needed to know. The knowledge had gotten me into enough trouble as it was. My only dilemma was I didn't know which would turn me on more; his fingers in my mouth or another twenty swats with the paddle. All I wanted to do was crawl into a dark place, calm my hammering thoughts, and hide from the world.

"I'll take that as a no." The paddle flew down on my backside once more, and this time its touch was scalding. Although I tried my best to wriggle away from its unerring aim, he still managed to hit the same spots. My breath now came in fast little pants, and my clit had a pulse all of its own. *Fight it*. But there was no fighting this. After he'd delivered another ten strikes my body ignited in the worst way.

"Stings, doesn't it?" His hand came down to squeeze my ass again, and I jumped. "Thought so. Want another ten or do you want to suck my fingers? It's your choice, Harper. One way or another you'll suck them before the evening's over." He sounded very sure of himself, but then, why shouldn't he? Everything was in his favour. "Going to stay mute, Harper?" There was another squeeze of my ass that had me gasping before the paddle began again with renewed vigour. Each smack went straight to my clit, and all I could think about was climaxing there and then. All I would need was the tiniest bit of stimulation, and the thought began to take over my head. *Fight it, fight it, fight it*. I didn't want to fight it, though. I wanted to embrace it, live in the moment, and accept the consequences later. Burning up with need, when the paddle finally stopped I almost mewled in disappointment.

Brandt moved around to the side of the bed, staring at me. I stared straight back at him. He'd removed his shirt, and all I could see was a wall of muscle... and the ink. Oh my God, the ink. His arms and torso swirled with a thousand intricate black lines, forming Celtic knots and patterns, dragons, eagles... I could have studied his body for days on end and still not found each and every design that decorated his skin.

"Like what you see?" he drawled. Swallowing gently, I slowly risked a glance upwards to see him glowering at me again. "You put these here," he said, pointing to his chest. "You and your lies."

My eyes closed in response as guilt flooded my body. I had done so much damage. This Brandt was almost unrecognisable to the man I'd known five years ago. There was no excuse for what I'd done, and now I'd ruined two people's lives rather than one. Why hadn't I been stronger?

"Look at me, Harper. Look at me." His hand closed around my neck, putting pressure against my windpipe, and my eyes shot open, wondering what he was about to do next. "Ahh, that's caught your attention, hasn't it?" His thumb feathered over my Adam's apple, and the glint in his eye was dangerous. "How easy would it be for me to end your life, Harper?" My pulse went mad under his fingertips, and breathable air became a very important commodity. Remaining as still as a mouse, I waited to see would he would do next.

"Tomorrow you will go to a police station and testify that it was you, and not me who stole that package. Then maybe we can come to some arrangement around here." His fingers tightened, forming a rigid band around my throat. "Just one little word, Harper. That's all I need to stop this. One little word." When I didn't make a sound he raised his voice and barked, "Say it!"

"No." The truth wasn't something I could give him without scarring myself. If he wanted to strangle me, so be it, but I would not be confessing all at a police station. That was how bad a mess I was in.

His eyes darkened at my defiance. He hadn't expected it. He had thought I would bend over backwards to get out of this situation and had it been anything else other than a confession, then he might have been right. Looking ready to commit murder he was now so angry his hands were shaking, and I had reason to be afraid. His control was snapping.

His next move surprised me. His other hand shot between my legs, plunging deep inside me, moving back and forth with vicious speed. I had to bite my lip to keep a lid on my moan. Then just before I thought I would climax he withdrew his hand and thrust it in front of my face.

"Open that mouth and taste yourself, little Liar, before I decide to cut off your air supply permanently." The fingers around my neck tightened sharply, as if in warning. A single tear fell down my cheek as I open my lips. If I wanted to live I would have to play his game, and I'd already antagonised him enough this evening.

"Wider." Opening my mouth as wide as I could, I waited to see what he would do. The back of my throat went dry as the seconds ticked past in silence.

Shaking his head, he blinked a couple of times, and then his eyes narrowed. Thrusting three gloved digits toward me, he slowly slid them along my tongue. Deeper and deeper, his fingers didn't stop until they'd reached the back of my throat and I almost gagged.

"Taste nice?" He looked at me intently.

The plastic coating on the gloves made me want to retch, but the subtle musky taste that was me was not so bad.

"Close your mouth around me, Harper. Suck my fingers." Doing as he asked, I took him as deep inside my mouth as I was able and sucked hard.

"Yessss," he hissed. "Exactly like that." At first he let me take the initiative, but it wasn't long before he began thrusting his fingers into me as hard and as fast as he could. I gagged helplessly and tears ran freely down my face. If he continued what he was doing for much longer I was going to vomit.

Then just as I thought I could take no more he pulled his hand away from me. Slowly, finger by finger, he released his hold around my neck, and then walked silently away. I took a few shaky breaths, but I was pretty sure I was still in one piece. Whether I would still be in a few minutes was another matter entirely.

"Imagine my cock inside that mouth, slamming away at you until you choke. That's what's going to happen unless you testify, Harper. Why put yourself through all this pain, when a simple statement will have me out of your life for good?" His fingers tugged at my hair, and he pressed his body into my back until I could feel his massive erection pressed up against me.

"No." The word was firmer this time, without the threat of his hands around my neck, but there was still a breathless quality to it.

"So be it. His foot slammed into the side of the ottoman, and I heard the sound of splintering wood. I didn't make the mistake of moving, though. "After five years with me you'll wish you did the jail time, Harper. That's a promise." His hand crashed down upon my backside, and I shrieked in shock as my flesh burned. Once again I had to contend with hormones and fear. They were jumping around my body like a bunch of grasshoppers in mating season.

"Any guess as to where the last hole is?" Oh God. I'd forgotten all about that.

"Has anyone taken your ass, Little Thief, or will I be the one to steal something for a change? I think I would very much like to steal something from you."

He parted my cheeks. My face went beetroot. *No, no, no.*

"I don't need you to answer that question, because I'll know in the next few seconds." There was the sound of pumping, and my face went from beetroot to scarlet. He was using the lube. Burying my face into the duvet I wanted to scream.

Another part of me almost agreed with him. Perhaps I did deserve this. The list of things he must have endured in prison for my lies would be long and horrific. Why shouldn't I experience some of them? It was a fitting punishment, really.

When his cold finger began smearing the lube around my last hole I prepared for the worst. This was not going to be pleasant, which was probably one of the reasons he saved it until last.

"Brace yourself, Little Thief." Pushing the tip of his finger inside me, I tensed hard and the immediate pain of having my anal walls dilated hit me hard. The crushing weight of desire I'd felt earlier also came back in full glory. Pain does weird things to me. I can't help it.

"It's rather invasive, isn't it? But you haven't seen or felt anything yet."

Brandt pushed his finger further inside me, and I half sobbed, half hiccupped into the duvet. My body was a mess after this evening's antics, and even I didn't know what I wanted. As he stretched his digit to its full length he pushed, moving the finger from left to right, causing me to gasp out loud.

"I don't think there's anything inside here, but I'd better make sure, Little Thief."

He did no so such thing. Pulling his finger out gently, he then proceeded to ease it slowly back and forth. It was a dangerous, heady mix of chemicals that now floated around my body, and my legs were so weak they flopped beneath me.

"How do you think it would feel if I put my cock inside there, Harper? Do you think it would fit? Do you think it would hurt? Or do you think you'd enjoy it?" The finger continued pumping, and I groaned against him. I couldn't help it. The sound escaped of its own accord.

"I guess we'll find out soon enough, huh?" Withdrawing his finger suddenly, I heard the snap of the gloves as he removed them and then the thud of shoes as he walked over to the corner of the room to put them in the bin. There was the squeak of a drawer sliding open, and then the jangle of a chain. Pressing my head into the bed miserably, I wondered what he had in store for me now. It didn't take me long to find out.

Grabbing a handful of my hair again, he yanked my head back before snapping a thick band of leather around my neck. It must have been around three inches in thickness and was unpleasantly uncomfortable, although thankfully not too tight. There was then the snick of something being attached to it, and then another yank, causing me to stumble backwards off the ottoman and onto the floor.

"I was treated like a dog in prison, Harper. So for the first few weeks, until you learn to obey my every word, that's what you're going to be: my little pet. That means you're not going to speak, because quite frankly I don't want to hear a word you have to say, and you will crawl everywhere unless instructed otherwise. If you understand me, nod your head."

The horror of that little speech took my breath away, but I nodded numbly.

"Good. As you don't like using your voice much it shouldn't be a problem, but if it is, I'll gag you. You should also be aware that the collar around your neck is fastened with a padlock, so don't bother trying to take it off. It also has a leash that I can use to pull you around, so I have a feeling your running days are over. Now put your hands out in front of you." When I didn't automatically comply he barked, "Now!"

It had the desired effect. Two shaking arms were thrust out in front of me, and I waited to see what would happen next.

Brandt grabbed my left arm and pulled out two steel cuffs from his pocket. There was a length of chain between them, perhaps a metre in length, maybe a little less. There was a soft clink, as cold metal embraced my left wrist and another as my right was given the same treatment. All I could do was stare.

"Get down on all fours."

"No." A tiny spark of defiance burst from inside me. "No. You can't do this to me." I held my arms out in front of him, shaking the chain madly, my eyes demanding he take them off immediately.

"You've just earned yourself a punishment, Harper. Pets don't talk. Get down on your hands and knees or I'll lock you in the basement, in the dark, for forty-eight hours straight. I'll also pin you to the wall by your chain like an animal, and there'll be nothing bar a bucket for company. Your choice." He smiled darkly. "It's an old house. You'll have to take your chances with the spiders... and rats."

My whole body shook as I lowered myself to the floor. I did not doubt that he would do exactly as he threatened, and if there were any other option I'd take it. If he wanted to punish me, wasn't this punishment enough?

When my feet connected with the wooden floor of the bedroom he wasted no time securing similar cuffs to my ankles. Now he had me well and truly trapped.

I could feel my body going into panic mode, my breathing shallow as a feeling of light-headedness crept over me. If I weren't careful I'd faint, and with Brandt in the mood he was in that could be disastrous.

Breathe, Harper. Just breathe.

"You have no idea how happy it makes me, seeing you trussed up like that." Brandt began rolling the end of the metal chain of my collar around his wrist, shortening the length, and then he tugged it as he walked towards the door. I had no choice but to follow him unless I wanted to add strangulation to my list of woes.

"Well, my Little Thief, it's high time I show you to your accommodation. What kind of host am I?" His feet clipped quickly over the wooden parquet floor, and it wasn't long before we were going down the stairs again, which was an almost impossible feat for me on my hands and knees.

"Seeing as how your first day in prison isn't complete without the appearance of bars, I've had some installed in your room for you. I'm going to try and make your experience as authentic as possible because it's only fair that you see exactly what I went through on your behalf. Don't you agree?"

I kept silent. It was clear he didn't want me to speak, and I had no desire to anger him further.

"Obviously you'll get a much easier ride than me because you won't have to deal with inmates, but I'll make things more challenging for you in my own way. I expect you to suffer under this roof, Harper. I want you to suffer just as much as I did. Until you appreciate what I went through for your lies, you are going nowhere. When you do leave, the first place we'll be visiting is the nearest police station where you can give a full statement regarding your guilt and my innocence."

That will never happen, I thought grimly, trying my best to keep up with him.

"I suspect you won't be under this roof long, Harper. Unless you're much tougher than you look you'll crack within a week."

There wasn't an option to 'crack', as he put it. My only choices were to stay alive or to die, and both of those looked equally unpleasant at the moment. But at some point Brandt would calm down enough that he could be reasoned with. Maybe.

The chain pulled continuously at my neck, the collar almost suffocating as I was propelled forward through the house. When we reached the ground floor I was dragged back the way we had come and then led down some rickety wooden stairs that went below ground level. Tripping over the first uneven stair, Brandt yanked me to a standstill by pulling the collar upward, and I gurgled for air.

"Take it slowly, Harper. We're in no rush. Five years is a long time. Trust me."

Somehow I managed to traverse the rest of the worn staircase without further incident. It had seen countless use over the years, judging by the worn indentations in the middle of each step where the footfalls of many servants had scurried in the past. The light above us was dim, just a few incandescent bulbs scattered here and there, and the feeling was eerie. When we reached the bottom of the staircase I sat back on my haunches on the cold terracotta-tiled floor and refused to move any further. I had a bad feeling about this.

"Don't make me drag you, Harper. If you want to add cuts, scrapes and bruises to your first night here, that's your choice, but there are no pain meds in the house. Getting meds in prison is notoriously difficult, so if you have a headache or joint pain, generally you suffer. I think you're going to suffer enough this evening, but if you want to add to your woes, be my guest." He then gripped my chain with two hands and yanked hard.

My body immediately began to slide and bump along the uneven tiles, and it was not a pleasant experience. The immense power behind Brandt's biceps was scary as he started walking, and I didn't doubt that he could drag me anywhere he wanted to. This had been another foolish move on my behalf.

"Stop. I'll crawl. Stop. Please. Stop."

After another couple of steps he waited for me to get back on all fours, and then we moved along again. My head was spinning, but I wasn't allowed a chance to assimilate my thoughts. As we rounded the corner, there, right in front of my eyes was a concrete cell. Steel bars had been set up to separate half of the room, complete with a door and a lock. Inside the cell embedded into the wall, there was a single steel slab for a bed, and a thin plastic mattress on top. The only other feature of the room was a plastic bucket. I backed up immediately.

"No. I got down on all fours. I've done exactly what you asked. I even crawled. You can't do this." My voice neared hysteria. There was a single blanket upon the mattress, and the room was already bitterly cold. As the night progressed it would be freezing down here.

Brandt looked down at me, his smile laden with irony. "I lied. It's something you should be very familiar with."

Dragging my chain he half led me half pulled me towards the cell. He almost had to carry me through the open door, because at that point I lost it. Clawing and kicking, biting and scratching, I went nuts as the reality of my situation began to sink in. He was going to do this. There was no mercy in those eyes, and things would only get worse from here on in.

Dumping me on the thin plastic mattress, he retrieved another steel padlock from his pocket. With this he fastened the chain to an eyebolt in the wall just above the bed, which sent me into a frenzy of histrionics, before he stepped back out of my reach to admire his efforts.

"You're going to have forty-eight hours down here in the dark with nothing but a bucket for company. I think it will give you some valuable thinking time, Harper Wilkinson. Let's see how you feel after two days in the dark, freezing your ass off." The door clanged ominously shut, and there was the sound of a lock being fastened. But I barely heard it. I was still frantically trying to pull the chain out of the wall.

When the room plunged into darkness I screamed. The sound of Brandt's receding footsteps on the stairs could be heard as he called back, "Welcome to hell, Little Thief."

My forty-eight hours of solitary confinement had begun.

Chapter 13 - Brandt

When the door slammed shut on Harper, I turned around and nearly ran from the room. Why the fuck had I asked her to strip naked? Why, why, why? I'd barely been able to concentrate from then on in, and I needed my wits about me.

Striding to the kitchen I began my search for alcohol. When I'd bought this place I'd still been in prison, so it was as new to me as it was to Harper. Having no idea where anything was I began to hunt through cupboards and drawers, but there were a lot more than I'd bargained for. The house had eight bedrooms, three bathrooms, a kitchen, dining room, drawing room, morning room, library, scullery, and more. Whilst I knew the layout from the floor plan I'd been given, it would take some time before I was comfortable with it. Right now I was just desperate for something to take the edge off things.

Harper was still as beautiful as ever. Hell, even her tears were beautiful. I wanted to taste them, suck on them and devour them. Even though she was way too thin, she had a fragile kind of beauty that floored me. The number of times I had to stop myself from slamming her against the wall and fucking her senseless were too numerous to count. Back in that bedroom I had barely been able to see straight. If I intended to show her everything I went through I was going to have to learn to focus, else I might as well give up now.

Perhaps five years of blue balls had taken its toll. Maybe I needed to go easy on myself. Adjusting to normality was going to take a little time if you could call this normal, and I was pretty sure you couldn't. But she deserved it. My conscience stopped attacking me. I had no reason to feel guilty. The woman had done a number on me, and it wouldn't hurt her to taste a little of what I had.

Now I'd given Harper two nights in her cell it was time to relax a little. There was CCTV down there, so if I needed to check up on her I could, though the picture wouldn't be great in the dark. Still, I could at least see what she was doing.

Where was the damn alcohol? The fridge had been well stocked as per my instructions, but there was no wine or beer inside it. On the plus side, there was plenty of food, so I grabbed myself a slice of quiche and a sausage roll. This wasn't the type of food I could eat too often if I wanted to maintain some muscle, but I probably deserved a week off my usual routine. The ability to choose whatever I wanted and eat when I liked was deliciously liberating, and one of the things I had missed most whilst inside. Food in prison had held no excitement for me, and though it was perfectly acceptable it had quickly become monotonous. Then there was alcohol. Oh, how I could murder a beer right now. There was no alcohol in prison, and with good reason. If we were the dregs of society, unable to be tolerated on the streets, just imagine how much fun we'd be after a few pints. It didn't bear thinking about. That was one rule that had my respect. As much as I missed the occasional beer, there was no way I'd want that stuff floating around the clink. You'd have to have eyes in the back of your head, and that wasn't an understatement. Take my word for it.

When I'd exhausted my search of the kitchen I decided to check out the rest of the house, grabbing a bottle of mineral water instead. Harper had a similar bottle left on the edge of her bed that she'd find soon enough, and a box containing a sandwich, apple, portion of cheese and a plain yogurt. If they weren't eaten by the time I went in there tomorrow, she'd get another paddling. The woman was far too thin and whilst I wanted to punish her, I certainly didn't want her fainting or dying on my watch. What was it with women these days? Having a healthy appetite was not a crime.

My next stop was the sitting room, so I rooted through the sideboard and a few other cubbyholes with no more success. To be fair, I hadn't specifically requested alcohol, I'd just asked the cleaning team to make sure the house had enough supplies for at least a month. Memo to me: be more specific in future. Swearing away to myself, I headed towards the library. Tomorrow I was going to have to make a stop in the nearest town, and as we were in the middle of the Scottish Highlands, it was going to be quite a drive. An hour or two at least, if I wasn't much mistaken. It wasn't a problem; Harper certainly wasn't going anywhere, but it was still a risk leaving her on her own. Mind you, I could hardly take her with me, could I?

Flicking through some leather-bound tomes in the floor to ceiling mahogany bookcase that encircled the room, I was amused to discover Little Women, Pride and Prejudice, Great Expectations, The Count of Monte Christo and Treasure Island all neatly nestled away in front of me. It seemed as if things hadn't changed much here since Queen Victoria had taken to the throne. Looking around me, I found high-backed leather armchairs with velvet-covered card tables placed at strategic intervals. Everything had been lovingly restored with great care and attention to detail. Oh, to be a fly on the wall one hundred and fifty years ago. Did they still spank women in Victorian England? Of course they did. If the ancient Greeks and Romans did it, then the Victorians would have been mad not to carry on the tradition. Even the Kama Sutra contained instructions on spanking women, and that text must be hundreds of years old. Funnily enough, in the sixteenth century there was a theory that whipping would make barren women fertile and it became a popular pastime of the French court. As you can see, I had no small fascination with the subject.

My mind wandered back to the paddle. Had Harper enjoyed her spanking, propped up at the foot of the four-poster bed? If I was a betting man, and I wasn't, I'd say she had. The trouble was, she was already wet before we started, so I couldn't be sure that spanking turned her on. The woman hadn't started bawling, but she'd had experience with BDSM before. This wasn't new to her. My conscience be damned, I was going to have fun unravelling her, piece by piece, before sinking deep inside her - anywhere inside her. The thought made me crazy. But not for another six days. Well, how hard could that be? For the next two days I wasn't going anywhere near her except to deliver food, and after that the trials would begin in earnest. I had so many great things planned for her. She should count herself lucky that I was giving her forty-eight hours to catch up on some sleep. She'd need it. The woman wasn't going to get much rest after that.

Turning around, wondering what room I should explore next, a circular piece of furniture caught my eye. Propped up on four artfully curved legs, it was a small cabinet surrounded by wooden slats and glass panelling. The top was just a round oak tray. Delightful as it was, that wasn't what had caught my eye. The interior was full to bursting with every spirit imaginable. Hallelujah! I'd just won the jackpot. Searching around for a bottle of whisky, I grabbed a Scottish malt by the neck and hightailed it back to the kitchen. All I needed now was a glass and a decent helping of ice. Who needed beer when they had a bottle of the good stuff nearby? Now I just had to find a working television.

Chapter 14 - Harper

When the lights went out I nearly had a fit. Today's events had been mind-blowing by anyone's standards, but to be left naked down a cellar in the pitch-black darkness had just about finished me off. My left arm still throbbed miserably and the utter humiliation I'd felt as Brandt had put his hands all over me still hadn't left me. I felt hot and cold, all at the same time. What was that all about?

I pulled frantically at the chain around my neck when he left me, desperately trying to wrench the thing from the wall, but the metal refused to budge and the padlock was going nowhere. I finally accepted I was here until Brandt chose to release me, and that was a scary thought. What if there was a fire and the house burned down to the ground? Mind you, it was so damp and cold down here that the fire would have to have a serious attitude problem before it took hold. But that wasn't exactly a comforting thought.

After I had exhausted myself trying to escape, there was little to do bar sit and think. The only thing I wanted to do was burst into floods of tears and drown in self-pity. It was also the one thing I couldn't do. At some point a chance to escape would present itself. It might not be for a year, maybe even two, but that point would come, and I was going to be ready.

Snatching the thin blanket I wrapped it twice around me. It didn't provide much protection from the cold, but anything was better than nothing. Brandt intended to make me suffer in every way, it appeared.

Wondering if there were rats down here, or if Brandt was trying to scare me, I scanned the floor in front of me. I could barely see past the bars in front of my nose, so I held out little hope that I'd see anything smaller. He was probably lying, anyway. There might be the odd spider, but I didn't think the previous owners would have left the house infested with rats. I crossed my fingers, just to be on the safe side.

My stomach chose that moment to growl. It wanted food. When was the last time I had eaten? I could hardly count yesterday evening because I'd immediately brought up my meal with the stress of being homeless. Now I faced a whole two days without food. What about drink? Surely he wouldn't leave me without some water? Hysteria started bubbling up my throat again. I must try and look at things positively.

Well, I had a roof over my head and very cheap lodgings for the next five years. He hadn't murdered me yet, which was another plus. Oh, and he was drop-dead gorgeous, although I think that was more of a curse than a blessing. Then there was the fact that he turned me on, and it appeared he might like depraved sex. Was that a positive? The jury was out on that; it depended upon how depraved he was. But by the looks of things, I estimated he was at the higher end of the scale.

Shuffling towards the wall, my back connected with a box of some sort. Squinting my eyes to try and decipher what it was, I tried to reach it with my arms, only to find that the chain didn't allow me enough movement. Damn Brandt and his bloody revenge. How long did he intend to keep me tied up like an animal? He didn't seriously expect to stow me down here for five years, surely? Would he grow bored of the game eventually? Time would tell.

Putting my foot on top of the box, which appeared to be made of cardboard, I dragged it towards me until it was within grasping distance. Anything he might have decided to leave for me was sure to be vile, so when the box was finally underneath my fingertips I was unsure whether to open it or not. Picking it up, I sniffed at it and then shook it. The only thing I managed to figure out was that there were several items inside. What could he possibly want to give me, other than a heart attack?

Opening the box slowly and with a good deal of trepidation, it was with surprise that I found food inside it. I had to run my hands over the items several times, to make sure I didn't imagine them. Sure enough, there was a sandwich, a bottle of water, a yogurt, a small squidgy rectangle that I guessed was cheese, and an apple. Tears pooled in my eyes. An apple. How long ago had it been since I'd had a piece of fruit all to myself? Putting the apple up to my nose, I just sat there and inhaled it for a few minutes. Wanting to smile and cry at the same time, I breathed in my apple for the better part of five minutes. It was one of the crisp, green, crunchy varieties, and probably a Granny Smith. The last time I'd had one would have been several months ago. When you don't have much money, expensive things like fruit are the first things to go. I'd filled up on bread, noodles, rice and soup for months. There was the occasional tin of beans, some potatoes, and some cheap crackers when they were on offer. I wasn't sure I even remembered what an apple tasted like.

Worshipping my prize for the better part of half an hour as I mulled over the day's events, I finally got around to taking a bite. It was my first taste of heaven in what seemed like a very dark couple of years. The fact that it happened in a makeshift prison cell didn't deter me from my enjoyment. Tart, fragrant acidity exploded on my tongue. It was a taste of summer, of better times, of childhood and play. Memories came flooding back to me, bittersweet, those of kinder times and softer landings. These days I felt like a walking disaster. It was almost as if every time I moved I was destined for failure.

Sitting back on the bed, almost shivering under my blanket, I wondered what lengths Brandt would go to in order to gain my testimony. Would he still release me after five years without it? He looked like a man on the edge, and that didn't bode well. That was the least of my worries, though. I was naked and in chains. Soon my body was going to be his plaything, however much he might hate me. Would he use sex as a weapon? Of course he would. I had no right to expect otherwise. Could I endure that for any length of time? He would use me ruthlessly, there was no question about that. When I ultimately didn't do what he wanted, would he snap? Was it right for me to deny him the life he was entitled to, in order to save mine? What was my life worth anyway? I was beginning to wonder if I might as well put everyone out of their misery. *You can't think like that. You've come too far*. I hadn't come far enough. I was going around in circles.

I ate every last bite of that apple, and by that I mean I ate it all. The core, the seeds, the stalk, everything was too precious to waste. Mind you, I was careful not to chew the seeds. I'd read somewhere that apple seeds released cyanide when chewed or crushed. That's how I amused myself when I had no money; books. The library down the road was free, so my favourite pastime became reading. Whatever the subject I could read for hours on end, and my mind was adrift with all sorts of wonderful, and for the most part useless knowledge.

Rummaging about in the box, I tackled the yogurt next. Snapping off the plastic spoon attached to the lid, I peeled back the foil and inhaled. It was nothing fancy, just plain yogurt, but even that was magical to me. Thick and creamy on my tongue, with the faintest aftertaste of lemon, it wasn't long before I was completely full. Had I not been jumpy with nerves I might have been able to eat something else, but with just one bucket for company I had no desire to make myself sick. I could eat the rest of the box when I woke up in the morning. Besides, just because Brandt had fed me today, there was no guarantee that he would tomorrow. Drinking half of the water I then refastened the top tightly. Today's waterworks had left me dehydrated, but I wanted to ration my supplies until the morning. I wasn't sure if I would see Brandt in the next two days, so it made sense to be cautious.

Grabbing the bucket beside the bed, I quickly relieved myself and then placed it as far out of reach as I dared. If I pushed it too far away there was a risk I wouldn't be able to reach it or would kick it over when I next needed it. Life was bad enough as it was, so I didn't intend to make it any worse.

Rolling into a tight ball on the hard mattress I tried my best to relax. After the events of the day it was almost impossible, but somehow, despite my shivers, I eventually manage to get a few fitful hours of sleep. My dreams, when they came, were angry, nasty and filled with terror. The nightmares were back in vengeance.

Chapter 15 - Brandt

Hitting the gym at 5:30am, I welcomed the chance to expend some energy. Harper had been playing on my mind all evening, and I'd barely gotten any sleep because of the girl. My cock was having fantasies it couldn't cash. One moment I was telling myself that under no circumstances was I going to go near her, and in the next my hands were all over her. She didn't deserve me, or my body, even in the basest sense, but my control was a fragile thing. Blame it on five years of celibacy. Perhaps I should have gone wild with Liam in London, back when I had the chance.

As soon as the thought entered my head, I dismissed it. There was only one woman who would be able to take what I had to offer, and that was mainly because she had no choice. Some days I felt as if the darkness was taking over. The constant battle to keep my desires in check was growing, and soon, unless I was very careful, I would snap. That couldn't happen for at least another week.

Finishing my tenth set of presses on the flat bench, I then began some cable crossovers. I'd wondered if my enthusiasm for fitness would diminish once I left prison, but the opposite appeared to be true. With Harper under my roof I seemed to have more energy than ever, and the small gym I'd had installed on the ground floor was getting a hammering. Maybe, I'd go out for a run later. With the hills around here that was sure to help me calm down a little.

After I'd played around with some free weights and a set of eighteen-kilogram kettlebells, I decided enough was enough. It was time to get something to eat and a much-needed cup of coffee.

Breakfast was just a protein shake with a scoop of oatmeal and a banana. It took no more than a couple of minutes to prepare, and then I was sitting in front of my computer screen, reviewing last night's footage of my captive. I was going to learn everything there was to learn about Harper Wilkinson, and then I would exploit each and every detail to its fullest extent.

Watching the video in front of me, I was surprised to find that Harper had not dissolved into a puddle beneath her bed. Women are different to men, in my opinion. They don't feel the need to hide and box up their emotions, and when upset, they generally let it show. Harper had not succumbed to tears last night, although she had several times in the van. I almost felt cheated. I wanted her tears, freely flowing, and I wanted that pretty face to be sobbing its heart out. I'd never thought of tears as beautiful before, but on Harper they were something simply astounding. A tortured form of beauty or bruised beauty perhaps, but no less magnificent for it. Tears were something my family were never allowed to indulge in. My father always said they were a form of weakness; an indulgence he wouldn't permit. If we wanted to survive in the real world we would need to be strong, he said. That was good enough advice, I guessed, but a little on the harsh side at six years of age when you'd just taken a tumble. Sighing, I pushed my thoughts forward and stared at the screen.

Bar the tears, everything progressed as I'd thought it would. She scrabbled around madly for a bit, starting clawing the walls, and tested the strength of the metal chain she wore by tugging at it ferociously. For such a small thing, she certainly had a lot of grit and determination. I couldn't help but admire her spirit. Then she wrapped herself up in the blanket and sat there rocking for a moment or two until she spotted the food parcel I'd left her. At first she seemed reluctant to open it, and I guess I was responsible for that. But did she honestly think I was going to starve her? Yes, I might be a monster, one of her creation I might add, but there was still some humanity left in me somewhere.

When she finally gathered the courage to open the parcel, I watched as she hugged the apple close to her chest, almost as if inhaling its scent. Was it comforting, perhaps? A familiar scent, the smell of home? Whatever it was, it certainly meant something to her, because that apple stayed in front of her nose for what seemed like forever. When she finally did get around to eating it, she ate like a starving man. A yogurt quickly followed, with a few sips of water and then she pushed the box away. I didn't get it. How could you be hungry enough to eat an entire apple, pips and all, and then not eat everything in front of you? Sure, she ate the yogurt, but I was damned if I could figure her out. Was she on one of those faddy diets? Paleo, low-carb, something like that? When I went in there in a few minutes' time with her breakfast, I'd make her eat the rest of the contents of that box, and then she could have the meal I'd just prepared for her. She was not starving herself on my watch.

The rest of the video was mainly fractured sleep. She obviously had a nightmare because there was wailing and thrashing about, and I was probably to blame for that too. But I refused to feel guilty. I'd had my fair share of nightmares on the other side, and my only crime had been to befriend Harper Wilkinson. It was a mistake I would not make again. Under no circumstances was I getting close to her. Everything would be done at arm's length, and after I'd got her to testify she'd be out of my life for good. There was no way that woman had five years of imprisonment inside her. She'd crack in under a week, two at the most. I just needed to be patient.

Putting a pan of oatmeal on the stove to boil, I then began loading up the dishwasher. The cereal was nothing special, literally one cup of rolled oats and two cups of milk, but the woman was going to eat it. She'd also get a banana, and that should see her through to lunchtime, giving me plenty of time for a run. I was wired to explode at any second, and I felt like a grenade that someone had already hooked their finger into. The hard physical activity would relax me, and a run through the Scottish hills was pretty magical to boot. It would allow me a chance to scout out the surrounding area and make sure there was no way Harper could escape. After her two days was up I'd give her a little more freedom, but anything extra would be dependent on good behaviour. I didn't expect much of that for the next few days, though. She'd be testing boundaries at first. Smirking, I scooped the softened oatmeal into a plastic bowl. She could test me all she liked. There was little chance she'd be winning any battles. Grabbing a plastic spork, I laid it on the tray with the banana and added another bottle of water. A spork was a cross between a spoon and a fork, and prison issue because it was really hard to do any damage with it. She wouldn't be chiselling any marks on the walls with this beast, that was for sure.

Making my way down to the cellar, I wondered what kind of mood Harper would be in when she saw me. It was either going to be anger or fear. Thankfully she didn't have much to throw at me, bar an empty bottle of water or a cardboard box. Heaven help her if she decided to throw the bucket. I would let her know, in no uncertain terms, who was boss around here and she wouldn't like my methods much.

When I turned on the light and began descending the stairs, I listened carefully for any signs of life. There was nothing. She'd been asleep when I turned my laptop off, so I guessed she still was now. If that were the case, I'd just drop the oatmeal and run. We could discuss eating everything I put in front of her later. Besides, I wasn't supposed to be doing much in the way of interaction for the next thirty-six hours, but if it came down to eating properly, I would put my foot down.

Rounding the corner my eyes immediately centred on the bed, but Harper wasn't where I expected her to be. In the few minutes since I'd turned my computer off, she was now awake and... jumping up and down. It was probably to keep warm because it seemed to be bitterly cold down here. I made a mental note to get her another blanket. While I wanted her to suffer, I didn't want her to come down with hypothermia.

Her face turned around to meet mine as soon as she heard my footsteps. Clutching the blanket tighter around her body she began backing away from me, though she had virtually nowhere to go.

"Pass me the box and you can have breakfast," I barked. So much for my no interaction rule; I'd kept it up for less than twelve hours. Oh well, I suspected things were going to get worse before they got better. Heaven help the woman if that box had any food left in it.

Harper gave me a mutinous look. I wondered whether I was about to get the bucket thrown at me, but then she grabbed the box from the end of her mattress and looked at me, shrugging her shoulders. She hadn't spotted the slot I'd had specially made under the door, and that was no great surprise, seeing as how the room had been in darkness for most of her time here.

"Kick it under the door.

Her eyes narrowed, but she did as I said. Carefully folding it back together to make it smaller, she slid it towards the opening and waited, eyeing me warily. So far she hadn't said a word to me; perhaps she was taking last night's threat seriously.

Laying the breakfast tray down on the floor, I then picked up the box and examined the contents. My gaze centred on the untouched sandwich and cheese. They'd been the bulk of the meal. Even the bottle of water was only half-finished. What was she playing at?

"Why haven't you eaten this? It was a small meal, Harper, and I expect you to eat everything I put in front of you." I glared at her furiously. When she glared back just as angrily, folding her arms across her chest, she ran her fingers lightly over her mouth in a zip-like motion. She had remembered. Christ.

"Permission to talk. Answer me, woman."

"I didn't know if you were coming back. If that was the only food I was going to have for two days, I wanted to make it last." Her hands shook by her sides, and she clenched and unclenched them as if to hide the fact.

That floored me. I blinked a couple of times. Seriously, though, what had I expected? I'd kidnapped her, dislocated her arm and then paddled her ass, and all in the space of a day. She wasn't going to be likening me to Gandhi any time soon.

My voice softened. "I'm not going to starve you. I will bring you breakfast, dinner and lunch. You will eat what I bring you, or there will be consequences. Do you understand?"

"Yes," she whispered, her eyes fluttering down to the floor. She wouldn't get away with that in a few days' time, but for now, I let it fly.

Placing the sandwich, cheese and half-filled bottle of water on the breakfast tray along with everything else, I slid it under the bars and shoved it towards her. "See you eat all that before I return, or there will be trouble. Are we clear?" My voice was still soft, but it held a hint of threat. In response she nodded mutely. Satisfied, I turned on my heel and left.

I needed to get out running. The temperature in the cellar had notched up twenty degrees, and all I could focus on was that damn blanket and what Harper wasn't wearing underneath it. My libido might have been asleep for the last five years, but there was nothing wrong with it after all. It seemed to have jolted into life with a pair of rocket boosters, and the feeling made my blood sing.

You can't have sex with her. You can't get close to her.

That was the voice of reason. All the other voices in my head screamed exactly the opposite.

Chapter 16 - Harper

Jumping up and down hadn't warmed me up much, but a visit from Brandt had finally done the trick. I now felt like a kettle. Someone had pressed my buttons and steam was escaping everywhere in thick clouds. Damn the man. Who was he to tell me to eat? He was probably only concerned for himself anyway. It wouldn't be any fun if I didn't have enough energy to fight him, right? That was all he cared about. If he wanted to torment me, obviously I'd need to be hale and hearty. We'd see about that. I didn't care two hoots for his demands. If I ate all he'd left me just now, I'd be sick. My stomach wouldn't be able to take that much food after having been denied so long.

For all my protestations of not eating, it wasn't long before the breakfast tray was sitting in front of me. Food wasn't something I was going to refuse in a hurry. The bowl of oatmeal still had wisps of steam coming from it, and anything with heat was welcome. Using the odd-shaped utensil he left me, I devoured it with gusto.

It was almost entertaining to think that Brandt thought he was giving me the no-frills experience with his bland meals. In reality this was more food than I'd seen for a long time, and from my point of view, almost fit for a princess. I wouldn't have been able to eat anything rich, anyway. The scraps of pizza I'd had back at the Italian made my stomach roil more often than not. It would take me a while to get used to eating again, but I had no doubt I'd be right as rain within a few weeks or so. *Well, Goldilocks, he got the porridge part right. Shame about the bed and the non-existent chair, though.*

As soon as I'd scraped the bowl clean and licked the spoon, I put the tray down beside the bed and huddled back in my corner. My stomach was once again full, and I felt reasonably warm, contented, and sleepy. Now the room was back in darkness it was a perfect time to catch up on all the sleep I hadn't managed to get last night. Thankfully, I was far too tired to worry about the miserable angst that had plagued me earlier. I'd fret over Brandt when I woke up. For now I just needed to escape my miserable life for a few hours, and sleep seemed to be the only thing that worked.

When I woke the place was flooded with light, and a quick glance around confirmed what I had already suspected. Brandt was in the room with me. Startling myself upright, I clutched my blanket tightly and tried to melt into the background.

"Good afternoon, Harper." His voice was lazy and relaxed, but there was a certain edge to it. "Did you sleep well?"

Rubbing my eyes, I yawned, and my stomach filled with dread. What was he doing down here and what did he want? I also wondered how long the animal had been watching me while I was asleep. It made my skin crawl.

"Did you eat everything on the tray I left you?" He regarded me casually, but I didn't make the mistake of letting down my guard. The man was a tiger, and he was waiting for the perfect time to strike.

"No, because—"

His voice rang out loudly above mine and I quickly compressed my lips together.

"Did I say you're allowed to speak? The time for speaking is gone, I think. Give me your tray."

Sullenly, I pushed the tray towards him. If he wouldn't give me a chance to explain, then I had better prepare myself for his temper.

Examining the leftover food in his hands, Brandt frowned in displeasure when he saw that his previous instructions had not been adhered to.

"If this is the way you want to play it, so be it, but don't say I didn't warn you." He fished in his pocket for a bunch of keys, before locating the one he needed, and then placed it in the lock. The small click it made as the cylinder turned seemed unpleasantly loud to me. He then locked us both back inside the cell. That didn't bode well.

Walking to me, he flipped through the keys in his hand and found another one, much smaller this time. He used it to unfasten the padlock from the wall. It was enough to send alarm bells ringing through my brain.

"Wait. If you'll just let me expl—"

"Another word, Harper, and I'll gag you just like I promised." Pulling a small black ball out of his pocket, with leather straps attached, I immediately shut up.

"Lie across my lap, with your backside facing upwards. A decent spanking ought to make sure you follow basic orders from now on."

"You can't do that," I wailed, before instantly realising my mistake. In less than a heartbeat the man grabbed hold of me, sat down on the bed and slung me over his knees. The ease at which he did so made me wince. He'd picked me up as if I weighed no more than a bag of sugar and when his hand pressed into the small of my back, keeping me down, there was no fighting it. He was so damn heavy, he felt like he was crushing me.

"Open wide," he whispered, bringing the black rubber ball to my mouth.

"No, I'll be quiet, I promise," I whimpered.

"If you want to do things the hard way, that's fine by me." It took him two sharp tugs to wrestle the blanket away from my body, and then his hand came down sharply on my right buttock. The crack that sounded made me jump, and just as the sting began to bloom another followed in its wake.

"When you're ready to wear the gag, you let me know. My hand isn't going to stop until that unpleasant mouth of yours is rendered mute. After you're gagged, we'll begin your punishment properly." He managed to say all of that while peppering my ass with swats left, right and centre. As my butt was still sore from yesterday, it wasn't long before I was wriggling madly on his lap. His hand was heavy, firm and unyielding. I also knew this was a far cry from what he was capable of and it scared me.

"You can't make me wear that," I howled, trying my best to squirm off his lap. Unfortunately, the grip he had on my body was unshakeable, and I already knew this was a war I wouldn't win.

"Oh, I think you'll find I can." To demonstrate his point, he began to spank me a little harder and the fiery intensity his hand imparted had my face glowing bright red, so God only knew what my ass looked like. The man didn't pause for breath as he continued to deliver molten fire down upon me, and slowly but surely insidious heat began blazing through my insides.

At first I fought it. Pain was just mind over matter, I told myself. That worked for all of two minutes. It might have helped if I had a little more meat on my bones, but every single smack he delivered went right through me, searing my skin and sending tendrils of stinging agony all through my body. Each one was less bearable than the last, and no matter how much I squirmed his hand always managed to connect with my backside.

It wasn't long before I realised it was just a matter of time until I gave in. No matter how hard I tried to focus on the gag and how much I didn't want to wear it, my backside was screaming the opposite. *Be strong. You can fight this*. My ass disagreed.

Sobbing in pain as his tireless hand came down, again and again, I finally realised he wasn't going to stop unless I told him to, and the longer I put off that irrefutable fact, the worse it would be for me. Sheer stubbornness made me hold out for another five minutes though, but finally, when I could bear it no longer, I bleated, "Stop. Please stop." His hand continued to crash down as if he hadn't heard me. "I'll wear the gag. Please stop!" My voice was torn and rough-edged from crying, but he had to have heard that. I'd yelled as loud as I could.

There was a pause as his hand stopped in mid-air, and then it slowly came down to rest on my burning ass cheeks. My body trembled under the warm heat of his hand, and I held my breath as I waited to see what he would do next.

"Say 'can I please wear the gag', and I'll think about it." Brandt's voice was low and lazy. He knew he had me. When I made him wait for an answer he squeezed my ass sharply, causing me to shoot up in pain and gasp out loud. "Say it," he reiterated, his hand moving to the other cheek.

I didn't want a repeat reminder. "Can I please wear the gag?" I whispered softly.

"Louder. I can't hear you." He squeezed me roughly again and I cried out, my legs flailing behind me before another spank hit. I swear I saw stars.

"Can I please wear the gag?" I cried out. At that point I would have said anything to stop that vicious hand in its tracks. Thankfully, this time it seemed to have done the trick. His hand settled down on my back, giving it a few soft caresses before he gently moved me off him.

"Kneel on the floor in front of me." It was another humiliation, designed to anger me, but this time I immediately did as he asked. My legs were stiff as I lowered them, and my knees protested at the contact with the cold, hard floor, but eventually I was where he wanted me. If Brandt wished to see me humbled, so be it. I had no fight left. If being on my knees would make him happy, then I would embrace this new life of worshipping the damn floor.

"Open wide, Little Thief."

The moment I had been dreading had arrived, but my mouth opened as ordered. Closing my eyes in defeat, I waited for the inevitable to happen. My body was almost vibrating with rage, but somehow I remained still for him.

"Open those eyes." The words were softly spoken, but I didn't mistake them for anything but a command. Reluctantly I obeyed, though animosity must have been bleeding from them.

Brandt looked straight at me and smiled. The fingers of his left hand strayed from the straps of the gag and moved to caress my face, sliding through the tracks of my tears to stroke my cheekbone. "You're beginning to feel a little of the resentment and fury I felt when you put me behind bars. It eats away at you, turning your insides to ashes and dust. At the moment you only think you hate me, Little Thief. Give it a few days and you'll begin to understand some of what I went through."

His fingers moved higher, tracing my eyebrows and then fluttering softly over my eyelashes. "Keep those eyes open at all times when you're with me. If you close them you'll earn yourself a punishment. That's another thing I had to do in prison, by the way. You can't let your guard down for a single second else someone will shove a knife into your back, or worse." His face closed off from me, hardening, and his fingers reached again for the strap of the gag. Bringing it up to my face, he gently slotted it in between my teeth and then fastened the leather strap behind my head. Please let us be finished for today, I thought. I wasn't sure my brittle nerves could take much more of his presence.

"You have no idea how beautiful you look, Harper Wilkinson. When I look at you, naked, kneeling at my feet and gagged, I could almost forgive you. Almost." His features softened again, and I wondered if I was off the hook for today at least.

"Right. Back over my lap. It's time to address your eating habits."

I wanted to scream at him. How could he do this to me? My ass couldn't take any more of this. If all he was going to do was spank me over and over again until I was crying and screaming, what was the point of the gag? He might as well have just continued what he was doing. Why hadn't I been stronger and refused to give in? This was madness.

My immediate instinct was to bolt, and I followed it, although I knew the action would be futile. I had seen him lock the door and there was no other way out unless I'd suddenly managed to become the invisible woman. My hands scrabbled at the steel bars in front of me, trying to rock them in my fingers, but they only confirmed what I already knew. The door was locked. As Brandt slowly stood up and walked towards me I banged against them, screaming for someone to help me. Nothing but a garbled mess escaped the gag, and my pleas were met with deaf ears. The silence of the house was resolute and unyielding, and it was also my undoing. Hysteria took over once again, and he had to flatten me against the bars with his body, holding my hands over my head, until the kicking and screaming stopped.

When I had finally quietened down he picked me up in his arms and carried me back to the bed. I didn't struggle. Exhaustion had taken over. If he wanted to spank me, so be it. I couldn't fight him, and I couldn't escape this. Somehow I would have to accept the consequences. Quiet tears of misery seeped from my eyes as he laid my backside back over his knees. Not even bothering to tense my muscles, I lay there motionless, just waiting for the agony to begin.

When his hand came down again I was in for a surprise. It was not the spank I was expecting, just a gentle circular rub. Using his right hand he began to soothe the inflamed skin, round and round, and the heat slowly began to dissipate into a more manageable, dull throb. Desire seemed to be pooling between my legs with every circuit his fingers made, but whether that was the massage, or just being near Brandt, was up for debate.

I waited in terror, waiting for the first strike to hit my flesh, waiting for well over five minutes. When none were forthcoming I gradually began to relax, degree by stiff degree. When he had me languid and sleepy upon his lap, consciously straining for the next touch of his hand, he decided to reveal his punishment.

"Are you listening, Little Thief?" When I didn't immediately respond he slapped my ass lightly.

Grunting through the gag, I watched a long line of drool drop to the floor. Great; yet another humiliation to add to my tally.

"Good." He went back to massaging my ass. "Punishment won't always be delivered in the methods you expect, and punishment doesn't have to hurt to make a statement, trust me."

I didn't trust him. What was he going to do to me? Was it going to hurt? How long would it take and could I endure it? There was a multitude of questions flitting through my head that I couldn't voice.

"Spread your legs wide, Harper."

I immediately went rigid once more. What was he planning on doing now?

"Relax. I'm going to bring you to the edge of orgasm three times, but you are not allowed to come. Nod if you understand me."

That seemed simple enough, so I nodded.

"You'll have to concentrate. If you fail, we'll have to go back to spanking. Do you understand me?"

I nodded again. Unfortunately I understood him all too well. This would be a different kind of torture, and one that was somewhere between heaven and hell. Still, it would be better than being spanked. Or so I thought.

"Spread those legs, Harper. Don't make me tell you again." There was a thread of steel through his voice, so I didn't make the mistake of disobeying him. Spreading my legs shoulder width apart I felt horribly exposed and vulnerable, but then that was the point, I guessed. He would exploit my body in every way possible until I gave into his demands.

"Wider. Spread those legs as far apart as you can."

My face burned brighter than my ass as I tried my best to comply with his order. When I'd finally stretched both legs as wide as they would go I felt decidedly off balance, in both senses of the word.

"Good girl, that's perfect." His hand dipped down into the valley between my ass cheeks, and using both hands he spread them wide. Even though I couldn't see his face, I could feel the heat of his gaze upon me. There was the longest pause, and I couldn't help but wonder what was going through his head as he looked at me *there*. If his hormones were anywhere near as crazy as mine, I'd better brace myself for madness.

The silence went on and on until I thought I couldn't bear the tension that froze the room solid. Then just as I got ready to bolt again, the spanking be damned, his fingers began to move.

Chapter 17 - Harper

His fingers were firm and assured, and knew exactly what they were doing. How many women had he had before me? I almost choked on the thought. He would have had plenty. They'd all been lining up for the good-looking rich kid, and who didn't need a Cinderella story in their lives? If they could just see him now they'd be flocking towards him in droves. Bad boys are even more popular than rich kids, aren't they? *He's not a bad boy. You did that to him.* Hell, however you looked at it, he was a bad boy now.

Initially his fingers did little more than flutter around my sex. Those light little touches were incredibly annoying because I wanted more - so much more. My whole body was throbbing with need, in part due to Brandt's closeness, and also because of the spanking. Bizarrely enough those firm smacks seemed to have rewired my undercarriage because all I wanted to do was hump his leg. What was wrong with me? Ha! I knew exactly what was wrong with me, and I was yet to find a cure.

"Are you wet for me, Little Thief?"

Hopefully he didn't expect me to answer that. Nothing intelligible was coming out of my mouth for the time being. Anyway, I was wriggling like a demented caterpillar in his lap, so that should have been answer enough.

After his fingers had teased my entrance for what seemed like forever and a very long century to boot, he pushed a finger inside me. Hallelujah! Except it wasn't what I'd been hoping for. It was just the tip of his finger, and he dipped it inside me again and again until I was panting with need.

"When you're close to coming, move your feet or shake your head. That's your signal to stop me. If you come without permission on my watch, I promise you I will make your life hell on wheels. Do. You. Understand. Me. Harper?" Those last words were bitten out with terrifying venom, and there was no way I was going to test him on them. So I nodded.

"Good. I don't think you could take another spanking today."

My ass was still swearing about his earlier treatment, but it paled in comparison to what other parts were doing right now. My insides were beginning to churn, my pulse rate had ratcheted up to near marathon-like levels, and my hormones, well, they were off the damn scale. It was as if someone had turned me inside out and hung me upside down. A thousand butterflies were wriggling inside me, and the persistent fluttering of their wings was a drug more dangerous than heroin.

Finally, he buried his finger in me up to the hilt. It felt so good I moaned long and hard. The damn man laughed.

"Desire is a fickle thing, Harper. You might like me now, but in less than half an hour you will detest me with every fibre of your being." I wasn't entirely sure about that. As much as I might want to hate him, actually being able to do it was another thing entirely. But five years is a long time. If he wanted to make me hate him I daresay he could - eventually.

The finger inside me began to move - a slow, slippery dance that had me gasping. One finger became two, two fingers became three, and before I knew what was happening the tempo had increased and I was humping his leg. There was no stopping them; my body was just doing what it was programmed to do. Up, and up, and up I flew, higher and higher. I could feel everything tightening, hardening, and getting ready for a mass explosion.

Somehow, through all that madness, I managed to wiggle my feet. Don't ask me how I did it, because it took almost more willpower than I had, but I'd done what he'd asked of me. Heaving through my gag, dragging in great gulps of air through my nose, I nearly wailed in despair when his fingers stopped instantly. The pain of being denied that kind of release was almost too much to bear.

"Good girl. It's nice to see that you can do as you're told. Maybe you won't have to spend your whole time here in shackles and chains. Mind you, it's early days yet. You've still got two to do, haven't you?"

I didn't want to think about that. My head was awash with misery and throbbing in pain, albeit a different kind of pain than the one the spanking had produced. It was hard to say which one was worse.

To calm me down he went back to his circling. Around and around his hand went, caressing my butt, easing one type of throb while making the other worse. All I could do was breathe and endure. In and out, deep, comforting breaths, as slowly but surely the painful ebb of desire began to flow out of me.

Brandt was in no hurry to get started on near orgasm number two. He was very content to stroke my back and the insides of my legs for what felt like an age before he slowly began to move back up to the apex between my thighs. I was trembling before he got halfway. It was a good job the bulk of my weight was supported on his knees, else I'd be flat on my face. Mind you, that might be preferable to where I was going to go.

"Ready to start again, Little Thief?"

Staring sullenly down at the concrete floor beneath me, I tried to make patterns out of the grit and dirt. Anything to keep my mind off what he was about to do. It wasn't the easiest game, and I didn't have a great deal to work with, but I was going to give it my best shot. I could fight this. I could beat the treacherous tide of rising desire, stamp it back down again, and remain utterly impervious to his touch. *In whose fantasy land? Yours? Not likely.*

Brandt wasn't waiting for an answer. His fingers swept down between my legs with even more enthusiasm than before, and I knew within the first two seconds that I was doomed to failure. My hips were already greedily bucking upwards to his touch, and my clit instantly surged to life, like a lily pad blooming on a hot summer's day. It was hungry, I was hungry, and we both demanded his attention using every trick in the book.

There were moans and groans, the grinding of hips, whimpers and desperate undulations of desire. Basically, I was trying to hump his leg, but he was having none of it. If I got carried away my ass got slapped firmly, and the resulting sting was enough to calm me down for a minute or two.

"Jesus, Harper, your body is so responsive. I swear you'd fucking fly given half a chance." Brandt sounded shocked, but it was nothing I hadn't already figured out. Whenever he was near me my body went into spontaneous combustion mode with minimal provocation, and the longer I seemed to be around him, the worse it got. This time, as soon as his fingers were inside me, I nearly shot up towards the roof. My breath was stuck solidly in my body, heavy and swollen with lust, and all I wanted to do was let go.

"Move those feet, Harper. If you climax without my permission you won't be able to sit on your ass for a week. That's a promise, by the way."

At first I disregarded his words. My body didn't want to hear them, so we completely ignored them. There was only one thing on my mind, and no one was going to distract me from my purpose.

Suddenly a loud slap rang down across my ass, making me bleat in agony.

"Harper! Move those feet or I'll spank you until you do." He was as good as his word. Spanks flew down, not curbing the agony of unspent desire in the slightest, just adding to it, in a tumultuous and almost monstrous intensity.

Squealing through my gag, I managed to waggle my feet almost right on the precipice of climaxing. The bastard stopped instantly, almost as if he had a sixth sense, and my clit pulsed painfully once, twice, and then settled down to a miserable and agonising throb.

My whole body was trembling from head to toe, and on a knife-edge. The slightest flutter of his fingertips would send me over. There was no way I would make it past round three. My clit was so revved up it felt like a Ferrari; one little press of the gas and it would shoot off at two hundred miles an hour.

When Brandt began rubbing my ass again I wanted to scream. Unfortunately, that would be a complete waste of my limited oxygen supply, so somehow I managed to keep it inside me.

"From now on in, you will eat everything I put in front of you. Nod your head if you understand." There was another squeeze of my ass and a playful tap. I nodded woodenly. There wasn't a lot else I could do.

"I don't care if you don't like the food, you will eat it. You look as if a stiff wind would blow you over at the moment, and you're so damn frail I'm afraid I might break you. Why you want to be so thin is beyond me, but it will not continue under my roof. You will eat, or there will be consequences. This one will be mild in comparison to the next one if you continue to defy me. Do you understand?"

Another nod followed, even less enthusiastic than the last. It looked like my existence was back to being miserable. If I ate all the food he'd left me I'd be violently sick, and I guessed he'd probably punish me for that too.

"Don't test me, Harper. I mean what I say." His fingers closed around my clit and squeezed cruelly. Immediately struggling in his lap, his elbow crashed into my back, keeping me exactly where he wanted me.

"That dampened your ardour somewhat?" He released his bruising grip, but instead of being cowed in submission my clitoris was hungry for more of the same. If my body hadn't already been clamouring for attention, now it was on its knees begging for more of the same. I wanted to put my head in my hands and weep.

"Time for round number three, Harper. Remember to move those feet at the right time, or there will be consequences."

Consequences, consequences... everything I did had consequences.

Brandt didn't mess about this time. He went straight in for the kill with both hands, and they were everywhere at once. Forking his middle and index fingers he brushed up and down my clit, in between the delicate petals of my labia. Desire spread slick and fast, all through my body, and its call was hot and heavy. Trying desperately hard to think of anything but sex I concentrated on the floor again, and the mess my drool was making upon it. A steady stream began to flow from my lips, heading towards the concrete in long, almost elasticated strings that bounced with each thrust of my hips.

My mind was mush, and it was all his fault. Thoughts swam in my head, faster and faster, almost in line with the desperate, burning pulse of my body. How long would he keep me here? Would he grow bored of trying to get me to confess? Would someone find me eventually? Would he fuck me? Did I want him to fuck me? Oh God, I think the answer to that question was yes.

Four fingers filled my pussy, stretching me wider and wider until the feeling of being completely filled was almost overwhelming. The contact on my clit disappeared almost entirely during this time, making me a needy, wanton mess. Brandt thrust inside me countless times before he spoke, but by then I was almost insensible. All I could think about was getting what I needed, and wondering what I could do to make it happen.

"Before the week is out you're going to be begging me to let you come, Little Thief. This is day one, and already you're grinding your hips against me, practically offering yourself to be taken. Imagine what you'll do after a week of this." His voice was rough and gravelly, and the sound did funny things to me. A week? Did he intend to torment me like this for a week? The horror of that thought drained right through me.

"Of course, there's always the possibility it could be more than a week. If you displease me it could be months or years." His fingers began moving upwards, searching for the other secret place he'd found yesterday, and I felt my body coiling up tightly, as if afraid to move a muscle.

"Right now I'm guessing you think it won't be a problem. As soon as I leave you'll be able to pleasure yourself silly, right?"

I hadn't thought any such thing, but I confess the idea would probably have come to me sooner rather than later. As his fingers circled my other, much tighter hole, I moaned. Did I want his fingers inside me there? The sad fact of the matter was that I did, desperately, and anywhere else he cared to insert them.

"Wrong, Harper. This room is rigged with cameras. You even think of touching yourself and I'll be down here like a shot. I'll pin you to the wall, hands above your head, legs spread wide open, and deliver punishments, one after the other until I think you've learned your lesson. Your pleasure is mine now, and I don't intend to be generous with you. I had to learn the hard way, and so you'll have to learn the hard way." He began to press his index finger against my sphincter, and my body had barely enough energy to fight him.

"Relax, Harper. It's worse if you tense. Trust me. That's something else I discovered in prison, thanks to you." His words were blunt and biting, but his finger at my entrance remained gentle, pushing through the tight ring of muscle until eventually I opened up and let him inside. All the anger I was feeling left me and gradually ebbed away until there was almost nothing left.

"That's it... just relax... let me in..."

As if I had any choice. Before I knew what was happening he was gently thrusting inside me, one finger inside my ass, his thumb on my clit, and if I thought I was aroused before, then this was something else.

"A little bit of pain tempers arousal, Harper. I can work your clit much longer doing this, and you still won't come. But when you do eventually make it past that annoying ache the orgasm is all the sweeter for it. Not that you'll be finding out anytime soon."

My eyes were rolling. If Brandt wanted me to beg I would have got down on my knees and licked his shoes. My whole body was vibrating with lust, and the painful drumbeat going through my body just got worse with each second he continued.

"Getting ready to move those feet, Harper?" His fingers became firmer and more insistent, almost as if they were trying to get me in trouble. Did he want me to fail? It wouldn't have surprised me.

Spiralling up and up, coils of desire running endless rings around my body, I wondered how long I could take being pinned to the wall. How long would he leave me there? And what sort of punishment would result? If this was a mild one in his estimation, it probably wasn't a good idea to test the theory, but my poor body demanded otherwise. Just give in, it whispered. *You've come too far now to back out at the last minute.* I was inclined to agree. Besides, I was barely capable of moving my feet now. Every limb had turned to liquid, and my whole body felt like a blancmange on a washing machine spin cycle.

"Move those feet, Harper."

I could barely summon up enough energy to breathe, let alone do anything else.

Tighter and tighter he wound my body until I was sure I would shatter and see stars. The moment loomed closer and closer, his fingers faster and faster, harder and harder, until he suddenly stopped and gave my backside an almighty slap. The agony of being denied a third time was so unbearable I began to sob.

"Oh dear. What a naughty, naughty girl you are. That greedy little body of yours isn't getting what it wants until I say so." Pushing me off his lap he left me in a tangled heap on the floor, still sobbing my heart out as he got to his feet. Looking down at me, the expression he wore was one of distaste.

"Up, Harper. On your knees."

When I didn't comply he grabbed a handful of my hair and pulled me upright. He didn't let go until I was on my knees, my back curled upwards in a painful arch.

"Looks to me like it will be a long time before you earn yourself an orgasm, Little Thief. I'd get used to disappointment if I were you." When he let my hair go I sighed in relief, but the sound was short-lived. Reaching into his pocket, he retrieved his set of keys and locating the smallest one, began to unfasten my handcuffs only to refasten them behind my back.

"Listen up. I'm going to remove the gag. You will not say a word, or I will put it straight back in. Do you understand?" His blue eyes were storm-dark and streaked with lightning, and his mouth was a cruel line. I nodded, stifling my cries, wondering what the madman was about to do next.

"You will sit there with your mouth wide open for the next ten minutes as I feed you all the food I've just brought you. At least this way I'll know you've eaten. If I have to do this every day for the next five years, Harper, you're going to have a very sore ass."

He walked behind me to unfasten the leather straps of the gag, and I winced as some strands of hair got tangled in his punishing fingers. Gentle Brandt had left the building. In his place was a fire-breathing dragon, and one I didn't want to mess with. When he pulled the gag free of my mouth with a sucking *pop* I gratefully breathed in great gulps of air.

"Mouth open wide, Harper," he barked at me, as he quickly retrieved the tray he'd left earlier. I didn't even think of disobeying him.

The sandwich was the first thing he got hold of, and he broke it into small bite-sized pieces. He fed them to me patiently, one at a time, giving me words of encouragement along the way. I barely heard him. My body felt as if the fires of hell had seared it, and my singed skin was still smoking. To make matters worse, my jaw ached from having worn the gag, and chewing quickly became a monotonous experience. To add insult to injury the sandwich tasted like sawdust because the adrenaline thundering through my veins had no time for mundane things like eating.

He fed me all of it, the cheese portion, and then the banana. I wondered briefly if he'd ram the thing down my throat, but no, he peeled it neatly and then broke it into bite-sized chunks. When all the food had disappeared from the tray I breathed a sigh of relief. Already feeling nauseous, I didn't think I could have managed another bite.

"Good girl. Wait there." Brandt patted me on the head like a dog and then left me kneeling on the floor as the door to my cell clanged shut. He didn't forget to lock it, although I'd have been the first to admit I was going nowhere. As his footsteps finally went out of air-shot I drew in a long slow breath. At the moment he wasn't the crazy madman I feared, but that would change as I continued to withhold what he wanted. This would be a delicate dance of willpower until someone snapped; either Brandt in a temper, or me in mind or body.

Moving from knee to knee, to try and increase the circulation through my dead limbs, I tipped my neck from side to side. I felt stiff as a board. The benefits of a crap night's sleep and a rock-hard bed. But even though the bed was terrible, as soon as he was out of my hair I was going to curl up and sleep for as long as I could. Every day I remained under his roof would get worse, and I was going to need some sleep if I intended to get out of here. The only thing I wanted right now was the sight of his back retreating into the distance. I would have to hope he had a busy day planned and that most of it didn't include me.

When footsteps began to descend again I started praying, but it made no difference. There he was, with yet another tray in hand. Oh God, not more food. If he wanted me to eat anything else I'd be sick.

He set the tray on the floor and opened the door. Shoving the keys back in his pocket he picked it back up and strode to the bed, setting it down carefully before taking a seat.

"Why is that mouth not open? Mouth open, Harper. This is lunch." He barked the command at me, and I didn't even try to argue. What would be the point? I'd rather be sick than have him come at me again with that gag.

Opening my mouth I watched as he stirred something in a bowl before bringing a large spoon up to my lips. The first taste revealed it was chicken soup, and though pleasant enough my stomach argued noisily. It was rich, creamy, and filled with vegetables. But it settled with the delicacy of lead, and I was rewarded with unpleasant cramps. As soon as I had swallowed one spoonful another followed, and he didn't stop until the bowl was empty.

"Now for the bread roll." He looked enormously pleased with himself as he tore the white granary roll into little pieces. Though little did he know, all his work would be for naught. Chewing woodenly on each piece of fluffy warm bread, I ate everything he put in front of me. I didn't complain once, and I didn't say a word. If this was the way the games were to be played, then so be it.

When he had finished feeding me, he motioned for me to stand up, and I did so slowly. I had no wish to be sick while he was still around. Some things were better done in private, cameras be damned.

Leading me by the chain on my collar, he padlocked me back to the wall and gathered up his tray.

"The next tray that comes in had better be empty when I come to collect it, Harper. I don't think you want me feeding you on a daily basis, nor do I think you'll want the punishments that come with defying me. I'll see you in a few hours, Little Thief. Get some rest. You'll be needing it." He ran three fingers of his right hand over my tear-stained cheeks and then left without another word.

A tide of nausea assaulted me as soon as the key turned in the lock, but I held it in. Waiting for the sound of his footsteps to disappear, I battled the wave of rising acid bursting up my throat. Keeping my lips tightly clamped, I reached out with my leg and slowly inched the bucket closer towards me, as quietly as I could. Counting silently to one hundred in my head, finally, I couldn't hold it in any longer. Grabbing the bucket with both hands I violently upended the contents of my stomach into it and retched until there was nothing left but stomach acid and water.

With shaking hands I placed the bucket back on the floor and wondered what Brandt would do when he saw it. Grabbing my blanket and curling into a comforting ball, I wiped the sweat from my forehead and laid one hot cheek into the cold mattress. My mouth tasted of bile, my eyes stung, and my body lay pulsing and weak. Sleep, when it finally came, was not the pleasant escape I had envisioned. Worry nagged at me, throwing me into vividly horrible nightmares that were another prison entirely, but from a different place in time.

Chapter 18 - Brandt

My hands were shaking when I left the room. My cock was still throbbing in my jeans, and I hadn't actually touched her the whole half hour I'd been feeding her. If I expected to be able to punish her like this on a daily basis I would need to get some release of my own, else I'd end up doing something I would regret.

Was she becoming an obsession of mine? As much as I wanted to deny it, she had filled my thoughts for five years of sleepless nights, and she'd also been the highlight of many of my days. Without those thoughts of revenge I might have considered giving up, but Harper had somehow kept me strong.

I should have been thinking about the best way to get her to confess all. That was the only thing that mattered right now. My mind invariably turned towards sex, though, and it was starting to drive me insane. Would fucking the girl get her out of my system? Did I even want to go there? It was a dangerous route to travel. Much better to take a long drive into town, hit the clubs, and pick up a nice distraction. That would settle the itch, let me focus, and then I could keep the hell away from Harper Wilkinson.

Other girls don't interest you, Brandt. You had your chance the other night, and you couldn't even be bothered to go the distance. Throwing my head back in frustration, I tried to think past the desire that was beginning to crush my internal organs, but coherent thought just wasn't possible right now. Slamming my fist into the wall so hard the plasterboard shook, I took a deep breath and tried to calm myself. Go take a shower; do what I needed to do and get a grip. At least there was a bit of privacy around these parts. If I wanted to paint the shower white, there wasn't anything or anyone going to stop me. The trouble was, I knew from experience that it would be a hollow victory. It might soothe the ache for a couple of hours, but the next time I walked back in that cell with her it would be just as bad, if not worse. What made it even harder was that I knew she wanted me. It would be oh-so-very-easy to take her, make her beg for it, and have her kneel at my feet. She was already half in love with me, and so far I'd been nothing but an utter bastard. There should be hate, mistrust, fear and disgust in her eyes whenever she looked my way. The only one of those emotions I'd seen so far was fear, and each time it had been warranted. I was turning into a crazy fucking monster. How could one person change so much in five years? Some days I felt like my humanity had been stripped bare, lacerated and shoved back inside my body, holes and all. The hardened beast that I'd become wasn't pretty, but he was a survivor. I wondered if Harper was.

Stomping up the stairs towards my ensuite, I pulled the shower door open and slammed the faucet on hot. Scalding hot, followed by ice cold water should do the trick. Stepping out of my black jeans and T-shirt, I slid my boxer shorts over my thighs and dove straight in. I wanted to get clean, feel clean, but first of all I needed relief, and that was only going down one way.

Pressing my back against the rear of the shower cubicle, I fisted my cock tightly and squeezed. A drop of pre-cum already glistened at the tip, and there wasn't enough pressure in the water sluicing down on me to wash it away. For a moment I was tempted to try and ignore the temptation of pleasuring myself. If I'd managed to do so for the past five years, I didn't think a few more days would kill me. The trouble was there hadn't been a Harper Wilkinson inside my jail cell. In the flesh the woman was incredible, and I had her naked and chained. All my fantasies had just been answered at once, and my cock demanded to be sated. And damned if I didn't deserve a little something nice in my life once in a while.

My fingers began to move; pulling, tugging and yanking. They weren't gentle, nor did I need them to be. This was a visceral and primeval need, and I set myself a frantic, urgent pace. My other hand gripped a handful of my sopping wet hair and tugged my head back, so I could feel the spray raining down on my face. My hips thrust forward, my fingers tightening, squeezing brutally hard, almost a cruel death grip as I moved my fist back and forth. Gasping out loud I swallowed a mouthful of water, and then it was all over - nothing more than several long strings of semen running down the shower wall.

Two minutes and I was done. Two fucking minutes! That was the Harper Wilkinson effect, apparently. Then again, perhaps it was because I had denied myself for so long. Maybe it was time to put that to rights. *Don't go there, Brandt.*

Grabbing the shampoo, I lathered up my hair and the rest of my body and rinsed quickly in freezing water. The burning ache had gone, but in its place was a dull emptiness that gnawed at me from the inside out. I knew what that emptiness was and I refused to feed it.

Grabbing a towel, I wrapped it around my waist while I looked for my clothes. In two seconds flat I was dressed and ready for anything. Sprinting back downstairs, I poured myself a large glass of water and necked the thing back in one. Shit. Water. I hadn't given Harper any. I'd have to go down there again. Grinding my teeth together I left a bottle out on the kitchen counter to remind myself in an hour or so, because I couldn't go down now. She'd just had soup. It was unlikely she'd dehydrate any time soon.

Meanwhile, I whipped up a quick omelette and settled down in the office, which was nothing more than a small room furnished with an oak desk and a comfy leather chair complete with castors. Rocking back and forth on them, I deleted an enormous pile of junk mail from my Mac. I was going to need to reset my spam filters at some point because everything seemed to be getting through these days. After I'd done that I briefly scanned the ones that were left, and there weren't many. Most people had conveniently forgotten about my existence, and that was just fine by me. If I could crawl under the woodwork for a few months, or at least until Harper confessed all, that would make my life much easier. The last thing I needed right now was people prying into my affairs.

Thankfully, it seemed that wasn't going to be a problem. The emails before me were from my friend Liam, Blake - who was an ex-con like myself, the hire car company, and my parents' solicitor. Blake and the hire car company wanted money, so they were easily dealt with. Opening Liam's mail, I got a *where-the-hell-are-you, Bro?* This was followed by a rant that I had cut short his playtime the last time we were out together, and that we needed to make up for lost time soon. I good-naturedly told him that it wasn't my fault he'd passed out on me and that the next time I was back in town I would look him up.

Saving the solicitor's email until last, I wondered what my parents were up to now. They'd made it clear they didn't want to talk to me. I'd tried to call them twice since I'd been released, and each time my call had been ignored. I knew they'd received them because I'd left an answerphone message, so I guess that was that. I wasn't surprised to have been ostracised by them. They'd already told me that if I went to prison it was the last they would see of me. My father was climbing up the political career ladder, and the last thing he needed was a slur next to the family name. I suspect he'd figured out that if he distanced himself now, he wouldn't have to worry about any more of my fuck ups. If I was honest, the thought of never seeing my father again wasn't as bad as it could be. What ate at me daily was the fact I'd probably never see either my mother or brother again. That still stung like an open wound, and was going to fester for some time. Harper had taken away my family with her lies, and the chances were I would never get them back.

Sighing, I clicked on the solicitor's letter and wondered what delights he had in store for me. There was a bad feeling in the pit of my stomach, so I braced myself for the worst. Were they going to cut me off? So far they hadn't, but it was always a possibility. If they did, I would have to sell this place pretty quickly and find myself a job. That wouldn't be particularly easy with no college education and a criminal record.

Closing my eyes, I could feel a headache developing. While I didn't particularly want my parents' money, it was necessary at the moment. I would need it if I ever wanted to extract a confession from Harper. If they took it away, I'd have to fast-track what I was doing and hope for the best. She wouldn't suffer as I had, but perhaps that wasn't such a bad thing. I wasn't sure I had a taste for torture; well, anything that wasn't sexual, anyway.

Scanning through the first paragraph, which was mostly polite niceties, we got down to the real nitty-gritty in section three. John Simmons awkwardly confirmed that he would be the go-between for any correspondence between my family and me. That was nothing I hadn't expected. He then went on to explain that my parents were prepared to continue my generous allowance provided that I didn't try to visit or contact them, and providing one other demand was met.

This should be good, I thought. What now? They probably wanted me to move to Outer Mongolia, or perhaps Siberia. That way they could forget all about me and move on with their lives.

My eyes flickered through the text, trying to get to the bottom of the matter. Mr Simmons attempted to hedge for as long as he could, but eventually I discovered the purpose of his extremely long-winded letter. In the end, it wasn't any of the possibilities that had quickly flown through my head. Oh no. It was a whole lot worse. No moving to the ends of the earth for me, apparently. That would have been far too easy. No, it seemed my parents wanted me out of the way, but they were prepared to go a different route about it. Marriage.

By some chance of fate, Helena Foster-Lyle, my proposed bride-to-be before disaster struck, had also managed to get herself into a spot of bother. She'd been caught shop-lifting less than three months ago, and even though Mr Foster-Lyle had thrown an awful lot of money at the problem, Harrods had refused to let it go away. At least the woman shoplifted in style. She'd been caught with approximately ten thousand pounds worth of goods! Anyway, the crux of the matter was that now she was a less than perfect specimen of society they were looking to marry her off on the quiet. And seeing as I had no real marriage prospects, I might be the ideal candidate after all.

Helena was quite fond of me, could cook a decent five-course lunch, and didn't mind that I'd probably never hold down a job. We'd be given an estate in Hampshire, a joint allowance, and would be required to keep our noses clean for the foreseeable future. If I chose not to comply with my parents' wishes, then I would be cut off entirely and left to fend for myself. He gave me two days in which to respond to his message. Actions would be taken accordingly if the answer was no.

"You fucking bastards!" I yelled, so loud the walls around me vibrated. Slamming the lid of my laptop down I pushed the chair back violently, and almost spun around the room as the castors slid everywhere. Pushing the thing away from me I heard it crash against the wall, but I was already in the hallway. Desperately needing thinking time, I grabbed a jacket and headed outdoors.

The day was miserable and wet, but it suited my mood perfectly. Embracing the fine sheets of drizzle that swept over me in large waves, I stormed off into the woods. My trainers were ill-equipped to deal with the boggy terrain, but they would have to do. I was on the warpath, and there was no going back.

Marriage! How could they ask that of me? And through a solicitor for fuck's sake! Was that how little they really thought of me? Perhaps they believed that if I settled down and had a flock of children I'd keep my nose out of trouble. Yes, that's probably exactly what they thought. Who knows, after five years or so perhaps I could re-enter society, albeit on its fringes, and be verbally acknowledged every now again. What were they going to do for the wedding? Ship us out to Barbados and do it under cover of darkness? Then they could smuggle us back to England, dump us in the middle of nowhere and leave us to get on with things.

And if that weren't bad enough, Helena Foster-Lyle was about as attractive as your average poodle and had the temperament to match. The lady was cunning and sly. I had no idea what had possessed her to shoplift, but I sensed that deeper forces were at work here.

Once upon a time I might have been the dutiful son who did as his parents asked. Once upon a time, I might have married someone out of obligation and responsibility. That time had passed. Right now I didn't feel I owed my parents anything, much less a death sentence in the form of marriage. I'd almost rather go back to prison, and that was saying something. But where the hell did I go from here?

Look at the bigger picture. Calm down and try to think rationally. That was nearly impossible after the morning I'd just had with Harper. So much for her forty-eight hours of no human interaction. Might as well cross that trial off the list. *Concentrate. Don't go back down that road.*

Well, there was only one way forward that I could see at this moment in time. I would stall. Mr Simmons would get his reply just before his cut off date, and I would say 'yes'. That didn't mean I had any intention of marrying the girl, but weddings took time to plan, and it would give me some valuable breathing space in which to explore my options, such as they were. If I got Harper to confess all quickly, this charade would come to nothing. If my name could be cleared, I'd be back off the blacklist and... married to someone else. I swore. After five years of having nearly all my decisions made for me I would not tolerate someone forcing me into marriage. It might be difficult, but somehow I would learn to stand on my own two feet and take care of myself. Money wasn't everything, and it wouldn't rule me. I would make sure of that.

In the end I must have rambled through the woods for hours, twisting and turning through the tall Scot's pine trees, while trying to avoid their errant scratchy branches as they came out at all angles to attack me. These were interspersed by the occasional birch, rowan, and aspen, but even when combined they did little to keep the rain off my head. By the time I headed back to the house I was soaked through, and the rain had even managed to make it past the collar of my jacket and drizzle down my neck.

Safe to say I was thoroughly annoyed by the day's events, and when I spied the bottle of water I'd left on the counter to take to Harper, I cursed. As much as I didn't want to go down there, I couldn't leave her without water. So shrugging off my jacket, I quickly changed my soggy T-shirt and headed back downstairs.

My mood had deteriorated from dark to black. It was now more important than ever that Harper started talking, so damned if I wasn't going to pull out all the stops to make my little canary sing. The woman had better brace herself because the devil himself was on her tail.

Chapter 19 - Harper

His footsteps woke me. I wasn't used to silence, having spent most of my life in London, and I found it completely unnerving. All these little noises now seemed like crashing cymbals to my ears, and wherever Brandt was concerned I never knew what to expect.

When he burst into the cellar his face was so dark it would have given a lump of coal a run for its money. Oh God, did he know I'd been sick? Was that why he was mad? Squirming back against the wall, with nowhere else to go, I watched as he rattled the key in the lock and burst through the door.

"Drink." He thrust a bottle of mineral water in my face and glowered down at me. I immediately obeyed. I was really thirsty now that my stomach had calmed down a little, and downed the whole bottle in seconds.

"What is that smell?" His face darkened further as he scanned the cell, his eyes finally coming to rest on the bucket beside the bed. There was a moment's silence before his eyes widened, his face curling into disbelief. The tension in the room upped several notches, and I watched him clench and then unclench his fists, which he held tightly at his waist. Cowering further, I waited for the eruption.

"You made yourself sick?" he asked me incredulously. "Why on earth would you do something like that? Do you like looking half-starved?" Slamming his fist into the wall beside my head I shrank in on myself. He was going to lose it. I didn't answer his question. I couldn't. I was too scared.

"Answer me, dammit!" His voice boomed around the walls, deafening my eardrums, but mine had frozen. I didn't even dare look up at him, although I knew he was looking down at me. I could feel his gaze searing through me. For some reason I was highly attuned to everything he did. Christ, whenever he walked into the room my skin prickled. Now all I could feel was fury, and it rippled off him in waves of malevolence. Should I beg him not to hurt me? Would it make any difference?

"So now that you have the chance to speak you choose to ignore me?" The question hung in the air, charged with rage and echoing inside my head. Yes, I could have told him that I didn't make myself sick, but would he listen to me? Unlikely. He'd already formed his own opinion. Besides, as I'd said, I couldn't have used my voice right now if my life depended on it. All I could do was wait, curled up tight in my blanket, and hope this didn't end the way I thought it would.

Holding my breath I tensed my body and waited. I would have bolted had I not been chained to the wall. And when his hand came down to grip my throat I swallowed tightly.

"Remember what I said I'd do if you defied me?" The fingers tightened, but they didn't cut off my air supply. He used his hand to push up my chin until I was forced to look at him. My eyes swam with tears. When one escaped its tremulous confines and trickled down my cheek his eyes were glued to it. He seemed fascinated. He scooped the droplet up and chased it all the way back to the corner of my eye. I shuddered.

"Do I look like a man you want to defy, Harper?" His voice was a deadly kind of quiet, and scared me much more than the earlier yelling. Still frozen into place, all I could do was stare at him in fear and shake my head.

"Stand up." His hand around my throat pulled me upright, and I had no choice but to obey. The blanket dropped from my body, leaving me naked and shivering. I had never felt so bereft in all my life. My legs were quivering like jelly as he walked me over to the far wall and I wondered what he was going to do to me. When my back was touching the wall he grabbed my cuffed hands and removed the chain that fastened them together. He then somehow managed to pin them above me, one by one, attaching them to metal loops embedded in the wall. When he had securely fastened them in a 'V' shape, he went to work on my feet.

The finished result was a wide and uncomfortable 'X' which left most of my body completely exposed. Rattling around in my chest, my heart was wondering whether to explode. Anxiety didn't even begin to describe the intense emotion that flooded me.

Leaving me hanging in more ways than one he then stormed from the room, leaving the door wide open as he charged up the stairs. Why had he left? What was he going to get? Something to hurt me with? Wriggling wildly in the restraints I tried my best to pull them from the wall, but neither the tough leather of the cuffs or the thick metal fastenings budged an inch. I was going nowhere.

I started screaming. I didn't expect anyone to come running, but it made me feel better to at least try. Anything was worth a shot. By the time he could be heard coming down the stairs again I was almost hoarse.

"Stop it or I'll gag you again." Brandt walked slowly towards me, carrying a small box under his arm. He began searching around in his pocket for something, and then pulled out the hated gag and waved it around menacingly.

That shut me up.

"Screaming won't do you any good. You earned this punishment, so you'll take it. If you want to avoid another you'd better be a good girl." Setting the box down on the floor and stuffing the gag back in his pocket, he came slowly towards me. The anger and violence of before had disappeared. In its place was cold hostility. It was even more unnerving. Biting my lip, to stop myself from pleading with him, I hung trembling, almost terrified of what his next move might be.

When his hand came up to gently caress the underside of my left breast, I jumped. Having expected pain, the pleasurable feel of his fingers against my naked flesh came as a shock. Standing in front of me, mere inches between us, the other hand rose to mirror the action on the right.

"You need to confess, Harper. I won't be responsible for my actions if you don't get yourself down to the station soon." His fingers fluttered around my nipples before his hands cupped and weighed each breast. Grinding my teeth I stayed silent, refusing to let a single gasp of pleasure past my lips. It annoyed him, and his touch hardened.

"If you stay, I'll make sure you endure everything I had to go through in prison, and more. As you might have guessed, I'm quite devious. You won't last more than a week under my roof. You have my personal guarantee. Turning yourself in will be far less painful."

If I went to a police station I'd put a ticking time bomb on my life, and my ending would be extremely nasty and messy. They'd make an example of me in order to send out a message to others. I'd rather take my chances with Brandt, any day. If we'd just been talking about years in prison, with no other consequences, then yes, I'd have been prepared to give him my confession. He deserved at least that much. Nothing was ever simple in my life, though.

A finger and thumb closed around each nipple and pinched tightly. "Do you want to hear about all the things that happened to me in prison? What do you think's going to happen to you if you stay here?" Grabbing hold of my shoulders he shook me. When he'd finished, and my eyeballs stopped bouncing around, I watched him as he leaned in towards me.

"Do you want to know how many times I've been jumped, Harper? How many times the bastards held me down, ripped my jumpsuit off and assaulted me? Or would you prefer to hear about when they tried to hurt me? Even though we're not allowed weapons in prison, that doesn't stop inmates from creating some of their own. Razor blades, toothbrushes, rusted steel from a bunk bed; anything they can get their hands on is sharpened and filed. When they weren't stabbing me, they entertained themselves by trying to strangle me. I've even been held down and fucking tattooed against my will. They love a pretty boy on the inside. It kinda helped that I was the rich kid without a clue. That made it far more entertaining for them. They also made a bet between themselves to see who would be the first to make me scream. Nice guys, huh? You want me to put you through all that? I don't think so. I guarantee you'll have an easier time of it on the inside, and you'll probably get less time than I did. All you have to do is flutter those eyelashes and shed a tear or two. Make up some cock and bull story as to why you did it. That's the easy way out, Harper. A nice detective, some quiet time all by yourself, and a clean conscience to boot. You owe me that, Harper. You owe me."

The words were bitten off violently and his sapphire eyes were nearly black. In this mood he terrified me, and the list of things he'd just threatened to do to me made my blood run cold. Was this what prison had done to him? Was this what I had done to him? Guilt ate at me. For some reason I thought he would have had a fairly easy time of it. His parents would have given him the best possible legal defence money could buy, and he would have spent most of his sentence in a low-security joint. What he was saying didn't match up with what I was hearing. It sounded like they had thrown the book at him and then made an example of him. This couldn't be true, could it? He'd just told me he'd been raped, and not once but several times. Oh my God. How was I going to live with myself now? Blinking just once, my mind lost in complete horror, another tear tracked down my cheek.

"I'm sorry," I whispered. "You're right. I do owe you." Taking a deep breath, I tried my best to keep my emotions in check. Trying not to think about what he had gone through, I looked straight at him and wondered what he would do next.

"Then you'll confess?" He tilted his head, a look of relief crossing his features as if he couldn't wait to be rid of me.

I shook my head, dashing those thoughts. "There is no way I'll confess. If that's your end goal, you may as well kill me now." I meant every word. I'd rather be killed by Brandt than the bastards my husband used to associate with. Brandt might have learned a few tricks in prison, but he had nothing on those guys.

His face hardened as all hope suddenly fled. Wrapping his fingers around my throat he pressed his thumb against my windpipe, waiting until I struggled for air. When I began panting he smiled.

"I don't want to kill you, Harper. That would be too easy. I want my confession, and you will give it to me. Sure, you might make it past a few days of intense torture, but there's no way you'll be able to take it all. You can't cope with what I'm about to throw at you. I know this because I only just managed to get out of that hole without killing myself. The only reason I didn't, was because of the injustice of it all. I told myself I'd live to see the day I brought you to your knees, and I mean that. One way or another, you will confess."

Picking up the small box, Brandt opened it in front of me to reveal a pile of wooden clothes pegs. My heart sank. I already had a rough idea of what he was going to do with them, and I knew with certainty that I wasn't going to like it.

"They don't look like much, do they?" He waved a peg around and smiled. "What possible harm could one little peg do?"

I already knew the answer to that question, but I wasn't going to risk opening my mouth. He was waiting for an excuse to gag me.

"They can be quite vicious when used properly. The pain starts slow, but builds to a beautiful crescendo when left for a few minutes or so. Of course, it depends where you put them, how long you leave them on for, and the method in which you choose to remove them. Normally, if you're a beginner, you might start on the inner arm, thigh, or nipple. Shall I demonstrate?"

Pulling out the innocuous looking peg he squeezed it until the jaws opened, and then with his finger and thumb grasped a section of my inner arm above my elbow. With one swift move he attached it there, and its mean bite sent a shockwave straight down to the parts that mattered. My face immediately went red.

"If I were a betting man, Little Thief, I'd almost say you like pain. Am I right?" He lifted my chin with his hand, and trying my best to keep my state of arousal a secret, I looked at him mutinously. I was damned if I'd say a word.

"You don't need to talk to me in order to confirm the matter. I can find out all by myself." Another peg attached to the soft skin of my upper arm before two followed on the opposite side. Heat pooled between my legs, and it was all I could do to stifle a moan.

"Hmm. Does Harper like pain? Is that why you defy me constantly? Perhaps you like being tossed over my lap and spanked?" He looked at me intently, as if trying to discern the answers to his questions from my facial expression. Careful to keep my features as neutral as I could I held his stare, but it wasn't easy with him almost breathing down my neck.

"Let's see if you're wet, shall we? Let's see if that body of yours is all hot and bothered at the thought of me playing with it." A single finger traced a path down my stomach, slowly meandering this way and that, before it reached my pubis, furrowing into the hair there, sliding down underneath me. I have never wanted to close my legs so badly. Each thigh trembled madly as the finger began to curve around my clit. Pressing gently he continued to stare at me, and I cursed myself when I felt my face flush. Brandt saw everything, of course. He

72

raised an eyebrow at me as his finger pulsed up and down on my clit and then he slid it forward. Gently teasing my entrance he pushed inside me a couple of times, before finally sliding it to the hilt and burying it inside me.

"So, it appears you are enjoying yourself, doesn't it?" Brandt chewed on his bottom lip and his gaze narrowed in on me. "I think we can do something about that, don't you, Little Thief?" Having no idea what he meant, I watched quietly as he withdrew his finger and then grabbed the box once more. This time he picked up a circular steel ring which had five wooden pegs attached by various lengths of steel wire.

"I call this the 'Ring of Pain'. Wanna guess where the five pegs go?"

I didn't.

"The first two are attached to each nipple, so I'd better get those nice and perky, hadn't I?" His hands immediately came up to my breasts, cupping them gently, while the pads of his thumbs ran lightly over my nipples. The soft abrasion of his calloused flesh running over mine made them instantly hard, and they strained madly for his touch. Closing my eyes, I wished my body didn't have to make everything so damn easy for him.

"Keep those eyes open, Harper." I got a little shake to make sure I did exactly as he said. "That's better. I want to see everything. I want desire, pain, fear, revulsion, and tears. I want everything you have to give, and what you don't give, I'll take." A clothes peg hovered over my straining nipple, and my eyes were drawn down to it.

"Look at me, Harper. Keep your eyes on me." Slowly my gaze returned upwards, and the anticipation of what was to come shone in my eyes.

"Such a greedy girl, aren't you? You're almost begging for this." The clothes peg slid down my body, another journey of coils, circles, and lines, running up and down before dipping between my legs to torment my clit. He wasn't doing it to pleasure me; he was doing it to torture me. He wanted all the parts that mattered nice and swollen, so his fiendish little pegs would hurt more. Brandt appeared to be a man who'd studied his craft in some depth.

Tilting my head, I tried to get my own back by examining him. Had he always been this dark? Was this kinky shit lurking in his head before he went to prison, or had he got a taste for it there? It seemed hard to marry up the old Brandt to the new. The old Brandt had been a joker, full of life, relatively innocent and mostly benign. The new Brandt was anything but. Mind you, if even half the stuff he'd told me had happened to him, I'd be bitter and twisted too. And what if everything he'd told me was true? What then?

"Brace yourself, Little Thief. The first one's coming for you."

That was all the warning I received before the vicious bite of the peg closed around my left nipple. The initial pain wasn't too bad, though. As the second peg came for my right I held my breath and tensed, and then it was all over. It might have been a little uncomfortable, but nothing I couldn't deal with - at the moment.

"If you think you can probably cope with this you'd be wrong, Harper. The initial burn is nothing to what you'll feel after they've been left on a few minutes, and when I take them off, well, I'll expect more tears."

Sucking in a deep breath, I saw that three more pegs dangled on the underside of the ring, and I had a feeling I knew where they were going. It appeared things were about to get worse before they got better.

"Oh, and by the way, the ones on your nipples will be nothing compared to the ones I place down here." His hand went between my legs and I immediately flinched, although no pain was forthcoming. His fingers were back, and they were sliding around my slippery flesh, teasing my little bud into life, making sure I was ripe and ready for torment. He needn't have bothered. I was already throbbing in need.

"Ready for this one, Harper?" I shook my head. I wasn't ready. I wasn't even remotely ready. It didn't make the slightest bit of difference though, because his hand was already in motion, grabbing the last three pegs on the ring and bringing them slowly downwards. The first one bit into my labia and I swear it wouldn't have hurt any more had a rabid animal bitten me. Before I had time to blink another one was pinned upon the other side, and the pain was really quite something.

"Ready for the last one? Have you figured out where it's going yet?" He waggled his eyebrows at me and squeezed the jaws of the last peg open. I didn't look at it. I kept my eyes on him and held my focus.

"How long are you going to leave them on?" I whispered. I figured if I had some kind of timeframe, maybe I could count away the seconds and stop myself from screaming the walls down.

"As long as it takes, Little Thief. I'll come back in ten minutes, and if you're not ready to talk we'll make it twenty. I'm in no rush, Sweetheart. I've got all day." With that, the last peg clamped down with a ferocity that made me gasp. I think I stared at him in horror for a moment, while he watched me with obvious amusement.

"A little more pain than you bargained for? You just let me know when you're ready to go to the police station. See you in ten." With that he gave me a cheery wave and sauntered lazily back up the stairs.

Counting to sixty, I somehow managed to hold my jaw firm against the howl of anguish that wanted to escape. There was no way I wanted Brandt to hear me. Only when I was confident he was out of earshot did I let forth a wail of absolute anguish. The pain was unbearable. Ten minutes was going to seem like a lifetime, and he'd threatened to leave me here until I confessed.

The only thought that could keep me sane right now was escape. I would get out of here. One way or another, he would eventually let his guard down and I would be gone. Until then I would have to be strong. This was only temporary. It couldn't last forever.

Disappearing inside myself I wished, not for the first time, that I had never met my husband. If I hadn't, my life might have been almost pleasant.

74

Chapter 20 - Brandt

Waiting at the top of the stairs, I listened very carefully. Call me sick and twisted, but I wanted to hear her screams. I needed some indication that she would crack, and sooner rather than later. The alternative didn't bear thinking about. As the seconds ticked by, each one quieter than the last, I began to wonder if the woman was made of sterner stuff than I thought. The kind of pain I'd just thrown at her was pretty miserable, and she should have been wailing and howling in fairly short order.

Finally I heard it. A long moan of misery lit up the dark room, echoing around the walls. Breathing in a sigh of relief, I relaxed. She was human after all, and she would fall. I just had to be patient. In no time at all I would be back home with my family. *Being married off to someone.* But without the prison tag hanging around my neck, perhaps they'd be more prepared to negotiate. There was always the chance I could finish my studies and somehow manage to get a decent job. Could I ever forgive my parents, though? They'd not once believed I was innocent. My pleas had fallen on deaf ears, and the look on my father's face as he realised what my incarceration had meant for his career told me everything I needed to know. I was a long way down the list of his priorities. Perhaps it was time to stand on my own two feet, one way or another.

But it didn't change anything. I still needed that confession. Why was Harper holding out on me? Was it the fear of going to prison? After what I'd just threatened her with I'd have been running towards the nearest police station. Besides, she'd be with women, in a low security joint. She'd have a breeze of a sentence compared to what I got, which was mostly down to my father. The asshole had a mountain of money, but when it came down to helping one of his sons with their legal battles, he had completely disowned me. I was left at the mercy of legal aid and a brand new employee who was so nervous he stuttered through the whole hearing. Needless to say, it had not gone well in court. Harper would be fine.

Rechecking my emails and cell, it was a relief to find that nothing new had happened. I didn't think my life could get any worse right now, but I didn't want to bet on it. Looking down at my watch, I realised that eight minutes had already passed since I'd been down with her, and it was time to go and see if she wanted to confess. My body was already pulsing with adrenaline, and I swear I'd have fucked anything in sight given half a chance, but that was not how it was going down. I would keep my distance. I would convince Harper Wilkinson that I meant business, and as soon as the opportunity presented itself I would get the hell out of here.

What will you do if she doesn't confess? It wasn't a question I had considered. If she didn't confess, I was going to be in trouble. While I'd threatened her with five years here, judging by the recent email I'd received that wasn't going to be an option. There was no way I could let her go, either. What if she ran back to the police and accused me of kidnapping? What then? I'd go straight back to jail. For all my thoughts of revenge, I hadn't considered the consequences of my actions very carefully.

Approaching the stairs to the cellar, I heard her sobs long before I actually saw her. The sound was both beautiful and horrific at the same time. A part of me never wanted to hurt her ever again, and the other part wanted to tear her limb from limb. The constant push and pull of emotions rattling through me was unsettling. I needed to focus and be clear on exactly what I wanted from her - except I wasn't sure what that was any more.

When I entered the cell her face was a mess. It was clear she'd been crying for most of the ten minutes I'd been absent because her face was a swollen, blotchy mess. Speaking of swollen, all the parts under my vicious wooden pegs were extremely red and swelling rather nicely. A fierce rush of desire shot through my body, and I had to stop walking for a moment in order to get myself together. It annoyed me. I didn't want to feel a thing where Harper Wilkinson was concerned, but my body felt differently.

Ignoring the thickening cock in my pants, I finished walking the last few steps inside the cell, until I was directly in front of her once more.

Lifting her chin with my finger, I raised her face until her eyes were level with mine. Then, because I couldn't resist them, I kissed her tears. Gently pressing my lips to her face over and over again, I didn't stop until I had mopped them all up.

"Anything you want to say, Little Thief?"

"P-please take them off me," she pleaded. Struggling madly in her cuffs for a moment, she eventually let her hands fall limp in defeat.

"That kind of pain is a bitch, isn't it? Although it's still not the same as being stabbed, take it from me."

"Take them off me," she wailed, and we were back to struggling again.

"Not until you give me what I want," I said, folding my arms across my chest. "You know what that is, Harper. Are we off to the police station or not?" I raised my eyebrow at her and felt sure she would say yes. It was obvious she wouldn't be able to take much more of this. As I waited patiently for my answer yet more tears squeezed from her eyes. They ran in rivulets down her face, splashing quietly to the floor below.

"No." Her voice was shaky, but the word was clear.

"No?" I had to repeat her answer to make sure I'd heard her correctly.

"No," she repeated.

"You want me to leave you here for another ten minutes?" I asked incredulously.

"If that's what it takes to get the message through to you, yes. I'm not going to the police station. I will not confess. No matter what type of pain you put me through, it's..."

"Silence!" I yelled. In less than three seconds I had gone from smug to furious. What was this woman trying to prove? "Fine, have it your way," I snarled. Turning around I began walking away from her. Another ten minutes would be sure to do the trick. She could only fight me for so long.

"Don't leave me like this," she wailed.

Spinning around to face her once more, I thought I'd leave her with a parting shot. "Just so you know, that ring comes off in one go. I get to pull it, nice and slow, until all of the five pegs are torn from your body. If you think the pain is bad now, you haven't seen anything yet. Sure you won't change your mind?" There was a single, determined shake of her head and that was all I needed to make sure I got the hell out of there, and fast.

The next ten minutes were spent pacing from one end of the house to the other. One minute I wanted to hear her scream, and in the next I couldn't think of anything worse. Where was my head at? I'm sure I didn't know. Having geared myself up for success, I decided I'd better prepare myself for defeat.

Running a shaking hand through my hair, I then massaged my neck, trying to ease some of the tightness there. This problem would go away. It would. I just needed to find the right incentive, and Harper would disappear from my life almost as if she had never entered it. *You keep telling yourself that, asshole.*

Pacing back towards the bathroom, I rifled through the medicine cabinet until I found the supply of birth control pills I'd ordered. Popping one out of the blister pack I closed my finger and thumb around the little white tablet. I shouldn't need to give her these. The woman was off limits, and I should be able to rely on myself to stay away from her. The truth was, I didn't trust myself one little bit around Harper. Even tearstained and drenched in sweat the woman was utterly stunning. Those big sable eyes of hers were my undoing. Her irises were ringed with shades of deep chocolate brown and vivid orange, and they were so expressive. She wore every thought on her face for the world to see. How could someone like that lie so expertly to a judge? I'd have put money on the fact that she'd have lost it. Mind you, I seemed to be underestimating her every step of the way.

Looking down at my watch, I was surprised to find that nine minutes had already passed. I didn't dare leave the clamps on for any longer than twenty minutes, so I began marching my way back to the cellar. I reached the old oak door long before I was prepared to go down the steps, but I had done the deed and now I needed to finish it.

My journey down should have met with lots of noise, but the opposite was true. Her sobs of distress were quieter now, and much more irregular than they had been before. That gave me reason to worry. Something wasn't right. Running down the last few steps, I burst into the room to find her head hanging down towards her chest, and it was clear she was going in and out of consciousness. Oh shit. I needed to get her horizontal and fast. Reaching for the keychain in my pocket I undid the locks on her wrists as fast as my shaking hands would allow, and let her body lean into my back whilst loosening her ankles. Carrying her over to the bed and lying her down, I reached for the half-finished water bottle beside it and pressed it to her lips.

"Drink."

Her earlier bout of sickness had cost her more than I thought, and if I'd been thinking clearly I'd have realised she hadn't drunk much at all in the last few days. I need to get water down her - lots of water.

"Harper, stay with me," I said, patting her cheek repeatedly as I wrapped her back in the blanket. It was no use, her eyes kept fluttering shut and her body was limp in my arms. Cradling her tightly to my chest, I grabbed the water bottle and rushed back upstairs. I didn't stop running until we reached the bedroom, where I deposited her quickly under a thick quilt. When she was back in the land of the living I'd run her a hot bath, but that would be too dangerous at this moment in time. Right now I needed to get her warm and free of pain, and the easiest way to do it would be to remove the clamps quickly. This wasn't going to be the kindest way to take them off, but speed was more important. Grabbing the ring I yanked. That caught her attention in reasonably short order.

Her eyes shot open, her fingers grabbed the edges of the duvet, and she made a loud keening sound that seemed to go on forever. I let her get it out of her system. Things weren't going to feel very pleasant for a few minutes, but she'd get over it. At least she was wide awake now.

"Drink." Raising the bottle to her lips, I lifted her up and supported the back of her neck. Pouring the water down her throat she didn't have much choice but to start swallowing quickly. When she'd drained the bottle I let out a long tired sigh.

"Thank you," she whispered.

"For the intense pain you're undergoing right now, or the water?"

"Very funny," she croaked, wiping a stray curl away from her soaked forehead. All that vomiting, sweating and crying had made her severely dehydrated, and I needed to get some fluids into her.

"How do you feel?" It was a stupid question, but it seemed like the right thing to ask.

"Oh, absolutely marvellous. Some bastard has just used me for a clothesline, and he left me hanging for ages." The sarcasm that dripped from her voice made my lips twitch.

"Nice to see you haven't lost your sense of humour," I remarked dryly, wiping a strand of hair away from her cheek.

"Nope, just the contents of my stomach. Everything else is just about in working order, though I could probably do with some more water."

There was no fear in Harper's eyes now. We'd gone past that. Although I was sure it would be back at some point, it wouldn't be resurfacing again today. She'd been through enough. I couldn't push any more without the risk of injuring her, and I wasn't about to play with her life.

"I'll go get some and then I'll come back and run a bath for you." She nodded. "Promise me you won't get up to mischief while I'm gone," I said, looking over my shoulder just before I went through the door. She nodded again, and I walked away, smiling to myself. The woman absolutely would get up to mischief, but I would have the last laugh.

Chapter 21 - Brandt

As I went downstairs to get another bottle of water, I wondered if Harper would try to run. As she hadn't been restrained in any way she might take the opportunity to bolt. Somehow, I didn't think so. She looked exhausted for starters, and by the time she'd looked around for something to wear she'd catch me coming back up the stairs. Little did she know, there was no escape route out of this house without a car, and that was safely locked up in the garage. The key to that car was in a combination safe, and the four-figure code to unlock it would take a while to figure out. She had lots of fun and games to look forward to.

On the way back to the room I walked very quietly, listening carefully for any noise that might indicate she was up to no good. The landing was quiet, and the door was still shut, exactly the way I had left it. So far, so good.

When my hand reached out for the patterned ceramic doorknob, I paused. Were there any weapons she could use against me in the room? Had she found time to go to my room and get something? It would make sense to prepare myself for the worst. If someone was keeping me captive, I know what I would have done. Setting the bottle of water down beside me, I took a deep breath and braced myself to go inside.

Standing back, I opened the door quickly. Finding nothing barring my entrance I stood smartly to the left and flung it shut, and sure enough, there was Harper to my right brandishing a candlestick and coming right at me. I had just enough time to get my forearm in front of my face before the massive bronze thing came flying at me. Thankfully she didn't swing it as hard as I anticipated, and although it hurt it wouldn't leave any permanent damage.

Wrestling the stick off her and throwing it to the other side of the room, I grabbed a handful of her hair and dragged her back over to the bed. She kicked and screamed the whole way. I was not amused, and I let her know it by laying my entire body weight on top of hers. Her nails raked into my skin, tore my T-shirt and probably managed to draw blood before lack of breath finally made her calm down.

"Get off me," she whispered. She couldn't yell, because she didn't have enough air in her lungs for the job.

"No." Lying like a dead weight on top of her I held her wrists above her head and waited for her to stop struggling.

"Get off me." She tried to push up with her hips, hoping to dislodge me, but I was far too heavy for that. After another couple of feeble attempts I eventually grew tired of her efforts.

"That shit turns me the hell on, Harper. Keep going and we might have some fun together very shortly." My erection was pressed tightly into her stomach, so she knew I wasn't kidding, and funnily enough the struggling stopped reasonably quickly. As much as I might turn her on, she wasn't keen to hop into bed with me yet, and that suited me just fine.

"Please, get off me. I'm sorry." Her voice was barely audible, and I could see on her face the grand effort required to pronounce those six small words.

"Are you finding it difficult to breathe?" I asked innocently. Her eyes darkened beautifully, the orange flecks igniting as she struggled against me once more. I knew I was goading her, but I was desperate to punish her and she gave me exactly the excuse I needed to unleash some of the violent storm contained within me.

Swooping down to kiss her, my mouth crashed into hers. Most people think of kisses as sweet, soft, delicate and sensual. Mine was none of those things. As I lunged down for her face she turned to avoid me, but not fast enough. My lips locked with hers and when she initially tried to deny me entrance to her mouth, I bit her. The bite wasn't hard enough to draw blood, but it did make her gasp, and that was all I needed to fight my way inside her.

Repeatedly slamming her wrists into the bed as she tried to break free, I let my tongue duel with hers, grinding my body into the soft, naked flesh beneath me. My lips were hard and brutal. They stole far more than they gave, and they kept coming back for more. Harper had no choice but to give in. There was no other option. Letting my fingers curl in her hair, I pressed her closer to me, as if I couldn't get enough of her. Then I tried to suck all the air out of her body, repeatedly stroking, flicking and tormenting her velvety soft tongue. She tasted divine. Having imagined this scenario in my head many times, the reality was even better than I'd hoped for. The hairs on the back of my neck stood on end, my pulse went into overdrive, and all the parts that mattered filled with blood and stood proudly to attention.

While her body was still rigid beneath me, I continued to pour fuel on the fire. Leaving her lips for a few seconds I kissed and suckled at her neck, before returning to her blood-red swollen lips, because I couldn't stay away from them. I wanted to eat her up and swallow her whole.

The minute she gave in to me I wanted to rejoice in my victory. When her neck relaxed into the down-filled pillow and her body began to soften beneath me, all I wanted to do was take more. Inserting a leg between her thighs, I spread them wide beneath me, and my hand came down between us to stroke her sex. Her clit was still beautifully engorged from the clothes peg, and she was so sensitive she nearly shot off the bed when I merely scraped my fingernails across her.

I pulled my lips away just long enough to utter, "Does it hurt?" Not overly worried about the answer, I drew my fingers away and began massaging her inner thigh. Kissing a path down her neck and then her breasts, I began to suckle upon her distended nipples, tormenting them with my lips and teeth. Just when I was sure she wasn't going to answer, she surprised me by grabbing my head in her hands and yanking it upwards.

"Yes," she said, enunciating the word very carefully. "Yes, it hurts, but whatever you do don't stop." She then let me go, but not before I'd seen the feral look in her eyes.

"You like pain," I added needlessly because I'd already figured that out.

"Fuck off," she groaned, "you're a sick bastard." She tried to get herself out from under me, but I was having none of it.

"You got that much right." I began stroking her slit with my fingers, a teasing caress, while I ground my cock into her thigh. The urge to bury myself in her was so strong all I wanted to do was rip my clothes off and dive in. No, I told myself sternly. That would be a terrible idea. My cock disagreed.

"I want to taste you, Harper. I want to put my tongue inside you, and I want to play with your clit. Open your legs." I waited to see if she would obey. She did, with barely a moment's hesitation, but mostly because she was so revved up she was about to burst.

Dipping my head between her thighs, I was surprised when she leaned forward to put her hands on my shoulders, stopping me.

"You want my tongue on your clit?"

She nodded, but her hands didn't move.

"So what's the problem?"

She looked up at me, her small pink tongue worrying away at the corner of her lips. For a moment I wondered if she would speak. The added pressure of my gaze finally inspired her.

"I want you naked. I want to see you, Brandt. Let me see you." She scrabbled at the torn neck of my T-shirt, but she didn't have the necessary leverage to get it over my head, so I did the job for her. I had no problem with being naked.

"Better?" As I said the word I watched her mouth form a large 'O' as she saw the mass of ink wrapping itself around my body. It isn't the kind of thing you see every day, but I'm so used to it I barely notice. The first tattoo I'd ever had was a result of a prison brawl gone wrong. I remember the boys holding me down, laughing as I almost cried with pain when the needle kept entering my flesh, over and over again. At the time I couldn't understand why it hurt so much. Later I discovered that inside the back of the knee was one of the most painful places to get tattooed, but I hadn't known that at the time. Four of the bastards held me down while they worked on me, and I thought my life was about to end. That was my first tattoo, but it certainly wasn't my last.

The boys got a taste for torturing me, and after that it became a regular occurrence until I learnt to take care of myself. Before my five years was up, I would learn how to make my own tattoo gun using a Walkman, guitar strings, nail clippers and a biro. This wasn't for my own personal use; it was to get my own back.

"Oh my God. How long did that take? Did you have it done while in prison?" Harper was still staring open-mouthed at my torso. If I'd suddenly come down to earth from outer space, I don't think she could have stared any harder.

My eyes pinned hers, before I said, "You find yourself with quite a bit of time to kill behind bars, Little Thief." Pushing her back down to the bed, I cut short her viewing time. I hadn't agreed to her request because I wanted her eyes all over me, I'd agreed because I wanted to feel her soft, smooth skin beneath mine. Placing my palm flat across her stomach, I held her down as my head began to examine the damage the clothes pegs had wrought. The result was one bright red, thickly swollen clit that appeared to be visibly pulsing with need. It was a fucking fantastic sight. When coupled with the fact she was so wet she was seeping onto the sheets below, I could have climaxed there and then, but I didn't. This wasn't about me. I needed to remember that.

Running a tongue down the side of her labia, she nearly took my head off as she shot up into the air. As far as foreplay went I'd give the clothes pegs nine out of ten.

Pushing her stomach with my hand, I growled. "Stay down, woman." I didn't give her any further chance to object, because my mouth clamped over her clit and that seemed to take all the air out of her sails, for a moment. I say for a moment because when I started moving my tongue all hell broke loose.

For such a small lady she was surprisingly strong. It took two hands to hold her down while I went to work. I suckled, I licked, I flicked and I nibbled. She fought my attentions at first, and I think she already knew what I intended to do, but it didn't stop her from eventually relaxing into me, her body going limp with desire and need. When she'd calmed down enough to lie still, I used my thumbs to spread her sex wide so my tongue had better access to all the places I wanted to go. Caressing her most intimate parts with my tongue and lips, she was writhing beneath me in no time. The pegs had done their work.

"Harder, faster, please Brandt," she moaned. I felt her fingers dive into my hair, and then gentle pressure on my head as if directing me to do as she asked. But she wasn't the one in control; I was. My tongue unleashed just enough pressure to titillate, but not enough for anything else. In less than three minutes I had her begging, and in four I had her almost sobbing with need. Pulling away and wiping a slow hand across my lips, I smiled at her.

"That was for coming at me with a candlestick," I said softly. "We'll address trying to escape in the bath." Her eyes widened in fury when she realised I wasn't going to continue, and her palm flew at me. A woman scorned is a truly amazing sight, and Harper's eyes went almost amber as they flashed fire and brimstone at me.

My arm shot out to grab her wrist before it had a chance to connect with my face and I then twisted it around, putting plenty of pressure on it. She gasped, tears of pain springing to her eyes. The tears didn't mask the desire still lurking there, they just emphasised it, and I wanted to fling her back on the bed and finish what I'd started. But I knew why I couldn't do that. The birth control pill. She still hadn't taken it. I wondered if it was still in my pocket. I'd check in a minute.

"Say sorry." My voice was clipped and my eyes dull with indifference. The pressure on her arm was all I would need for my apology.

"Fuck you," she spat. It wasn't a particularly intelligent move, as I just twisted her arm further and further until she screamed.

"Stop! I'm sorry. I'm sorry," she sobbed. It's amazing how quickly you can get someone to do something under intense pain. Evil memories of being held down and stripped surfaced, but I banished them to the back of my mind. This was not the time to dwell on the past.

"Put a couple of pillows behind your back and get ready to drink that bottle of water we were speaking about earlier," I said brusquely. Striding towards the door, I grabbed the bottle and searched around my jeans pocket for the tiny tablet I had forgotten to give her earlier. When I'd found her unconscious back in the cellar, I'd shoved it there for safekeeping and nearly forgot all about it. Pulling it free, I held it securely between my finger and thumb. Seriously, could the manufacturers have made them any smaller? If I dropped the thing it was a goner.

"Stick out your tongue." I passed the water to her.

Taking the bottle, she shook her head. "I'm not taking any more tablets unless I know what they are," she said firmly. Considering all that had happened, the girl had some considerable spunk.

"You'll take whatever I tell you, whenever I tell you to unless you want to face the consequences. I'm more than happy to hold you down and go another couple of rounds. Wanna try me?"

When she finally did stick her tongue out at me, she did so in the way of a little child, her eyes glazed with anger. That suited me just fine. Handing her the tiny white pill, I watched carefully as she took it with several slugs of water.

"Open." It was almost impossible that she'd be able to fake the act of swallowing, but I wanted to make sure, and I wasn't prepared to take any chances.

She looked at me sourly but did as told. The pill was nowhere to be seen. One less problem to worry about.

"Drink the rest of the bottle. Then I'll run you a bath. If you're a good girl I can play nice every once in a while." Waiting to see what she would do, I folded my arms across my chest. If she were stupid enough to misbehave she'd pay the consequences, but I figured she'd probably been through enough today.

Harper weighed up her options. I could see her eyes shooting this way and that as she thought about it. Wanting desperately to defy me, it took her a few moments to figure out that was not an option.

"My spanking hand feels all tingly, Harper." I held up my right hand and waggled it, to push the message home.

"You can't keep me here against my will," she said defiantly.

"Says who?" This should be an interesting conversation.

"One false move and that's all it will take to put you back inside. You'll need eyes in the back of your head every step of the way. What about your family? How will you leave me if you need to visit them? Shop for groceries? See your friends? What will you do if I escape and tell the police what you've done?"

My eyes took on a glazed, and decidedly bored look. This was the game she wanted to play? Really?

"What I've done? Let's talk about what you've done. What if I tell the police exactly what you've done?"

"They won't believe you," she insisted. "That's why you've been inside for the last five years. It's your word against mine."

"And that's exactly why we're here. We're going to change that, Little Thief." I smiled darkly. "At the moment you think you're strong. I'm here to tell you you're wrong. Now drink the fucking water, before I make you drink it, and believe me when I say that you will not like my methods." Fury wanted to consume me at her defiance, but I kept my calm. She would do exactly as I asked, one way or another, and if she wanted to do it the unpleasant way, that was her problem.

"Then go ahead and make me, asshole!" Throwing her hands up in the air, she let the large bottle of water drop from her hands. She didn't flinch when it bounced to the wooden floor below; just stared straight back at me. If I were a betting man, I'd say she was frustrated and searching for more pain. But that wasn't going to work this time. If she thought she could play me, she was about to be disappointed.

Walking around to the other side of the bed, I snatched the bottle back up from the floor and then grabbed hold of her hand. Yanking hard, I hauled her from the bed and marched her into the ensuite.

"Sit." I indicated the pine toilet seat near the bath. When she remained uncooperative I said, "Want me to dislocate the other shoulder after all?" That sentence did the trick. She sat down woodenly, but the look on her face was murderous. Too bad. I held all the cards in this relationship, and she would learn to obey me. Turning on the crosshead taps, I made short work of filling up the tub. She remained silent as she sat there, and that suited me just fine. The time for talking was over. I kept my face studiously occupied with the rising level of water, but I kept one eye on her the whole time.

When the tub was full I simply beckoned her over. Surprisingly enough, she managed to follow that instruction. Climbing into the bath, she sunk into its depths gracefully and for a moment, she closed her eyes.

I figured she was trying to block me out from the scene, but it wasn't going to work. Clearing my throat, I decided I'd try and be civil one last time.

"Are you going to drink this water?" I tapped the bottle with my index finger. She opened one eye in acknowledgement. Her tongue darted out to lick the corner of her lips, and I suspected she was going to regret her next move.

"What are you going to do if I say no? Pour it down my throat?"

Twisting the top off the bottle, I licked my own lip in return and said, "Buckle your seatbelt, Harper. It looks like you're about to find out."

Chapter 22 - Brandt

Raising the bottle up to my lips, I took a swig of the water myself. Was I delaying the inevitable, or just letting the tension in the air creep up a notch or two? Christ if it rose any higher I'd go up in flames. It wasn't anything I couldn't handle. If I'd gone five years in prison without sex, what was another week between friends? A fucking long time, that's what it was.

It didn't help that Harper was staring at me again. Her eyes seemed to be glued to my body, and I was beginning to wish I'd never taken my shirt off. Inhaling a lungful of much needed air, I walked over to the bath and stared down at her for a moment. Time to turn the tables. As my cock stood rigidly to attention, I guess I could be glad I was still wearing my jeans.

"Seen enough?" The sarcasm in her voice would generally have elicited a response from me, but I was too focused on my task. Grabbing her chin with my right hand, I lifted it until she was staring at the ceiling, and before she knew what was happening, began pouring the bottle of water down upon her face. As suspected there was a moment of shocked stillness, and then all hell broke loose.

Water went in her mouth, down her nose, and all over her face. She couldn't avoid it; it was a two-litre bottle. She began splashing and struggling, but my grip held firm. I wasn't going to let go until the bottle was empty. One way or another the woman was going to learn that she couldn't defy me.

The harder she struggled the firmer my grip became, and I didn't release her until the last drop of water had dribbled out and the bottle was completely empty. She began making retching noises, trying to inhale great gasps of air whilst trying to expel a mass of water. It took her a minute or so of coughing and choking before she could direct her venom at me.

"And I'm supposed to believe that was something that happened to you in prison too?" Another blast of sarcasm so soon after the last was surprising, considering what had just happened. Was she trying to test my patience?

"As a matter of fact, it was. They didn't use a two-litre water bottle, but the effect was pretty much the same. Not very pleasant, is it?" Water was still dripping out of her nose and she had to sniff it back in order to answer me.

"I don't believe you. That kind of thing doesn't happen in a low-security prison. Why are you making all this stuff up? I get that you want to torture me, but I don't see why you have to lie about it." Her jaw stuck out indignantly, and the look in her eye was withering.

"Who told you I went to a low-security prison?" I sat on the toilet lid and passed her a white flannel. She'd better make good use of the wash facilities while she could; she wasn't getting another one for a while.

"Well, no one, but I assumed, what with your parents footing your legal bill—"

"Well you assumed wrong," I interrupted. "They disowned me as soon as the incident happened. My father's political career is far more important than little old me. They left me to my own devices, and I was allocated a legal aid lawyer fresh out of law school. The jury wasn't particularly impressed with his defence, and they were even less impressed with me. It gave the elderly judge the perfect excuse to make an example out of me."

"Oh my God," she whispered.

"Oh my God, indeed," I said tightly. "Especially as you get to look forward to everything that has happened to me in the last five years. Still sure you want to go the distance?"

She didn't answer me. Her face had gone white. She continued to wash with the flannel, moving it in the appropriate directions, but not paying any attention as to what she was doing. She appeared lost in thought.

When she'd finished soaping and rinsing herself, I grabbed a towel from the back of the door and held it up for her. She stood obediently and took it from me. Perhaps we were making progress after all.

"What now?" Her voice had lost its earlier anger. It was quiet and subdued, and her face looked tired. Damned if I wasn't feeling the same way. I think I just needed to distance myself from this mess. We'd been through enough today. I had no energy for anything else.

"Go pick up the duvet and we'll head back downstairs. I think that's enough for now. We'll get you another bottle of water, and this time you'd better drink it."

"Don't you mean blanket?" She gave me a confused look as she towelled herself down.

"If I meant blanket I would have said blanket." I sighed. "It's cold down there, and you won't get any sleep without a decent covering over you. Take the duvet. You've been through enough today."

A small smile ghosted around her lips. "You'll regret this leniency in the morning, you know."

"More than likely, so I'd hurry up and grab it before I change my mind." Turning her back to me, she did exactly that.

It took no time at all to get Harper back to her cell. She probably couldn't wait to be rid of me, so perhaps her eagerness to be caged was almost understandable. There was also the possibility that she just wanted a good night's sleep, and I could understand that, too. Some days I wondered if I'd ever sleep properly again. My dreams seemed to be permanently haunted by the last five years of my life. I wanted to lay them to rest, and I would, after the last obstacle in my way was dealt with.

"Drink the water." Handing her the bottle, I raised an eyebrow and waited to see if she'd obey.

Taking it, she twisted the cap off and then looked at me.

"Can I drink half now and the rest through the evening? I don't want to be sick again, and my stomach is still sore."

She had a good point. Replacing her old bucket with the new one I'd just brought, I nodded. She did as instructed, carefully replacing the cap and placing it within arm's reach of the bed. Handing her a small sandwich box similar to the one she'd been given yesterday evening, I watched her place it beside the bottle. Then she snuggled under the duvet and rolled on her side. She looked exhausted. While I knew I was to blame, I hadn't counted on her being this stubborn.

Hopefully she would learn her lesson this time. Unless she was stupid, she would not want to go through that ordeal again any time soon. As much as I didn't want her to fear me, I needed that from her. How else would I get her to confess?

"Is there anything else you need?" I had no idea why I asked the question, but now I had I felt curiously interested in the answer.

She rolled onto her back, and her head peeped up from under the duvet. "We need to talk. I know you don't want to, but until we do you'll be going around in circles. Goodnight, Brandt." She rolled away from me again.

What the hell did that mean? It felt decidedly strange to be dismissed from the inside of a prison cell. As much as I wanted to challenge her on that last statement, my need to get away from her was greater, so I bolted. I may have carefully locked the door to her cell, before walking quietly and calmly up the stairs, but I knew damn well I was running away.

After another shower, where I brought myself to climax not once, but three fucking times, I finally managed to take the edge off things. Why did Harper have such an effect on me? One minute I wanted to wring her neck, and in the next I wanted to stick my tongue down her throat. What was wrong with me? I needed to get a grip and focus on my end goal.

We needed to talk? The hell we did. I wouldn't trust a word that came out of her mouth, so what was the point? There would be no talking. I rolled my eyes heavenward and tried to think of something else other than Harper. It wasn't as easy as it should have been. Eventually I settled on getting myself some food. For some reason I was starving. Looking down at my watch, I realised it was just past seven o'clock. That would explain it, especially as I couldn't remember if I'd had lunch or not. Oh well. There was a steak in the freezer, and it would only take a few minutes to defrost it.

In no time at all I had an eight-ounce lump of meat defrosting in the microwave. While I was waiting for that I grabbed a glass of orange juice and sat at the table. It gave me some much-needed thinking time. The first thing I needed to do was fire off a reply to the solicitor. While I had no intention of marrying Ms Foster-Lyle, I did need to buy some time. That time would be used to make Harper squawk.

In a sick and twisted kind of way, I was glad she hadn't spilled the beans today. If she had, I'm pretty sure I would have been disappointed. Having spent years plotting and planning all the things I wanted to do to her when I got out, having her under my roof for just a few scant hours would have been deflating. It wasn't just revenge though, was it? If I was going to be honest with myself, I might as well admit that I desperately wanted to fuck her. Even while every brain cell I possessed told me it would be a really bad idea, that didn't stop me from craving it with every pore of my being. She was right; I was a sick bastard.

The steak was tough and unappetising, but I ate it anyway. I still hadn't managed to find any wine in the place, so I had a glass of whisky to finish it off. The afterburn seared a path down my throat, but it wasn't an unwelcome heat. Anything that made me feel alive was good because I'd been dead for far too long. Yeah, excuse the hyperbole, but it was true. That's how prison makes you feel. Your free will is pretty much extinguished the second you enter, and the only thing you really have any control over is when you get to piss. Everything else is dictated to you. When you eat, what you eat, when you get to exercise, when you sleep, what you read, where you read... It had nearly destroyed me.

Everyone needed something to live for when they got sent down. Some had a wife or family, some had a life they wanted to return to, or a business they'd created... but everyone had something or someone waiting for them on the other side. All I had was Harper. I'd become fixated on the woman, and it wasn't healthy. Did I need therapy? Probably. I also needed a whole heap of justice and several years of my life back. Would I get them? No. But I might get something else instead. Except I didn't know quite what that was, nor did I want to examine it too carefully.

Grinding the last bite of steak in my mouth, I swallowed it down with a finger of whisky. It made it almost palatable. Thankfully the French fries and green beans that accompanied it were perfectly edible, and I made the best of them. When I'd scraped my plate clean I headed back into the office and sank heavily into my chair. It was time to form some kind of reply to my parents' solicitor. Studying the ceiling above me I considered my options again, and realised, wearily, that I had none. I'd been neatly backed into a corner, and without their money I would quickly have to learn to fend for myself. This was something I was quite prepared to do, but not while Harper was under my roof. I couldn't trust her not to run off and spill the beans, nor would I be able to find anyone to look after her for any length of time. Well, someone who wouldn't ask questions, anyway. This meant I was between a rock and a hard place for the time being.

Flexing my fingers, I curled them into claws in frustration. It seemed like the whole world was against me, and I just needed a little bit of luck to get through this major hiccup and out the other side. Although it pained me to do so, I replied that I would be happy to meet Helena and discuss the situation. This way I hadn't actually lied, because I had no intention of marrying her. It wasn't unreasonable to take a little time to think about something as big as marriage, was it? I was pretty sure I'd manage to get to the bottom of Harper's lies by that time. All I wanted was a week or two. That would be more than enough time. How difficult could it be? I'd just have to meet the woman, wine and dine her, and pretend to be on board with the situation. If I could put that meeting off until Harper was out of my hair, then I might not even need to meet her at all. I'd play it by ear for now and wait to see what he came back with.

Thankfully the rest of my inbox was mostly junk, so I deleted all the rubbish and decided to finish up for the evening. My hand hovered on the lid of my laptop, pausing as my fingers bent down to touch the cover. Should I check in on Harper before I headed upstairs? How much trouble could she get into anyway? She'd be sleeping by now, and even if she wasn't, I'd locked the door. She was going nowhere fast. I urged my fingers to draw the lid closed. They did no such thing. Instead, they clicked on the camera app at the bottom of the screen, and I settled back down into my chair. *You're obsessed with the woman. This can only end badly.* My subconscious had a point, but I chose to ignore it.

When the footage began to stream on my laptop, I was pleased to see my first initial assessment had been correct. She was asleep, curled on her side, and the water bottle remained close by her bed. Nothing of interest to note there. I didn't shut down the laptop, though. Going back through the earlier footage I stared intently at the screen, desperately trying to figure the woman out. It wasn't a particularly interesting tale, especially as I'd left her chained to the wall, and I kept my finger on the rewind button for most of the time. Then just as I was about to lose interest, I saw something that made me pause. My eyes narrowed, and I hit fast-forward so I could watch it again in real time.

The reason I'd stopped the video was because I saw Harper vomiting into the bucket, but the video didn't play out as I expected. I assumed she'd stuck two fingers down her throat and made herself sick, but that didn't appear to be the case. She'd grabbed at the bucket with an urgency that suggested she'd been genuinely ill. I spent some more time staring at the ceiling. How did that work? I knew damn well I hadn't poisoned her, but perhaps the sandwich I'd made her eat had been left out too long. Shit. Now it was my turn to feel bad. Had I inadvertently given her food poisoning? No wait, it was freezing down there. It seemed unlikely - not impossible, but unlikely. Well, what other reason could there be? My brain cells tried to gather together some possibilities. She could be allergic to something I'd fed her, or she could be anorexic. If she were anorexic I'd probably overloaded her stomach.

I rewound the footage and observed her. She seemed uncomfortable nearly as soon as I'd left her. Her face looked strained, and her hand kept stroking her stomach as if she almost knew was what about to happen. I was still none the wiser to the reason behind her sickness, but I did know one thing. She hadn't made herself ill. I'd just spent most of the afternoon punishing her for something she hadn't done. Slamming the lid of the laptop shut, I put my hands over my eyes and sighed long and hard. I felt absurdly guilty. She'd tried to tell me, and I hadn't wanted to listen. *This is the woman who lied to put you behind bars for ten years.* Yes, but what if she was allergic to something? I could have killed her. I wanted to do many things to Harper Wilkinson, but I didn't want her death on my hands. She was right. We did need to talk. Perhaps not about the things she wanted to talk about, but tomorrow we'd sit down and have a chat.

Chapter 23 - Harper

For the first time in what felt like forever, I actually slept. It helped that my neck wasn't chained to the wall and that the duvet kept me tolerably warm. I probably got a decent eight hours sleep, and my usual nightmares seemed to have been beaten into submission. Perhaps that was because I was living with my own personal nightmare, though he didn't scare me nearly as much as my husband had. Mind you, it was early days yet. If he didn't get what he wanted, there was a good chance Brandt might go psycho on me. There was no way I could go another round with a madman. I'd had my fair share of that.

I needed to get out of here. Yeah, and how did I intend to go about that? Unless I suddenly developed superpowers that would allow me to bend iron bars, I was going nowhere fast. There was no chance of squeezing through them, either. As thin as I was, I wasn't that thin. I also knew there was little to no chance I could reason with him because to do that we'd need to talk and he wasn't ready for that. He might never be ready for that because the scars he wore plunged deeper every day.

Okay, so what other options did I have? Hiding under the duvet, I tried to rack my brains for anything useful. Brandt was unpredictable at best, but there was one thing I might be able to use. For all his threats, I didn't think he meant to kill me. I think he fully believed I'd take myself down to the local police station and exonerate him, provided he gave me a good enough incentive to do so. That meant that whatever he was dishing out would get progressively worse, day-by-day until I got to the point where I couldn't take any more. I didn't want to wait around for that to happen, which meant I had to be smarter than him, which was going to prove a challenge.

Curling deeper into the warm duvet, I let a couple of escape scenarios cross my mind. They were both long shots, and they would both rely on luck. That was the one thing I'd never had a lot of, so neither idea boded well, but I couldn't just lie here and wait for the monster to emerge. I needed to do something. It would help if I had a rough idea of where I was being held, and the whereabouts of the nearest house or road, but if I had to walk twenty or thirty miles to find it, then that's what I'd do. I needed to be strong, and I'd had a whole lot of experience with that.

Not for the first time I wondered if anyone would come looking for me. As I didn't have any family to speak of, there were only a few options. There was a slim chance the restaurant might have raised the alarm when I didn't show up for my last shift, but that was unlikely. I'd been there less than a week, and a waitress was easily replaced. They'd have better things to do with their time. Someone would be coming to look for me with regards to the arrears on my flat, but that could be months away. I also didn't fancy their chances of locating me, with virtually no paper trail. They might manage to trace me to Nottingham, but they'd get no further. Would they launch a manhunt when they found I was missing? Unlikely.

The last set of people were my husband's friends, who checked in on me from time to time. They were probably my only hope. When they found the flat vacant they'd start asking questions. They wouldn't go to the police, but they'd have their sources. It was possible they'd look for me. They'd want to protect their interests, and if they suspected Brandt had taken me, then they'd be doubly keen to get me out from under his nose. That would be making a deal with the devil, though. They were the very people I was happy to escape from. I did not want to go back to that life. My cold little cell was far preferable to that. It didn't take a genius to figure out that my prospects were looking bleak.

Closing my eyes once again, I wondered if I might be able to go back to sleep. There was no guarantee that Brandt would let me have the duvet for a second night, and I wanted to make the best of this little piece of luxury. As soon as the thought entered my head, I could hear the sound of footsteps. Immediately panicking, mostly because I hadn't eaten my evening meal, I wondered whether

I'd get away with pretending to be asleep. Remaining as still as a statue, I tried hard not to breathe as he unlocked the cell door.

"You can stop the act, Harper. I know you're awake. Did you sleep well?"

He peeled the duvet back from my face, and I blinked back up at him. "Do you care?" His face hardened, but it was a reasonable question. Why bother with pleasantries when you don't mean a word of them?

"Don't push me, Harper."

Sitting up on the hard bed, I stretched my arms over my head and yawned. My nipples peaked above the cover, but I refused to feel self-conscious. Brandt was the one who had taken away my clothes, and he clearly didn't feel uncomfortable about it, so why should I?

"Have you eaten your sandwich?" Oh God, we were back to that again. I'd fallen asleep before I'd even thought about eating, so I guessed I was going to be in trouble again.

Brandt held his hand out for the box he had given me, so I handed it to him and wondered how long it would take him to go from Mr Nice Guy to Mr Fucking Scary.

He looked at the contents for a long time. They weren't particularly exciting, so I guessed he was thinking about all the evil things he would do to me. I wanted to shrink under the duvet and disappear into the floor, but I held my ground. If he wanted to dish out pain, I could take it.

"Why don't you eat very much?" His eyes attached themselves to mine, and I found myself squirming. How did I answer that? The most reasonable explanation was because I couldn't afford to eat very much and was in debt up to my eyeballs. It wasn't something I wanted to share with him. He'd probably turn his nose up, and be relieved that his white trash suspicions about me were correct.

"You need to let me go. People will come looking for me." It was a lie, but he didn't need to know that.

"No one is coming for you. You have no family to speak of, and I don't think you made too many friends in Nottingham in the few days you were there."

"How do you know that?" I asked suspiciously.

"I have my sources. Now answer the question."

He sounded impatient. I didn't care. "What are you going to do if I don't?" I thought I might as well know what I was letting myself in for before I started lying.

"Why are reluctant to eat? Are you anorexic? Or is it because you're allergic to something?"

"If I made myself sick I'd be bulimic, not anorexic," I pointed out.

"I saw the footage. I know you didn't make yourself sick." He raised a single eyebrow as if encouraging me to continue. Damn. I'd forgotten about the cameras. I wondered how long he'd been watching me and why he would even want to. It must have been a very boring video. There wasn't exactly a lot of things to do down here.

Trying to change the subject, I said, "I drank the water. All of it. If you give me a few moments I'll try and eat the food too. My stomach can't take very much at a time, but in a week or two I'll be back to eating reasonably normally. If you're intending to keep feeding me." The last sentence was rather quiet. My head was elsewhere remembering when my husband had told me he thought I was getting fat. He pushed me up against the wall, yanked my top up over my breasts, and then stared at my stomach in disgust. He then basically starved me until I'd lost the five offending pounds that were bothering him. And I don't mean by feeding me soup and salad for a few weeks. It was water. Two weeks of nothing but water. I lost every single one of those pounds, and more besides. I also gotten the flu in the process.

"If I intend to keep feeding you? What sort of crazy question is that? If I wanted you dead you'd be dead already. I'm not a killer, Harper. You might have made me a monster, but I'm not a killer."

He looked furious for a minute, and his anger made him start pacing the small length of my cell. With his head focused on the floor I happily ogled his torso, clearly defined within a plain black T-shirt. For the one-hundredth time, I wondered why I was so fucked up. I should hate this man, or at the very least despise him. He'd kidnapped me, after all. Instead, I lusted after him. Especially after he'd cuffed me to the wall. This was madness. Complete and utter madness.

"Are you anorexic? I want a yes or no answer, else there'll be trouble." He drummed his fingers against the wall, frustrated that he couldn't figure me out.

"Not through choice, no." Alex, my husband, had probably cultivated the complex after a few years of emotional abuse. That was made doubly worse when he left me virtually penniless after his death. Those were yet more gems that I wasn't prepared to share just yet. There were some things I didn't want to talk about with anyone, and my late husband was one of them.

"What's that supposed to mean?" He looked perplexed with my answer, and I was happy enough to keep his mind running around in circles.

"It means that if you're patient with your torture plans, I'll eat. If you gradually increase the portion sizes, my stomach will learn to tolerate them. If you force me to eat, the chances are I'll be sick, and that will put us back to square one."

Brandt stopped pacing and sat heavily on the steel bed. Turning to face me he said, "I'm not a patient man, Harper. You stole too much from me. However, having said that, I'll back down on the food issue. There's nothing to be gained from making you sick and weak."

Tell that to my husband. Apparently I was much easier to control when I hadn't had a lot to eat.

Picking up the box he handed me a sandwich. "Small meals and often. Will that work?"

I nodded. Taking a mouthful of brown bread and peanut butter, I almost sighed. It was one of my favourites. Somehow I suspected my meal might be the highlight of my day.

When I'd finished chewing the first mouthful I asked, "When's the next torture session scheduled for?" I would probably regret my little quip later, but I've always hated long silences. They usually mean something bad is going to happen.

Brandt's head turned slowly, and he stared at me long and hard. "This isn't a joke. Do you find this situation funny? I sure as hell don't. My parents, the ones who aren't speaking to me because they think I'm a criminal, are currently trying to marry me off to ensure I do no further damage to the family reputation. The chain of events you set off for me seems to be spiralling out of control. No one gives a fuck what I want any more. They just want to control me, one way or another. Do you know how that feels?"

I did, but I wasn't about to tell him so.

"You've ruined my life in nearly every way that matters, and you want to make jokes about it?" His irises were getting bigger and darker, and his mouth was a vivid slash of angry red. Why did I always have to babble my way through tense situations? If I wanted to survive, I was going to have to learn to shut up.

"But that's not even the worst of it. Do you know what I want to steal from you above all else? Want me to tell you exactly what it is?"

No. I didn't want him to say another word, already knowing I wouldn't like this very much. My lips stayed firmly closed in response, but I knew that wouldn't stop him talking.

"I'm going to steal the same thing you stole from me, Little Thief. A little piece of your soul. When I'm finished with you, you'll be damaged goods. No one wants damaged goods in their life. When your soul is as blackened and tarred as mine, then, and only then, will I let you go. Remember those words. They're going to come back to haunt you. Now eat the fucking sandwich."

It now tasted like sawdust in my mouth, and I was almost afraid to look up at him for fear of what he was going to do next. Me and my stupid mouth. When I'd finished he handed me another of his white pills, and I swallowed it obediently. After I'd drunk my fill of water from the new bottle he gave me, he stood up. Walking over to my cell door, he held it open and motioned for me to go through.

"On your knees." He pointed to the floor, and my heart sank. It appeared we were back to square one. Obediently following his command, I reluctantly shrugged out of my warm duvet and dropped to the floor. When my knees hit the cold concrete I wanted to gasp out loud, but I stoppered the sound. I'd get used to it in a moment or two. Brandt walked round to the side of me and picked up the metal leash. Wrapping it around his hand, he yanked it firmly and began striding off. That was my cue to follow.

Crawling up the stone steps was slightly better than crawling down them, but only just. My knees were going to be black and blue if he expected me to keep up with him, and judging by the pull he exerted on the leash, he did.

"I fail to see what's funny about your situation, Harper. You don't get to see daylight, you don't get to wash, you don't get to drink, and you don't get to eat unless I allow it. Hell, you have a bucket for a toilet and a chain around your neck that's regularly embedded in the wall. Did I miss something somewhere?"

"No," I whispered, though I think only the floor heard me.

"Answer me!" He repeated it at twice the original volume, making my ears ring.

"No. I'm sorry." This time I made sure he heard me.

"Damn right you're sorry, but you're not sorry enough." We finally reached the top of the stairs and sunlight filtered through the windows, blinding me for a second. I faltered on my hands and knees, but he yanked me brutally forward. "Do you think I give a fuck about you, after what you've put me through? Do you think you'd be here if I did?"

I couldn't respond to that statement, mostly because he was pulling the chain so hard he was almost choking me. Not for the first time I wished I could have just kept my mouth shut. Brandt had murder written all over his face; this was probably not going to end well for me. I wasn't even sure I had the stamina to survive another one of his sessions so soon, but it wasn't like I had a choice. He would keep coming for me until I gave him what he wanted, or he grew bored of me. But we were a long way from him getting bored. If I wanted to survive this ordeal I needed to improve my game. If I didn't he was going to break me, and I couldn't be broken again. There are only so many times you can be glued back together.

Chapter 24 - Brandt

I was pretty sure I'd be up for liar of the year award soon. Having told Harper I didn't give a flying fuck about her, I saw the statement for a lie as soon as it exited my mouth. I did care about her - a lot more than I wanted to admit. And it wasn't just that I needed her underneath me. The obsession was developing into something more, and the closer I got to her, the more I wanted to keep my distance. There was some kind of pull between us that I couldn't control, and I didn't like it. As much as it excited and enthralled me, I knew it was dangerous. Harper Wilkinson was a viper and should be treated as such.

You should let her go.

No matter how many times that inner voice called to me, I refused to listen to it. Even though I knew what I was doing was wrong, I wasn't going to let this go until I got what I wanted. The trouble was I wasn't sure if I knew what that was. Every instinct told me to make her suffer, exactly as I had for the last few years. I wanted her pain, her tears, her cries and her screams. That's all I'd dreamed about. I needed to reduce her to the same turbulent mess that I had been; almost unable to function or communicate because life in prison had been so bad. I guess I wanted an eye for an eye, but hell, some of the stuff that happened behind bars no sane person should ever have to go through. But she'd see sense soon enough. When she realised I was deadly serious about carrying through my threat, she'd be hightailing it to the police station as fast as her legs could carry her. I hadn't planned on taking her to my playroom so soon, but events had conspired to make her quick confession extremely important.

Stopping outside a plain pine door, I placed my hand on the handle and looked down at my captive. "Are you ready for an exciting day, my Little Thief?" She looked anything but. Scared eyes popped out of her head, and I could see her chest heaving from the exertion of having followed me. She didn't answer, which was probably wise considering the mood I was in.

"Good." My hand slowly turned the handle and pushed the door open. "Ladies first," I said, dropping her leash and motioning her to go in. She looked up me with loathing but did as I asked. Well, until she saw what was in there. When her head had finished doing a slow rotation of the contents, she got to her feet and made a dash for the door.

Too late.

Slamming it behind me, I leant against it and gave her a lazy smile.

"Were you thinking of going somewhere?"

Her mouth opened wide, but then snapped shut. The look of loathing had turned to one of fear. Good. I could work with that.

"Did anyone give you permission to stand?" The imperious look I gave her let her know I meant business. She blinked at me, staring stupidly for a second before she got back down on all fours. The girl was learning.

"So, welcome to my playroom. Feel free to take a look." I gestured all around me, but she didn't seem too eager to take me up on my offer. Funny that. It might have been due to the fact that whips, crops, paddles and canes lined the ivory walls of my favourite little room, or it might have been due to the various array of restraints I had dotted all over the place. There was a lot of black leather; maybe she took exception to that. Then again, it could have been the spanking bench, the cage, or perhaps the vast number of sex toys on display. It could have been any one of these things, but it was more than likely all of them together, and I had to admit they could be a bit overwhelming if you weren't used to them.

Stepping forward and making sure I crowded out her personal space, I said, "You've played around a bit. Surely you've seen some of this stuff before." She was as still as a mouse in the middle of the room, and I wondered if she'd managed to take a breath yet. If I were her I'd get as much oxygen in as possible, because in a few minutes it would be very hard to come by.

When there was no response I decided to take matters into my own hands. Grabbing a black leather crop from the wall, I swished it in the air so she'd have some idea of what was coming, and then I let it loose on her ass. When the whip landed smartly on her left buttock she shot up as if stung. Her eyes turned to stare at me, and she wore a haunted look that was remarkably at odds with the flutter of desire I saw there. I think I was just beginning to realise that Harper Wilkinson was an utter enigma from start to finish.

"Pretty vicious little number, isn't it?" Her immediate reaction was to cast her eyes downwards towards the floor, and for some reason the action angered me rather than pleased me. I guess that on some level I wanted her to fight me so I could feel justified for putting her firmly in her place. But it didn't look like that was going to happen. Too bad, I was going through with this one way or

95

another. I needed that confession.

"What are you going to do to me?" The voice was barely audible, especially when directed at the floor, but I got the gist of her question.

"If I told you, Little Thief, it would spoil the fun of the little session I have planned for you. So I'm not letting you in on a single detail. In fact, I have a blindfold and gag here, and some earplugs that are going to ensure you won't know what's coming until it hits you - quite literally, as it happens. That should make the proceedings a whole lot more exciting, don't you think?"

"Don't do this. I'll be good. I'll stay still. I won't say a word. I promise." Harper crawled over to my feet and looked up at me pleadingly. I won't lie and say the sight didn't arouse me, but it certainly didn't encourage me to go easy on her. It was quite the opposite, in fact. I wanted to push her to the absolute limit and watch her shatter. And I think I needed to prove to myself that I could do it.

"There's no question you'll be good once I've tied you up. It's hard to be naughty without the use of your arms and legs." Her face immediately lost its colour; I could see the healthy pink hue draining away. She did not like the way today was shaping up one little bit, and that suited me just fine.

"Can we talk? Just for a moment. I'll only need five minutes to explain..."

"I don't want to hear it. Whatever you need to say, you can say to the police down at the station. Now do you want to beg me to go easy on you, or are we good to go?"

She clamped her lips tightly shut, which was exactly what I'd been hoping for. Whilst I fully intended to gag her, I didn't want to do so just yet. There was a list of things that needed to be done first. Besides, if I gagged her there would be no moans of excitement or cries of pain, and I found myself anxious to hear them.

Walking over to an ornate Victorian armoire that rose gracefully upon four curved legs and had cherubs flying atop its doors, I slid my hand along its smooth cream panels, which were expertly outlined in gold gilt. I knew her eyes would be glued to whatever I pulled out, so I prolonged the moment.

"What sort of blindfold would you like, Harper? Black rubber, plastic, leather, silk, velvet or just plain old cotton?" Slowly opening the creaky door, I waited to see if she would answer me.

"Please, Brandt. You don't need to do this..."

"You're wrong. I do need to do this, but there's something else. I *want* to do it. I want to hear you suffer. I want to hear as you beg for mercy. Each little whimper, sob or cry of pain will be mine. I own your body, and I intend to do exactly as I like with it, until I get what I want."

"You'll never get that." Her trademark look of defiance was back, but I had a bet with myself that it wouldn't be there long.

Scanning the shelves of the armoire for a blindfold, I found the one I was looking for. It was a thick, oversized, black leather version. Once I'd put it over her head she wouldn't be able to see a thing. Plucking it from the shelf, I advanced towards her. Her eyes quickly zoomed in on the offending item, and she began backing away from me.

"Could I have the cotton one, please?" Her voice had lost several decibels, and she wasn't anywhere near as sure of herself as she had been.

"Too late," I said, placing the thick blindfold over her eyes and fastening it tightly at the back of her head.

"Give me your hands." After a moment's hesitation she shakily placed them out in front of her. "The fear that's written all over your face, Harper. It has every right to be there. Did you think about me in prison? After you lied and went back home, sat in your cosy armchair and had a nice cup of tea, did you think about what you'd done to me?"

She hung her head. It was answer enough.

"I bet you didn't even give me a moment's thought, did you? You simply filed the incident away in the back of your mind and forgot all about me. You thought I'd be out of your hair for ten years, so there was no reason to worry, was there?" Striding back to the armoire I grabbed a pair of police-grade steel cuffs and squatted down to twist her arms behind her back, before fastening them around her wrists.

"You're wrong. I had to live with that guilt every day." Her voice was tremulous and timid, but she was so close to me that I heard every word. Her head rocked gently on her shoulders.

"I don't believe you," I said, but there was a part of me that wanted to. Falling under her spell would be so easy.

"It's true," she sniffed.

"Enough, or I'll gag you sooner than I was planning to." My voice was sharp and cut hers dead. And it had the intended effect. No further lies were forthcoming.

"Get up." Pulling her roughly to her feet I half dragged, half carried her to the spanking bench. Directing her body downward, I positioned her stomach at one end and used two soft, black nylon straps to fasten her waist and torso firmly onto it. This seemed to be the last straw for her. She began kicking out at me and screaming, giving me the fight I wanted, but far too late for it to be a challenge. Sighing, I grasped one leg and fastened it into the awaiting cuff at the bottom of the bench, and the other quickly followed suit.

She didn't stop yelling, so I needed to snap her out of it, else my eardrums would be ringing for the rest of the day. Picking up the crop I took a hard swing at her right buttock. It produced a shocked gasp of pain and silenced her for a second. Excellent.

"Be quiet. There'll be reason enough to yell and scream later, so you might as well wait until then. If you choose to continue making that awful racket I'll have to get the cane off the wall, and believe me when I say you won't like that very much."

My threat had the desired effect, and thankfully she shut up. So giving her no time to get her bearings, I figured I'd begin the session. The sooner we started the more chance I'd have of getting exactly what I wanted by the end of the day. I was so sure of myself, in fact, I could almost smell the scent of victory and we'd barely begun. Time to get to it.

Using my palms to warm her up, I began sliding them across her skin; a soft caress of flesh upon flesh. It seemed like a good idea to calm her down before the fun started, and truth be told, I just wanted to get my hands on her. She was the stuff of dreams, and I intended to get my fill. My fingers were drawn to her skin like a magnet, and the silky soft feel of her flesh was the sweetest aphrodisiac. It was almost uncanny that I'd spent so much time fantasising about her in prison that my touch felt entirely natural and practiced. I'm sure she didn't see it the same way, but that was her problem.

"Do you want to hear a little story, Harper?" I waited for a few moments, but it appeared her silent side was back. So smacking her left buttock I asked the question again. "Do you want to hear a little story?"

There was a cough and a sound as she cleared her throat, and then she spoke. "Not really, but I have a feeling you're going to tell me one anyway."

Smacking her right buttock, in part for her impertinence, but mostly just because I wanted to, I smiled.

"For once your instincts are entirely correct, so settle down for the ride, Little Thief." Caressing her body once again, from the top of her neck and shoulder blades, all the way down to her calf muscles, I began warming her up. Kneading and massaging her muscles I wanted to get her blood moving - to all the parts that mattered. It would give me something to concentrate on while telling her my sad tale.

"My first night in prison turned out to be disastrous. When I accidentally trod on my cellmate's framed photo of his wife and daughter, breaking the glass, he went bat-shit crazy. Pinning me down on the floor his fists crashed into me for half an hour while he tried his best to break any bones he could lay his hands on. Thankfully I was pretty flexible and he only succeeded in dislocating my arm before the correctional officers finally broke us up. Hurts like a bastard, doesn't it?"

Her lack of reply earned her four sharp swats of my hand, and I was about to go with five before she piped up with a response.

"Yes," she bit out, "but I suspect you're going to rival that kind of pain by the time you're finished with me."

Staring at her backside, which was beginning to take on the first hue of a rosy blush, it took a moment for me to answer. The sight was mesmerising, and I could have stared at it all day given half a chance.

"Ahh. So that's how you want to play? Tit for tat? Well I'm more than happy to go down that route." My hand delivered another four spanks around her backside and upper thighs before I paused to continue with my story.

"Where was I? Ah yes, so after that first day in prison, when I was limping along with a sling around my arm and a black eye, I was identified as an easy target. Funny that, huh? I was young, green, and had no clue how to defend myself. Sure I could throw a few punches around, but the rest of the guys knew how to do a lot more than that. They knew where to hit, and they made damn sure it hurt."

I gave her another few swats with my hand and then moved away, deciding I needed to find something a little stronger. Perhaps it was time for the paddle again. I went to the wall behind her to inspect my collection. Glancing back at her quivering body, I wondered how long it would take her to reach out and say something. Not very long, I suspected, but we'd see.

Now, which paddle to choose? I wanted something light and flexible, but which would still deliver a decent sting. Leather or silicone were my choices, and I decided to go with leather. There was a nice rectangular Knoppler design in front of me with a comfortably grooved handle, and I'd be able to wield it for hours in relative comfort. Not that I intended to. We had a lot to get through, so I couldn't drag my heels.

"What are you doing?"

Ah, there was the little voice I had been waiting for. It was a cross between a mouse and a nightingale; tremulous and timid. Harper was pretty sure she shouldn't be speaking, but nerves had taken over. The blindfold covering her eyes didn't help, and I daresay the restraints added a nice edge to things.

I decided not to answer her. Let's see how she liked a dose of the silent treatment for a change.

Picking up the paddle that had caught my attention, I tapped it against my hand experimentally. Then, to get a feel for what it would do, I smacked it hard against my thigh. Out of the corner of my eye I saw her bolt up against the restraints, so I did it again. Sure enough, her body jerked again. I had a feeling this next session was going to be fun.

"Are you bracing yourself for the first swat, Harper? Are you wondering how much it will hurt?" My voice was directly over her ear now, and that alone made her shoot up in surprise. Bringing my hand between her legs to grasp her crotch, she gasped at the contact.

"Tell me to get off you. Tell me you don't like this." I waited patiently for the lie I knew would be forthcoming. It took her a few moments to get her breath back, but she soon found the courage to speak.

"Untie me. Get off me. I don't like this." Her voice was bolder, and it seemed I'd sparked a little core of defiance in her. It was a start.

"But I think you do. I think if my fingers dip between your legs I'll find that you like this very much. Unless I am much mistaken, you're already dripping wet." My fingers squeezed her pussy tightly, while the other hand drew the edge of the paddle slowly down her leg. "Why lie all the time, Little Thief? Why don't you try and tell the truth for a change? All your lying will achieve is a red, raw backside."

"You aren't interested in hearing the truth. You'd rather I remain silent. And for the record, I didn't lie. I don't like this. I might be aroused by it, but that wasn't the question you asked." Her body pulled against the restraints for a moment, before realising the action was futile, and with a hiss of air she settled back down on the bench.

So, my little cat did have claws. Maybe this session would be more interesting than I'd thought.

I reached with my left hand to tug her chestnut curls, pulling her head back. With the other hand I let the first sharp stroke of the paddle fly. She didn't flinch when the blow came down, so I guess she'd been expecting it. Deciding to let the paddle do its thing, I rained down swats from one ass cheek to the other. They struck quickly; I didn't even give her the chance to draw breath. Perhaps she'd behave a bit better once her rear was a hot mess. It was worth a try.

The paddle was a particularly good choice. Each swing delivered a very satisfying thwack, and it was effortless to wield. The amount of heat that could be achieved with the beast was pretty impressive, and it wouldn't be long before I had her exactly where I wanted her. But there was no rush. I had all day and a story to tell.

Letting the paddle wrap around her buttocks a few more times, to make sure there was a suitable burn and a decent fire in her belly, I decided it was time to take up where I'd left off.

"Are you listening, Harper?" This time when the paddle struck it merely fluttered across her skin, and she shivered at the unexpected touch.

"I'm listening," she gritted out.

I swatted her ass again with more force, and she hissed. The sound was almost beautiful, in a weird and utterly fucked up kind of way.

"Good. Then I can continue. Where was I? Ah yes, there was me in a sling with a black eye, not to mention a pissed off cellmate. Anyway, my cellmate was a Portuguese guy who didn't speak a word of English, but he took an instant dislike to me when I trod on his photo and proceeded to make my life hell from that moment on. At first he started small. When we'd go down to the prison canteen he'd steal my spork. No problem, I thought, I'll go and get another one. But as soon as I'd done that I got another black eye to match the first. He got one of his gang mates to tell me that I'd need to get used to eating like a dog until I could learn to behave. It took two broken ribs and a broken nose before I realised he was being deadly serious. For the next year I learned how to eat my food using nothing more than my hands. Spaghetti, rice, stew; you name it, I picked it up with my bare fingers. It gave Micas and his crew hours of entertainment, at my expense. The worst thing about it was the utter frustration I felt. There were at least ten of them, and I had no one. I'd made no friends, mainly down to my cellmate, and I was unlikely to while I was sharing a cell with him. Most of the other inmates just wanted to keep their noses clean, so they were happy to turn a blind eye. That's the thing about prison. No one's going to stick their neck out for you, unless you've already stuck your neck out for them. But I was never given a chance to do anyone a favour; Micas made sure of that. So, for all intents and purposes I was his bitch, but it took him a few months to realise what I already knew."

Figuring I'd done enough talking for a minute or two, I ran my fingers lightly over her pink ass. She jumped at the first soft flicker of my hand, like a nervy mare, but with a few gentle strokes she settled down nicely, relaxing into my touch.

"Do you prefer the soft stroke of my fingers or the sharp sting of the paddle?" Silence reigned. I hadn't been expecting anything else. "Sometimes the anticipation of wondering whether the touch will be pleasurable or not is the sweetest torment." My hands continued to explore her, familiarising themselves with her body and responses. Though she tried her best to keep them hidden from me, when I let my fingers explore some of her most intimate places she had little choice but to let me know exactly how she felt. At first there were soft whimpers and moans. They were bitten off almost as soon as she'd uttered them, but I heard them. When my fingers dipped inside her repeatedly and my thumb caressed her clit, the whimpers turned to sobs of frustration, and I watched her fists clench in her cuffs.

Squatting down behind her, I was in my element. I could do this for hours. Her body was so ripe and so exquisitely beautiful, I could literally gaze at her forever. The only problem was that it was tormenting me nearly as much as it was her, but I didn't let that stop me. I continued until her legs were trembling and her knees threatened to give out. Her whimpers and moans had long since changed to screaming, sometimes with the occasional swear word thrown in for added emphasis, and even then I didn't stop. All I did was make it far more interesting, going deeper inside her, finding that elusive little spot which would drive her wild.

I must have nearly brought her to orgasm about eleven or twelve times before I finally took pity on her. She'd been sobbing in frustration for quite a while, but that was music to my ears. It meant she was beginning to flag, and when people start to weaken you press your advantage home.

"Do you think it's time for a break, Little Thief?" My fingers tickled the pretty little folds of her pussy, and I gave her a swat with the paddle for good measure. The two beautiful globes of her ass shuddered and heaved, and her sobbing increased.

"No? Let's go for another half hour then. I'm up for the challenge if you are." Her voice miraculously managed to say something then.

"Please. Can I have a break, please?" There were plenty of hiccups, some coughing, and a good bout of sobbing between the words, but I got the message. Even so, I couldn't resist teasing her.

"Are you sure? My spanking hand is still feeling pretty good. I could go for a while longer yet." I smacked her ass to confirm the matter.

"Please. I. Need. A. Break." She had just about enough air to finish the words. She could do with time to get her breathing back under control. No matter; I had a few things I needed to get ready for round two anyway.

"Fine, you just sit tight for a few minutes. I could do with stretching my legs." I smiled evilly. I'd be stretching something else in a minute, and I was going to let her know about it very shortly. I figured that might get her blood pumping.

Standing up to my full height, I raised my shoulders a few times to work the kinks out of them. If only I could use that same trick with my head, I thought dryly. The truth of the matter, though, was that I didn't want to be cured. Having finally been able to accept who I was in prison, kinks and all, I wasn't going to let anyone dictate to me what I should or shouldn't be doing in my life. My parents had attempted to control me, with some success, but the last few years before I was put inside I was always pushing boundaries. Perhaps that's what happens when too many of your freedoms are curtailed. Most of the stuff they'd pressed upon me - attending this and that function, dating so and so's daughter, or being seen in a particular venue - hadn't been that bad. Although I generally protested at their requests, I played the part of the good son and did as I was told.

No one had asked me to get married before, though. For some reason, I'd expected a small measure of choice in that decision. When I'd initially been paired up with Helena, I'd figured it was all for show. My parents were humouring hers, and a few years down the line we'd go our separate ways, and all would be well. I remember bringing up the topic with my father one day. I can't recall exactly what I said, but it was somewhere along the lines of Helena was a lovely lady, but I didn't think she was the right woman for me. My father looked horrified and told me I would need to think differently. The right woman was whoever would give me a leg up with regards to my social status, and Helena would do nicely. My father also told me to stop thinking for myself. I should be thinking about the family. As long as the needs of the family were met, then I could begin to think on my own. Nice guy, my father.

"Okay, Harper, you get a ten minute recess. I'm going downstairs to get us both a drink and a snack, and after that the real fun will begin."

"What are you going to do to me?" she croaked. Her voice was still ragged from her earlier cries, and I had never heard anything so beautiful.

I squatted down in front of her and brushed a stray tendril of hair away from her face. "Do you really want to know?" My smile was lopsided. She didn't want to know, but she'd ask anyway.

"Just tell me."

Staring at the mottled red and peach tones to her cheeks, I traced a soft path over the tip of her upper lip with my index finger.

"Have you ever been fucked in the ass before?" Her pretty pouting lips caught me captive under their spell, but I still managed to catch the stiffening of her body and watched as she drew in a slow, tortured breath. I didn't need to wait for her to speak to know the answer to my question. "Are you going to go all quiet on me, Little Thief?"

We were back to silence again. I didn't have a problem with that. I patted her head and left her to contemplate her fate.

Chapter 25 - Brandt

It didn't take me long to gather a couple of cartons of apple juice and pop a pre-packaged lasagne in the microwave. I figured she'd need a few calories to get through the afternoon ahead. Cutting up a few salad vegetables to go with it, I figured we were on track for her five a day - if I could get her to eat them.

Then I had a coffee and relaxed on the sofa for a few minutes until the timer went off. You can't beat the smell of freshly baked Italian food. My mouth was watering as soon as I dragged it out. So much for feeding her nothing but bland prison food; that idea had barely lasted a couple of days. I didn't seem to be doing a great job of sticking to my guns just lately. I guess I only had myself to blame. One moment I wanted to kill the witch for what she'd done to me, and in the next I wanted to fuck her into next year. The two didn't sit well together. Somehow I would have to find a way to control the attraction I felt for her, and file it somewhere far, far away. That was the only way this could work. A little voice in my head whispered that wasn't going to be an easy trick, but I ignored it.

With lunch in one hand and the drinks in the other, I made my way back to my prisoner. Funnily enough, she was in precisely the same place as I'd left her. Grabbing a black plastic chair, I sat down in front of her and pulled her blindfold down around her neck. Eating would be messy enough in her position, so I figured she could use her eyes for this one. Blinking up at me as she adjusted to the light, she spied the food in my hand and sighed. I ignored her. Digging my fork into the lasagne, I scooped up a small mouthful and held it out towards her.

"Are we back to this again?"

"Open wide." I waited a few seconds for her to comply, and when she didn't I frowned. "Open wide, or I'll get out the riding crop and whip you until you feel inclined to do as you're told." It was her turn to frown.

"Didn't we agree on small meals?" Her voice was almost pleading. It appeared that food was the last thing on her mind. That was too bad because there wasn't going to be any fainting on my shift.

"Do you want the riding crop or not?" My tone was terse.

"Fine. Feed me." Her mouth opened and she rolled her eyes at me. The woman was a cheeky little monster. Popping a small chunk of lasagne between her lips, I waited patiently for her to chew. She did so reluctantly.

"And yes, we did agree on small meals. Half of this is for me." When she'd finished chewing, I placed another forkful in front of her.

"I don't get you at all." She shook her head in puzzlement.

"Eat the food." The last thing I needed was conversation. I just wanted her to eat as quickly as possible so we could get on with things.

"One minute you can't wait to torture me, and in the next you're worried about feeding me."

"You're half-starved, and I don't want you to faint. Eat." She did.

Then I let her have some juice. Placing the straw gently on her bottom lip, I watched as she drank the carton dry.

"So, seeing as I have your attention, and you're going to be reasonably quiet while you finish your meal, I guess I might as well finish my story. Now, where was I? Ah yes, Micas, my Portuguese cellmate." I shovelled another forkful of pasta into her mouth as I considered what I wanted to say.

"So, Micas and his crew played with me for a few months. They treated me like a dog, making me crawl about for their entertainment, and occasionally carry things in my teeth, like a newspaper or magazine. Some days I fought them, others I made sure I got put in solitary, but some days I couldn't bear the thought of another beating. Pain is a funny thing. It comes upon you in waves. The first one or two aren't too bad, but the more layers of pain you have to endure, the more you weaken. Give a person too many layers, and they'll do anything to avoid getting any more of it. More often than not, that's where I was at. But it didn't stop me from working out. Every damn day, no matter how much pain I was in, I hit the gym and worked my ass off. I knew the only way I was going to get out from under my cellmate's clutches was if I managed to knock the bastard out, but it would take at least another year before I was strong enough to attempt it. This was mainly because I wasn't getting enough to eat. Micas had decided I didn't need as much food as the rest of them, so everyone got to pick what they wanted from my tray, and I got to finish up whatever was left. It wasn't a great deal."

"Oh God, I can't listen to this," Harper whispered. I blinked in surprise. Bar feeding her the odd forkful of lasagne, I'd almost forgotten she was there. I'd become lost in my own dark little world. It wasn't somewhere I liked to dwell, but I wanted her to know the results of her actions and why I was treating her this way. While I might be a kinky fuck, I'm not generally sadistic, but a lot of things had changed since I'd been in prison.

"You'd better. The only way I'll shut up is when you ask to be taken to the police station. Are we at that point yet?" She shook her head obstinately, but if I wasn't mistaken her eyes had filled with tears. For me? Surely not.

"No." I barely let her get that word out before I shoved another mouthful of food her way. I was sick and tired of hearing "no" and time was running out, but neither did I want to do something I'd later regret. As much as I wanted to hate the woman in front of me, for some reason I couldn't. It almost angered me to the point of madness.

"Then shut up and listen." Putting the dish of food down, as I didn't want to overdo it, I reached up and smoothed back the hair from either side of her face. It was soft and silky in my hands. Anything sweet and feminine would feel good right now, my brain argued, but I was inclined to disagree. Looking her straight in the eye, I made sure I had her attention before I began the second half of my story.

"So, Micas was a bastard, and he tried to starve me. I was aware that I'd need to find some way of eating, else I'd end up getting sick, but my options were limited. There were only three ways to score extra rations in prison. One was to buy them from the tuck shop, but even though my parents didn't cut my allowance, it went straight into a savings account that wasn't easily accessible from the inside. Basically, I had what was in my bank account, and when that ran out I needed to be more resourceful.

"Now you can work in prison, doing laundry, kitchen duties, using basic machinery - all sorts of things. But you can't with the threat of a good beating at the end of your shift. I was effectively stuck between a rock and an extremely hard place. The only time I got completely free of Micas and his goons was when they took their bricklaying class, which was every Thursday afternoon, and they only did that under duress to appease the prison warden who wanted all his detainees to try and do something 'constructive' with their time. After they'd left, I would head straight down to the tuck shop and try to stuff as much chocolate down my face as I could, but as I said, I had limited resources. I figured I had three months' worth of money at best."

The whole time I'd been speaking, Harper's eyes were glued to mine. It was slightly unnerving. Although there was a reason I was sharing my innermost secrets with her, the constant eye contact was beginning to freak me out, so I stood up and began pacing. But walking behind her was a mistake. With those two beautifully red globes staring back at me from above the leather spanking bench, my cock immediately began to beat a tune against the zipper of my jeans. Running my hand slowly over the pink abraded flesh, I watched her squirm. It was nothing compared to what she'd be doing in a few minutes, but I was happy to enjoy the moment.

"Still aroused from that spanking?" I asked casually. When there was no reply I deliver four sharp spanks, two on either side of her ass. "Want some more?"

"Yes," she hissed. "Yes, I'm still aroused, and I know that you know that I'm still aroused."

"That may be true, but it's still nice to hear you say it." My index finger centred in the valley between her ass cheeks and took a leisurely ride downwards. Yes, I was about to confirm what I already knew, but I couldn't resist tormenting her further. When my fingers found her entrance, it was with great satisfaction that I still found her dripping wet. "Is it just me, or is it the kinky sex that's turning you on?"

"Fuck you," she spat.

I tutted with mock severity. "Nice girls shouldn't be saying words like that."

"Who said I'm nice?" She tried to turn her head to look at me, but the restraints wouldn't let her.

"Good point. Maybe I should just whip you instead." I plunged two fingers inside her as deep as they would go. That shut her up for a moment.

"Oh, God!" I wasn't sure if it was a whimper of protest or a plea to continue. I took it as the latter.

"Besides, Little Thief, it's me who'll be fucking you, over and over, until you scream yourself hoarse. I think I'm in that kind of mood today." Letting my fingers move a little quicker I pushed harder and deeper, sliding effortlessly into her soft, silken folds. This time she ground her teeth together, to make sure I didn't hear a sound, but she'd only be able to do that for so long. I was going to push her to the limit. Swapping digits, I began to fuck her with my thumb, while two fingers tormented her clit. She'd want to be aroused for what I planned next, and while I'm the first to admit I was a bastard, I wasn't ready to destroy her just yet. Yes, I was in a hurry, but I wasn't in that much of a hurry.

"Shall we put the blindfold back on?" Pulling it back up over her eyes, I led her back into a world of thoughts, tactile sensations, and emotions. It was far more beautiful than lines and colours. Every feeling would be far more intense without the use of her eyes, namely because her other senses would make up for the loss.

"No, I'd..." But it was too late, the blindfold was back over her eyes and I wasn't about to remove it. She must have known it too, because she didn't try and finish her sentence.

"Okay, so there I was running out of money or food, take your pick, and there wasn't much I could do about it. I could have requested a transfer, but that was unlikely to be granted, or I could have started punching various inmates hoping it would result in a spell in solitary. The trouble was, if I did that too often I'd add time to my sentence. Short of hoping that Micas and his mates suddenly dropped down dead, my options were limited. I needed an ally.

"Anyway, so one Thursday I'm visiting the tuck shop, stuffing my face with potato crisps and chocolate, when Gabriel Rodriguez walks in. The guy was a badass son of a bitch, who easily rivalled Micas, so I made short work of stuffing my remaining treats into my gob and made to get the hell out of there as quickly as possible. As I was leaving though, he grabs hold of my arm and spins me round to face him. I'm thinking I'm about to get the shit kicked out of me again, although I have no idea why when the guy takes his hand off my arm and strokes my face with his finger. A little like this." I curled my index finger into a knuckle and ran it gently down Harper's cheek, and with the added sensation of my thumb pumping inside her, she couldn't help a moan. It was an adorable little sound and I wanted to hear more of them, but I needed to finish my story.

"He tells me that if I want his help, all I have to do is suck his cock. If I can do that, he'll get the goons off my back and make sure I eat proper food. My face must have shown my complete revulsion because he laughed. He advised me to think about it. Said I wasn't going to last long in there unless I did. Said Micas and his crew were thinking the same, and that I'd either get fucked by them or him, and my time was running out. He brought his face close to my ear, so close I nearly wet myself, and told me to make the right decision, that if I wanted to get through my term there was only one way to do it. Then he left, my mind in turmoil. It was a damned if I did, damned if I didn't situation. Know what one of those feels like, Harper?"

"I'm beginning to have an idea," she said stiffly.

"So," I continued, "I saw fit to ignore Gabriel for the next three weeks. I kept my head down, did as I was told, and made no sudden movements. Bar the constant hunger pangs that loomed wherever I went, life in prison was just about bearable. But all good things must come to an end. Just as Gabriel had predicted, Micas was beginning to suggest he wanted more from me. He'd been giving me long, leering looks, making me even more uncomfortable than usual, and the violence he unleashed was increasing. I'm not sure if he was fighting himself, or just unleashing his frustration, but I knew this couldn't continue. I'd been in the infirmary three times in a week, twice for stitches, and I realised that if I didn't want to come home in bits and pieces - or a body bag - I would have to take matters into my own hands. While the thought was abhorrent, it was clear that no other options were coming my way and if I wanted to survive, I was going to have to make some hard choices." My fingers stopped moving because judging by her breathing, I knew she was close to exploding.

She made an angry sound in her throat. A cross between a roar and a scream, but to her credit she didn't beg me to finish the job. She knew what my game was. We'd played this before.

Bending over her ear, I whispered, "It came to a head a couple of days later. After the cell doors closed for the evening, Micas began his staring thing. He motioned for me to come over to him, but I pretended I hadn't seen it and headed straight for my bunk. This just pissed him off and he grabbed my arm, spinning me round to face him. Pressing his crotch up against mine, he let me feel his growing erection as he said, 'Maybe it's about time I make you my bitch, what you think, Browning?' I told him that if he put his cock anywhere near me I'd make sure he ate the thing the next day. If he wanted to fuck me he'd need at least two of his cronies to hold me down, and I told him so. This pleased him rather than angered him, so I think he was relishing the idea of a fight. Pushing me away he merely smiled and said, 'tomorrow'. That was probably the only thing that saved me from a fate worse than death, but now I knew with certainty that my time was running out.

"As luck would have it, next day was Thursday and I found myself searching for Gabriel. He was easy enough to locate. I saw him lounging against the pool table in the common room, lazily watching the TV whilst waiting for his next shot. At first he didn't see me, far too intent on whatever was happening on the box, but eventually his eyes wandered and when they latched on to me, he smiled. Finishing up the game quickly, he handed the cue to another inmate and sauntered over.

"'You look like you've had a rough week, pretty boy', he said. He frowned and ran a finger over the scar and seven stitches above my eyebrow. 'That Micas is a bastard, no?' I didn't want his platitudes. I needed help, and quickly. There was no point beating about the bush, so I came right out and asked if his offer was still on the table. He raised an eyebrow and asked what if it wasn't, so I said I'd have to find someone else to fuck, with far more bravado than I felt, but you have to play the game in prison. Picking up one of his tight dark curls in my fingertips, I said, 'Pity. I was almost looking forward to sucking your cock'. It was one of the hardest things I've ever had to do. If I'd thought begging would work I'd have gotten down on my knees and begged, but I knew Gabriel would take that as a sign of weakness, and he wasn't looking for a little bitch to fuck. If he was he could have had his choice from hundreds of others, most of whom would have loved a chance to hump one of the most notorious guys in the joint. It also helped that he looked like a God. Oh well, I'd tried and failed. There was little more I could do but go back to my cell with my tail between my legs. Slowly counting to twenty as I walked from the room, I could feel tears of stress well up. He wasn't going to change his mind, and my life was just about to implode in a really unpleasant fashion. There's no wonder the suicide rate in prison is sky-high. My last and only option for a life preserver had just sunk to the bottom of the ocean.

"'Wait, wait, wait', I heard behind me. 'Where you going so fast? I only teasing you. The offer is still there if you want it. Do you want it?' The rubber ring exploded back up to the surface, and I felt like a drowning man who'd finally managed to get a breath of fresh air. There was still a feeling of dread deep in the pit of my stomach, but at least there was a little ray of hope trying to break through the God-awful mess I'd found myself in. Blinking rapidly, to dash away the tears, I took a moment to calm myself before turning around to face him. The last thing I needed was for him to see me in tears.

"'Do you promise to knock the fucking shit out of him?' I asked. Gabriel gave me a sly look and promised to do that and a lot more, but said he needed a taster of what I was offering, giving me a leisurely head to toe examination. My stomach sunk again. What was I offering? Whatever he wanted, I guessed. Although I'd never done this before and didn't want to start now, the alternative was even worse. Besides, how bad could it be? All I had to do was suck. I could close my eyes and pretend none of this shit was happening to me. The key was staying alive in there. You kept me alive in there, Harper. You and no one else."

I paused for a moment, waiting to see if I'd get a response, but the room was so unnaturally quiet I wondered if she'd fallen asleep. Thankfully she hadn't. I could just make out the soft sounds of her breathing, but I smacked her ass to make sure she was paying attention.

"I'm listening," she growled. Damn, the woman could read minds. Placing my thumb back inside her, deciding that she needed another round with an almost orgasm, I continued with my story.

"'Do you know how to fuck a man?' Gabriel asked, brushing his hand through my hair, pushing my head back so I had no choice but to look up at him. I told him no, and asked him to show me what to do. There was no point being anything but honest. Besides, I'm pretty sure Rodriguez knew I'm straight. That was half of the fun of it, for him.

"He told me to meet him in cell 302 in ten minutes. We'd seal the deal there. With that, he released his fingers from my hair and sauntered back to the common room as if nothing had happened. I, on the other hand, felt like my whole world had just split down the middle. There was now a massive crack in my life that I would never be able to repair.

"But hey, I was the one who'd got myself put inside. I deserved all this, isn't that right, Little Thief?" This time I waited for her reply. It took a long time to come, but when it did her voice was strangled with emotion.

"Stop. Just stop. I don't want to hear this. Do what you're going to do, make it as painful as you like, but spare me the backstory."

"Ah, but I've lived these past five years solely for the purpose of delivering my story... to you." My thumb pumped a little harder as my fingers worked her over. I couldn't care less whether she wanted to hear my story or not; I'd made myself a promise to deliver it, and that's exactly what I was going to do. "Besides, your opinion carries little weight here, let's face it." There was a sniff and a hiccup, but then she quietened down. Well, all bar the heavy panting.

"Where were we? Ah, yes, cell 302. Funnily enough it looked a lot like mine. There was a stainless steel basin and toilet, and an elderly bunk bed with greying sheets. Not terribly romantic for my first time, huh? I remember sitting down on that bed and feeling my legs shake at the thought of what was to come. A million questions buzzed in my head. Why had God put me here? Why was I being punished? What had I done to make you hate me so bad you'd put an innocent man in jail? Of course, there were no answers and the misery of not knowing continued to spin round in my head. It took me a good ten minutes to get a hold of myself because I'd started to hyperventilate. I tried to tell myself this would all be over in a couple of hours. The deed would be done, and I'd have to hope that Rodriguez would honour his side of the bargain. Yep, here I was, trusting a convicted criminal with my life. How fucked up was that? As the minutes ticked by, I tried to keep myself occupied by examining the contents of his cell. There was nothing of particular interest. A couple of magazines and pictures were dotted around, and a battered old library book lay on the bed. When I turned it over I would have been amused to find it was Huckleberry Finn, had I not been so nervous. I heard footsteps and spun around with my heart in my mouth, to find Gabriel moving slowly towards me.

"'When I got in here', he said, 'I didn't know a word of English. One of the volunteers taught me, mainly by reading. The first couple of years were hard, but I've been in here fifteen years now. After all this time I could speak the Queen's English if I wanted to, but I have a reputation to uphold, you understand'. He winked at me. That was the first inkling I had that Gabriel Rodriguez was a lot more than he seemed. I already knew he was dangerous, and now he was doubly so. Curiosity got the better of me. I asked what he'd done. If he'd been locked up that long it must have been pretty bad.

"'You should be more concerned with what I'm about to do', he said, 'rather than what I've done, Querido'. He took my hand in his and rubbed his thumb across my palm, studying me carefully. He was far too close, but I guessed that was the idea. 'Do I make you nervous?'.

"'Yes' I said, 'and you're enjoying the fact immensely'. Looking him in the eye to prove I wasn't afraid of him, I held my ground.

"'You're not quite as stupid as you look, you know'. He yanked the collar of my jumpsuit and brought my lips to within inches of his. 'You've been bugging me for months, you know that? I've wanted to fuck you since the moment I laid eyes on you, and while I'm a patient man, I was beginning to think all hope was lost'. Pressing his nose to my neck, he said nothing as he leaned close and inhaled my scent.

"'If you don't hurry up with whatever it is you're going to do I'm going to run, so get on with it'. I meant it. I don't think I had ever been more nervous about something in my life.

"He laughed at me, said it was no fun to hurry, that I wouldn't like it if he rushed his end of the bargain, that he was sure I'd want whatever he did to Micas to be nice and slow. He put a lot of emphasis on the word *slow*.

"'Okay', I said, 'just so I know, what exactly am I signing up for here?' I figured I might as well know in advance, and I wasn't very good with surprises. He told me not to worry, that he'd be gentle, unlike my cellmate. He'd also make sure I ate and got to the gym unscathed. That there were perks to being with him. 'And what if I decide later down the line that I can't do this any more?' I asked. I needed to know if there was a get out clause, or if I'd be beholden to the man forever.

"'Give me six months. I think that's fair. After that, I'll probably be bored of you anyway. But before I get rid of you I'll make sure you can take care of yourself. Do we have a deal?' I could feel his warm breath on my cheek and the smell of mint. My pulse was beating so heavily I feared I might have a heart attack, but somehow I managed to breathe through the crashing cymbal in my chest. 'Do we have a deal?' he repeated. My heart felt heavy as lead as I said, 'Yes, we have a deal'.

"And with that he pushed me away and told me to get down on my knees."

Chapter 26 - Brandt

My fingers hadn't stopped tormenting her the whole time I was retelling my tale. After the last sentence I heard her stifle a sob, so I stopped what I was doing. I hadn't expected her to get aroused so quickly after the last time. Was she going to go off like a firecracker, left, right and centre? There was another snuffle, and then a sniff. Hang on a minute.

Walking around in front of her, I was amazed to see tears running freely down her cheeks. She wasn't about to orgasm at all. She was feeling sorry for me. How was that possible? Did she have some kind of Jekyll and Hyde syndrome?

"Are you crying for me?" I asked. "Surely not. I was under the impression there isn't an inch of compassion anywhere in your whole body. Don't tell me I'm beginning to get through to you?" Squatting in front of her, I pressed up close against her face so close I could smell the salt of her tears. Inhaling the beautiful scent, I used my tongue to trace the intricate little tracks they had made. She tasted divine. "Don't you want to hear how my tale ends?" I caressed her wet, blotchy face with my finger, and smiled at her coldly.

"Stop it. You're torturing both yourself and me with this retelling. Just do what you need to do, and let's get it over with." There were a few cute snuffles and the odd hiccup, but she managed to finish her sentence.

"Ah, but being tortured is good for the soul. Think of all the great things that never would have come to fruition without a little pain or heartbreak. The movies that make you cry, the books that stay with you for weeks, the songs that drive you wild; they aren't the happy-go-lucky type, are they? We're all hooked on a wild emotional ride. Especially you women. Isn't that right, Harper?"

"Fine. I'll start singing until I block you out. I can't listen to this any more. I won't."

The next thing I knew she was belting out a song, out of tune, but I don't think that deterred her any. She was giving me everything her lungs were capable of, and it was quite unpleasant. Striding back behind her, I picked up the riding crop and shook my head. When would the girl learn that she couldn't fight me? I was a force of nature at this moment in time, and nothing was going to stop me

110

until she broke.

Ten viciously sharp slices with the riding crop stopped the singing in its tracks. She screamed at me to stop, but I chose not to hear her. Each stroke was less than a second apart, and I let my fury rule me. I felt the beast rear its ugly head. If I wasn't careful I'd break her just like I'd been broken. She'd shatter like a wine glass under a crushing fist, and the trouble with glass is that there are only so many fragments you can find afterwards, and most of those you can't glue together again. That was me. That was my life.

"I'm listening."

Grabbing a handful of her hair, I yanked her head back and said, "Damn right you are." Bending my head down low, I growled, "Next time you try to interrupt me it'll be twenty strokes, and then thirty. I think you get the idea." I pushed her face back into the bench. Her tears had lost their appeal. It was time to finish what I'd started.

"Let's get back to my story, shall we? So, there I was, down on my knees, trembling like a leaf, wondering if I'd be able to live with myself when it was all over. Even though I knew it was the only way I was likely to get rid of Micas, it seemed like a bitter consolation when I knelt in front of Gabriel's crotch, watching him slowly pull his jumpsuit down. All I wanted to do was bolt. The idea of doing this with another man was pretty fucking hideous, but if I ever wanted to get out and clear my name, it seemed like a necessary evil." Placing my thumb back inside Harper, I began pumping again. Watching her squirm on my fingers gave me pleasure. She aroused me more than I cared to admit, and resisting her was becoming more and more difficult.

"When he grabbed his cock it was already erect. My eyes were immediately glued to it. Knowing it would be in my mouth in just a few seconds, I swallowed tightly. I kept telling myself there was still time to run, even though there wasn't. I was doing this. Casting all revulsion aside, I took a deep breath and waited for his move. But Gabriel was in no hurry. Stroking himself, he brought it up close to my face and said, 'Lick. Softly. Just the tip'. He then pressed against my mouth, and even though I wanted to gag, I did as he wanted. I expected the taste to be awful, but it wasn't as bad as I'd feared. 'Now up and down. Get your tongue on me. Lick all the way up and then all the way down. Slowly. Make me believe you want it, even though you don't'. He laughed at me, and I knew he was enjoying my struggle. I guessed I wasn't the first inmate he'd toyed with, and I certainly wouldn't be the last. 'Don't disappoint me, Browning. If you want my protection, you're gonna need to show me a little enthusiasm'. That was the sharp edge I'd been expecting. Gabriel wasn't going to mess around. This was a one-time deal, and I figured I'd better give it my best shot because the alternative wasn't pretty. So I licked, and then I sucked, nothing more than a little light teasing, but it had the desired effect. He closed his eyes and moaned, and that was all I needed to hear. He didn't have to prompt me again. I'd already compartmentalised what I was doing to the far corners of my brain, and now all I wanted was to make the bastard come. If I was going to have to do this regularly, I had to find the quickest way to pull his chain. As his eyes were on me I knew he wanted to watch, so I gave him as much of a show as I could. Raising my eyes to his, I let him stare at my face as my lips wrapped around his cock. This seemed to work him up quite quickly because his soulless black eyes filled with light. That light was lust. My body had a bizarre kind of power over his, but it would take me a few months to learn that. In the beginning, all I could think about was pleasing him, though I didn't trust him an inch. There was a good chance I'd just destroyed what little sanity I had left for nothing. Gabriel could easily go back on his word, and there would be nothing I could do about it. He wasn't stupid. If he decided I was too much of a risky prospect he wouldn't think twice about reneging on our deal, and all I'd done for him would be for naught. So it was important I made the bastard want more of what I was offering, and to do that I needed to show the man a good time. So I decided to reverse engineer my project. I would give him what I liked. Thinking back to when women have gone down on me, I did everything to him that I enjoy. That included taking his whole fucking cock down my throat, which made me gag, but it didn't stop me. I'd had it done to me a fair few times, so surely it couldn't be that hard?

"It was nearly impossible. I have no idea how you women do it. Add to the fact that my head was all over the place and I almost destroyed any chance of getting him to help me within the first ten minutes. Thankfully, Gabriel took pity on me. He told me not to think so hard. Not to over analyse it. Just feel. Feel his cock sliding down my throat, and lubricate it with my saliva. Then he could move inside me. His voice in my head made everything worse, rather than better. I had to block it out entirely and concentrate on relaxing. He was right, everything had gone to shit because I was nervous and thinking too hard, but it was too difficult to do anything else. I was a hairbreadth from a breakdown, and I think he knew it. Putting his hands on either side of my head, he guided my mouth back and forth along his cock with increasing speed and power. I couldn't do a thing. I knelt on my knees and watched him slam into me over and over again, bruising the soft tissue of my throat until he hissed and pressed my face tightly into his crotch. It was all over in less than five minutes.

"He told me to swallow it all down like a good boy. He stood over me and watched to make sure I did as I was told, and when I had, he patted me on the head and walked from the room without another glance in my direction. I remember pressing my head to the cold concrete floor and wondering what the fuck had just happened. I then banged it against that floor. Did we still have a deal? Would he hold up his end of the bargain, or had I just prostituted myself for no apparent reason? Time would tell. Oh fuck.

"The taste of him bubbled up my throat, and I got to my feet on wobbly legs. Then I had no choice but to run. I was about to be violently sick, and I didn't want to risk doing so in Gabriel's cell. There were enough problems in my life without adding any more to them. Thankfully I made it to my cell with seconds to spare before I vomited up the contents of my stomach, which I really couldn't afford to lose. Sitting on the edge of my bunk, shivering, I stayed there for what could have been ten minutes or two hours; I honestly don't remember. What I do remember is that Micas never came back to the cell that night. The next day I would discover that he'd been so badly beaten he'd had broken four ribs, an arm, and his collarbone. He'd also been stabbed multiple times with a makeshift shiv - made from a toothbrush - and further complications to that brutal stabbing would later result in his death. As much of a bastard as Micas was, having his death on my conscience was a nightmare I wouldn't wish on my worst enemy. Over the next few years it drove me to insanity and back, several times over. But that's another story."

Harper was breathing heavily. My fingers were playing a tune her body could not resist, and we were quickly reaching the moment of truth. She was keeping very still and trying her best not to give me any indication of her level of arousal, but I had a lot of experience at this game. While in prison my skills hadn't dropped any; they'd just deferred to a different gender. Stopping just as she was about to tip over the edge, I waited for the verbal explosion that was sure to follow. She didn't disappoint me.

"Are you taking great pleasure in doing that? How many times has it been now, ten? I've lost count. Don't think I'm going to beg you for an orgasm. I know what a waste of time that is. So you keep on playing your games and telling your story. It's going in one ear and straight out of the other." Her voice was a beast of fury, rising in volume until she'd finished her sentence.

"You're wrong on both accounts. I can tell you're listening just by looking at you, and by the time I've edged you along the path to orgasm nineteen or twenty, you'll do almost anything to achieve one."

"If you think I'm off down the station, you're wrong. You can play this little number as many times as you like and the end result will always be the same." If it were possible, she was even more gorgeous when angry. The emotion and passion that poured out of her was a joy to see, namely because I had seen so little of it in prison. Everyone tried to keep their thoughts and feelings hidden behind bars.

"Who says that's what I want from you this time? I think you might have misread this round, Little Thief, but you'll figure it out soon enough." Picking up the crop, I gave her backside another couple of shots to focus her, before I went back to my pretty little armoire. There was something I wanted hiding in its depths, and it was going to make our fight a very interesting one.

"What are you doing?" Her voice was softer now, and more unsure of itself. Good. There was nothing wrong with a little panic and adrenaline flowing through her. It would make what I was about to do so much easier. Pulling a drawer open, I saw what I wanted and let my fingers close around it. Perfect.

When I sat back down on my chair, I brought the oversized rabbit vibrator up between her legs. It was still cold, so it made her jump. I smiled darkly. She'd warm it up soon enough.

"What is that?" she whispered.

"It's ten inches of pure jelly-powered orgasmic bliss. It's also known as a rabbit vibrator. Unfortunately for you, I'm not going to let you climax, but you'll still have fun. According to the instructions, this baby has a little extra girth to your average vibrator, with seven modes of vibration, pulsation, and escalation. The good news is, we're going to test them all. Then we have a rotating head that moves in two directions and twenty rotating beads for deep internal stimulation, apparently, and if that wasn't enough the bunny ears are going to give your clit a workout like you would not believe. Have you used one of these before, by any chance?"

"I hope your testicles shrivel up and drop off, Brandt Browning. Go ahead and have your fun. It looks like I'll be hanging around for a while."

"It's nice to see you haven't lost your sense of humour." I smacked her ass hard, but she didn't even flinch. Switching the vibrator on, I put it on its lowest setting and began to pulse it towards the source of the sticky wet heat that was freely dribbling from her body. Although the vibrator was oversized, I didn't think it would take me too long to get it inside her, judging by her level of arousal. Sliding the beast in inch by slow inch, it took me some time, but I finally managed to sheath the whole length. "How does that feel?" I asked, letting the little bunny ears touch her clit.

"I thought you were supposed to be torturing me. You'll need to work harder."

"Oh, I've only just started. We'll get there, I promise."

I was true to my word. Each time I edged her towards orgasm and stopped just short of the prize, I gave her five minutes rest before I upped the vibrations and started over again. We played this dance through all seven settings until she was sobbing with exhaustion and the most intense, exquisitely unpleasant frustration I suspect she'd ever experienced.

"Now I'm going to give you a choice, Little Thief. I'm going to play the same kind of mind games with you that Gabriel played with me. So the deal is this: you can either suck my cock, or we can do all seven settings over again. I'm happy with either option, just so you know."

Harper snapped something unrepeatable at me in response, and when she finally got her fury under control, her next words surprised me. It told me she was far sharper than I'd given her credit for.

"And after we do all seven settings again, you'll ask me the same question? Do you take me for an idiot? Right now you're wondering whether I'll cave in to your demands or drop from exhaustion trying to defy you. I've played these games before, Brandt. They nearly killed me the first time around. I can't do it again. If you want me to suck your cock that badly, you need only have asked. I'm done fighting you for today."

Well, didn't that spoil all my fun? She'd accurately predicted what I was about to do to her, and my growing excitement about finally getting a little of what I wanted evaporated on the wind. I needed to be in her mouth and surging down her throat so badly I could have cried, but my goal had been to take the choice from her, giving her no other option but to suck me. The ultimate control I'd been searching for had just backfired in my face.

"I do want to know one thing, though," Harper purred, and the sound shocked me. Up until now she hadn't done anything except whisper or talk quietly. "Did Gabriel suck your cock? Did he make you shoot your load?"

As soon as those two small sentences were out of her mouth I saw red and wanted to thrash her to within an inch of her life. I couldn't help but wonder if that was what she was after, though it seemed ridiculous; why would she provoke me like that? Ah yes, I remembered, she liked pain. But there's pain and there's pain. She needed to be careful; she wasn't just playing with fire, she was playing with an inferno. If she thought an overload of the stuff would get her what my fingers were not prepared to let her have, she was wrong.

"All in good time, Little Thief." My voice was soft and calm. The number one rule of prison is never to let your enemy rattle you. That would be another of Gabriel's lessons I would learn too late, but better late than never. Letting out a long slow breath of air that I hadn't realised I'd been holding, I stood up and stretched. Did I want Harper Wilkinson to suck my cock? Yes and no. Yes, almost more than life itself, and no, because if she did, I wasn't sure I'd be able to stop there, and this wasn't what it was all about. I wasn't doing this to satisfy my base desires; I was doing this for justice.

"Do you ever lose your temper?" Harper sounded exasperated, as well she might be.

"No." I used to, frequently, but I've tried to learn from my mistakes. "Having said that, it's not a particularly clever idea to annoy a man who's got you tied up in chains and has access to a whip."

"I've never been particularly clever around you, Brandt." Hell, that sentence echoed around my brain a few times.

"You don't need to tell me that." I threw my head back and stared at the ceiling. Why did this have to be so difficult?

"So am I going to suck your cock?"

"No. I'm going to finish my story and then fuck your ass like I promised."

"So women aren't the only ones that change their mind every five seconds." There was a note of smugness in her voice that I didn't like, but I chose to ignore it for now. We needed to get a move on.

Standing up, I stretched slowly and strode back to the armoire. I needed a few more things to complete the day's session. The first was a box of three black rubber butt plugs. The second was a pair of headphones. The idea was to shut off the world around her, so she would feel more acutely every movement I made. Without my voice helping her through it was probably going to hurt, but I wasn't here to be Mr Nice Guy. I was here to get results and a confession.

Time to get to work.

Chapter 27 - Harper

When the soft leather headphones came down over my head, they made me jump. Covering my ears entirely, I instantly hated them, but I wasn't really in a position to complain. All I could do was dread the next part of Brandt's attempt to destroy me. He wanted to show me what he'd been put through in prison, and judging by what he'd told me earlier, today's session was just a drop in the ocean. Some small part of me was honest enough to admit that I deserved it. Other parts wanted to shout from the rooftops that I had no choice. But wasn't there always a choice? Perhaps I had never been smart enough to figure that out.

By now I had decided I would run as soon as an opportunity presented itself, and my lack of clothes was not going to be a barrier. But every second would count if there was any hope of outrunning Brandt, and I intended to make use of them all.

When music exploded in my ears I jumped again. It was classical and dark. I recognised it, but the name of the piece would remain elusive. What I wanted to know, though, was how did he intend to finish his story if I couldn't hear it? Didn't having me in headphones defeat the object of his purpose?

The next thing that would make me jump was Brandt's fingers, covered in cold lubricant, circling their sticky wet fluid around my tight little hole, before trying to gain entrance. As much as I might have wanted to deny them, they were insistent, and it wasn't long before he was pumping away inside me, one finger at first before it was swiftly joined with another. The feeling was uncomfortable and slightly painful at first, but it eased the longer he carried on. He seemed determined to push as much lubricant inside me as he could, and he took his time doing so.

At first, I tried to deny him the sound of my voice. I clamped my mouth tightly shut, refusing to let the slightest little noise escape. This was a battle I would try very hard to win, but like all good battles, there is a winner and a loser. I wasn't destined to be the former.

When his fingers finally stopped tormenting me, something hard cold and wet pressed against my backside. Was it the vibrator or something else? No, I quickly realised it wasn't the vibrator as its tip was tapered. It was a butt plug. A feeling of dread consumed me. He'd meant to do exactly as he'd threatened, but not in the way I was expecting.

Initially all he did was circle my anus and repeatedly slip the tip of the plug inside me. There was the occasional swat with the crop, to keep me on my toes, but the sensation wasn't really painful. Just a little annoying and uncomfortable. That meant he was toying with me because I was under no illusion that the day would end in pain. Still, at least I was getting a breather. There was no way I could have gone another round with the vibrator. Thankfully I had been spared that.

Disappearing into my own little bubble, the music helped my mind drift away for a time, and though I felt his hands on my body, tormenting, teasing, rubbing and kneading, I did my best not to pay him too much attention. I succeeded for a time, even managed to relax for a couple of minutes, but like all good things my precious few moments of quiet time were destined to end.

As the piece of music increased in tempo and volume, so too did Brandt's movements, and that was when things became... somewhat challenging. The little plug might have had a tiny tapered tip, but as he began to push it a little further inside me it wasn't quite as small as I'd hoped. The thing had a vicious bite as it delved deeper inside me, and the promise I'd made to myself to stay quiet was tested. It didn't seem to matter how tightly I squeezed my buttocks to try and keep the thing out, the plug still managed to make its way past my defences. All I received for my troubles was a smart crack from the crop every now and again.

Brandt was relentless, of course. He kept pushing and pulling, stretching and widening my little hole, making me grunt as he tested my pain threshold. When he'd finally buried the plug inside me I let out a long slow hiss of relief. Thank God. There was only so much of that kind of thing a girl can take.

When the headphones came off I wondered if he would release me, but that hope was quickly dashed.

"You've taken the smallest plug, but you still have two to go. I figure I might as well get on with my story while you take a breather and your ass prepares for the next round."

Another two? I could barely take one. He was going to stretch me apart. Perhaps that was the plan. Was this how he envisioned me running off to the police station? Nothing would surprise me. By the end of this there was no question he'd have me in tears. The cycle would be repeated day in, day out until he got what he wanted. Was I strong enough to go through it? Was there any chance I could somehow make him see sense? Maybe the Brandt I'd known and loved was gone forever. Maybe...

"Ready for me to continue, Little Thief?"

"No," I said sullenly, knowing it wouldn't make any difference.

"Good, then let's begin. So, there I was in a cell all by myself, half filled with joy at the knowledge that Micas wasn't coming back, half filled with guilt that I'd pretty much put him in his grave. It was an odd combination, and one I'd never completely come to terms with, but there it was. For the time being I was on my own. You'd think I'd be happy about that, wouldn't you?" When he didn't get a response he twisted the plug sharply in my ass, making me jump. Beneath the blindfold I clamped my eyes shut but kept my silence. He didn't really expect me to say anything. He just wanted to annoy me.

"I wasn't. Prisons are too overcrowded for an inmate to have a cell to himself for long and that meant I would be getting a new flatmate. There was a chance he would be better than Micas, of course, but there was also a chance he could be a lot worse. I remember being restless that night when they turned the lights out. It was almost as if I had a premonition that I wasn't going to like what my future would bring.

"The next day started innocently enough. I walked to the mess hall, gathered my tray, and for a change I was allowed to eat in unmolested peace. This was a novelty for me. Even Micas' goons were unusually quiet. I was fully expecting to get a crack on the nose and someone's foot in my rib, but no one was looking my way. Something was up. Then again, maybe it was just a period of mourning for their beloved boss. The guys had to have some morals, right? Keeping my head down and making sure I didn't engage eye contact with anyone, I quickly finished up and put my tray away. Deciding I was being paranoid, I wandered around in silence for a bit, but I was left alone. When I hit the gym that afternoon I managed a reasonably decent workout, due to the fact I had some food in my belly. It was a nice feeling, but one that came with a bitter aftertaste. I knew Gabriel had not finished with me. I knew it wouldn't be long before he sought me out. What I didn't know, was that those thoughts would be the least of my worries in approximately half an hour's time."

He paused and twisted the plug inside me. He reached his fingers underneath me and found my pulsing core, the one that wouldn't stop bleating for attention whenever he was near. You'd think I'd have managed to cure myself of the attraction by now, but if anything it was worse. The constant level of arousal was beginning to do something pretty horrible to my hormones, and my body craved his with an addiction as dangerous as heroin. When he started to tug on the plug, teasing it from my rectum, I wanted to scream. I knew what was coming. I knew what we were building up to, and I was powerless to stop it.

"Imagine my surprise when I got back to my cell to find I already had another cellmate. Yep, I'd not even been given a whisper of warning that when I returned I'd already have a roomie waiting for me. Not just any roomie, though, but one that would put the fear of God into me."

There was a long pause.

"Gabriel," I whispered in horror, before clamping my mouth shut. I hadn't meant to say anything, but the name blurted out almost of its own volition. Christ. What had I done to the man?

"Gabriel," he confirmed in a hollow voice, as the plug inside my ass finally popped free, the feeling of relief short-lived because a new, bigger plug was already being inserted.

"Gabriel had friends everywhere, and they included the prison guards. The benefits of serving heavy-duty time, I guess. He'd managed to bribe one of them into letting him move into my cell. When I walked in he sat there staring at me, smiling slyly, and it didn't take me long to realise that all I'd managed to do was swap one empty-headed monster for one with a brain. I remember having this sinking feeling in the bottom of my gut that I was never going to make it through my five years. When the lights went out that evening and Gabriel ordered me to take off my pants and stand by the bunk bed, I remember thinking that hell had nothing on that place."

A sharp slap was delivered to my ass.

"Okay, Harper, I think it's time to try the second plug. It's still not as big as a cock, but you'll get the general idea of what it's like to be fucked in the ass. Believe me when I tell you the first time isn't pleasant." He paused, lost in his dark little world, as he began to lubricate my ass again. It didn't take him long to recommence my torment, and when the new rubber plug pressed for entry, I could feel it was quite a bit bigger than the last one. Biting my lip, I took a deep breath, in through the nose and out through the mouth. I would get through this, just like I got through everything else. All I needed to do was keep on breathing.

"The first time he bent me over the pain was intense. There was no lube in prison. Gabriel spat on his fingers, and that was my warm up. Let me tell you, it wasn't enough. When he began fucking me I wanted to scream, but I bit the back of my fist so hard I drew blood. That was probably one of my darkest moments in prison, and thinking I'd probably have to put up with much more for the next six months of my life, possibly more if Gabriel didn't hold to his end of the bargain. I remember wondering if I would last another day because the pain was that bad, but what I didn't know was that it would dull with time. In fact, I would barely blink an eye when it happened a week or two down the line. It's amazing how extraordinary things become ordinary when you've done them enough times."

All the while he was talking he was slowly twisting the plug further and further inside me. With the first one it had been a few seconds of pain, followed by relief when it found its way inside me. This one was pain from the word go, and I was panting in an effort to stop myself from crying out. I wondered if Brandt wanted me to scream or if he wanted me to keep quiet, just like he had been forced to do. As the plug twisted deeper I asked the question; anything to distract me for a second or two.

"I don't give a damn. All I want you to do is feel. Maybe I can't put you behind bars, but I can sure as hell show you what it felt like. That's what the purpose of this exercise is." With that he pushed the plug too deep too quickly, and I hissed. My whole body tightened to what felt like breaking point, and he retreated a centimetre or so, which was just about enough for me to halt the snapping of my bones.

"It's not pleasant, is it? Can you imagine taking this every day for months on end? Can you ever imagine enjoying this?"

"No," I whispered. He deserved an answer to that question even though I could barely talk. I was too busy trying to suck in as much air as possible before the next assault began.

"Ah, but there's the kicker, Harper. Not only would I learn to enjoy it, but I would come to crave Gabriel's attention, even long after he became bored of me." The plug pressed again, and I could feel myself getting lightheaded with fatigue. Was it possible to faint lying down? I had the strangest feeling I was about to find out.

The plug began to plunder my insides, and my back arched like a bowstring.

"Do you think I could make you enjoy this? Can you imagine screaming with ecstasy while my cock is filling your ass?"

"Nooo," I screamed, trying my best to push away from his insistent fingers, but with my ankles in cuffs I was going nowhere fast.

"I can do all that and more, Little Thief. I can make you fall at my feet, I can make you crawl, and I can make you beg. You are at my complete and utter mercy, and you haven't even managed a week of your five-year term." With a monstrous push he forced the plug home, and I went rigid with shock and then screamed. When I'd recovered I was almost shaking with fury.

"Stop it. For God's sake stop it." Although I didn't expect him to pay any attention to my pleas, I needed to voice them. Yelling whilst someone's trying to do you bodily harm is a little cathartic. It was also the only thing I could do.

"I'm only just getting started. We haven't torn skin yet." As if to prove a point

119

he twisted the plug inside me, and I nearly swallowed my own tongue. I was quickly approaching my pain threshold, and I desperately needed to get out of there. Digging my fingernails into my palms, I tried to focus my thoughts on something else. Anything else.

"Okay, let's have a few more swats of the crop while you get used to that one, and then we'll try the next beauty. Anything you want to say to me before I begin?"

What I wanted to say was unrepeatable and would probably only anger him further, so somehow I managed to keep a lid on all the horrible things I was feeling. When was this madness going to end?

The headphones going back over my ears was the first indication I had that Brandt was about to begin, but he made me wait for several agonising minutes before I felt anything. When the first touch of the crop came down, it was more of a kiss than a smack. It still made me jump, because with my eyes and ears out of action I had no indication of its presence, but it certainly wasn't as hard as expected. Was he going soft on me?

I soon found out that he wasn't, but the aim of his game was to keep me completely off balance. A caress of his fingers here, a lick of the crop there, the feel of his warm body between my legs, and then his hands moving all over me. He was gentle and hard, both at the same time, and my body wasn't sure what to do. One moment it was aroused, the next it was preparing for pain. Was this how Gabriel had made him feel? Never sure whether he would be rough or gentle? Always on edge? I couldn't help but wonder.

Brandt then went into beast mode. The crop struck sharply three times in quick succession, and my poor backside bleated in protest. I wasn't ready for it. "No, I can't do this again," I wailed pitifully. My poor bum was a mass of stinging, throbbing, burning flesh.

He chose that moment to caress my reddened flesh, and then the next plug dipped inside me. I nearly gasped in horror. Although I couldn't see it, I could easily feel it was much bigger than the two previous. Perhaps even as big as a... The headphones came off again, and Brandt's voice whispered in my ear.

"This will be pretty much like the real thing. Not quite as painful, because the rubber tends to be a little more forgiving than your average cock, but you'll feel it rather keenly." He pushed it to emphasise his point, and my eyes watered.

"You think there's no way it'll fit inside you, right? I know that's what I thought the first time. You'd be wrong, though. It will fit; every single last inch of it."

He was as good as his word. There was more lubricant, lots of twisting and turning, and the fingers of one hand were back underneath me again. My desire ebbed and waned with the thickening girth of the plug trying to burrow its way inside me, but he knew what he was doing. Even though he had to pull out all the stops before he got so much as a whimper from me, eventually he had me right where he wanted me; panting in heat and half delirious with a heady mixture of both pain and pleasure.

"Feels wonderful and awful all at the same time, doesn't it?" He had that right.

One moment I thought I was going to come, and the next I thought I might die. Sometimes it was hard to distinguish between the two. All I knew was that I wanted it to stop.

"I can make you want this, Harper. I can have you down on your knees begging for this, every single day for the next five years if I want to. If Gabriel could do it to me, when I found it utterly repugnant, you're doomed. It'll be incredibly easy to corrupt you."

His words floated about in my head unheeded. All I could concentrate on were the delicious swirls of his fingers and the evil twists of the plug. It felt like he was splitting me in two, but I couldn't fight him any more. I didn't have enough energy to raise my little finger, let alone kick and scream. My body went lax beneath me, and that was all the encouragement he needed. In one swift move he forced the entire length of the last plug inside me, and I climaxed instantly with a scream I couldn't hear - because I finally fainted.

I have no idea how long I'd been out, but when I came to I was no longer in Brandt's playroom. I was back in the four-poster room, minus all restraints except the collar around my neck. The light through the arched window was dimming, so I guessed it was around four o'clock, maybe a little later. Rolling over on the soft cotton sheets, I groaned. My body was rather tender in several places. I suspected it would be for a few days to come.

I couldn't help but wonder if he was mad at me. Had I spoilt his best laid plans by fainting? Would his vengeance continue the minute he knew I was awake? It was more than likely. Something had happened in the last day or so. There was a crazy gleam in his eyes that spoke of desperation, and I didn't understand it. The look hadn't been there when we'd first arrived at the house, but it was there now. He meant to get through to me quickly, and by whatever means possible. If he had morals once upon a time, they were no longer with him, and I guessed I was partly responsible for that. If the tales of prison woe were anything to go by, his time inside had been hell on wheels, and I had a feeling I hadn't gotten the whole story yet. Would I ever be able to live with the guilt of what I'd done? I didn't think so. If I'd felt bad before, it was nothing compared to what I felt now. I was beginning to crack on the inside, and it wouldn't be long before you could see sunlight through me. Couple that with having been in love with my captor before he went inside, and you had a recipe for disaster. He was right. He could do anything he wanted to me, and I would let him because even after all that had happened, I was still in love with him. If I could have taken his prison sentence away and served it for him, I would have. What on earth was wrong with me? Wait, I think I'd just spelt that out earlier.

Rubbing wearily at my eyes, I wondered how long it would be before Brandt came back up the stairs. I should check to see if the door was locked. Why hadn't that occurred to me sooner? Glancing over towards it I saw it was shut, so I suspected it was locked too, but I needed to make sure. If this was my one chance at escape, I intended to take it.

Easing my foot out of bed, I placed it on the wooden floorboards and crossed my fingers. Standing up, I winced as a soft squeak escaped. It couldn't be helped. If Brandt was waiting outside the door he was going to hear me whatever I did. Deciding speed rather than stealth was of the essence, I scampered the rest of the way to the door handle. Twisting it gently, the door opened.

An empty landing greeted my eyes, with several doors that might house something I could wear. I didn't bother with any of them. There were going to be no hesitations this time around. Whoever rescued me was just going to have to take me as they found me, because I no longer cared. The only thing that mattered was getting out fast.

My bare feet almost flew across the floorboards, and I was as light as a sparrow, so I didn't make as much noise as I thought I would. Racing down the stairs so fast I feared I might tumble down head first, I didn't see any sign of Brandt. My pulse quickened and adrenaline flowed through my veins as I set my sights on the door we'd come in through. I wasn't going to make the same mistake of exiting down the driveway this time, though. I knew he would easily catch me if I tried that tactic. This time I intended to go around to the front of the house and see if I could spot some sort of farmstead or road in the distance. Anything. I would take any chance at freedom, no matter how small.

My heart began to swell as the moment of freedom approached. Would the door be locked? Would this all be for nothing? Perhaps that was why he hadn't bothered to lock me in the bedroom. All this excitement would probably be for nothing, and then I would have earned myself yet another punishment. But I didn't care. At least I might deserve the next one.

When I reached the tiled hallway I skidded on the flagstones, but I didn't let it slow me down. I had to reach that door before Brandt caught me in order to stand a fighting chance of escape. Brushing against the velvet wallpaper in my hurry to barrel through to the outside world, I finally managed to reach the porch. My hand twisted the handle sharply downward, and I prayed with everything I had. Someone must have heard me, thank God, because the door opened.

There was an effervescent, bubbling sense of victory erupting through me as I burst out of the house. It was quickly dashed when I heard a shout from behind me, but I didn't let him slow me down. Running as fast as my legs would carry me, I pelted across the lawn aiming to run past the tennis courts and outbuildings I'd seen at the rear of the property. Although there might not be any hope of escape at the front of the house, with my limited time, maybe there would be another house or cottage near the rear. Even if Brandt caught me as we were running, perhaps there was a chance someone would see us and raise the alarm. Especially if I screamed loud enough.

By the time he was close to catching up with me I'd managed to get clear of the grounds and begun running through the thick undergrowth that encircled the back of the stables. More pine trees, lots of moss, and plenty of prickly thorns greeted me. The stones beneath my feet were ripping me to shreds, but that barely registered on my pain scale. I had a goal, and that was to find out what was behind the trees. I'd spotted nothing that was going to help me, but there would be something beyond this little forest. I just knew it.

Ignoring the heavy, ominous thuds of Brandt's feet gaining ground with every second, I ran like the wind. Bark shredded my skin, knotted ropes of ivy sent me sprawling, and my hair was being torn out by prickly trees, but I didn't let any of them slow me down. My lungs were burning but adrenaline fuelled them. Stopping wasn't an option. Until the end of the world met me, that was.

Chapter 28 - Harper

The end of the world comes in various shapes, sizes, and designs - but mine came in the form of a rocky cliff top. For three scary seconds I toyed between jumping or slowing down. This was the first time I had ever considered suicide, and it scared the shit out of me. When I sensed Brandt slowing behind me, I didn't turn around to face him. I already knew I'd lost this battle, but I was going to have a hard time acknowledging it to myself. My feet continued to stumble forward, and suddenly the world tilted on its axis.

"Harper. Stop. You'll kill yourself!"

Following Brandt's command, for some reason unknown to myself, I skidded to a halt less than a foot from the edge of the cliff. When I got there all I could see were brutal, craggy mountains spiralling for miles below me. Vertigo hit me in dizzying, suffocating waves and I wobbled, my arms wind-milling to keep my balance. Oh, God. Maybe I would die anyway.

"Harper, for God's sake step backwards."

No such luck. My sore backside fell with a heavy thud into the rough stone below, and I put my head in my hands. This was yet another pointless dead-end; the story of my life.

"Jesus, Harper, what were you thinking? You could have died." The thundering feet behind me had slowed, but they were still advancing and there was nowhere to go. For the first time since he'd kidnapped me, I thought I heard fear in his voice. Maybe the bastard did care about me after all.

"What do you want from me?" The question was a horrified whisper, and for a moment I didn't think he'd heard me. The wind whistled around us with formidable fury and sliced straight through my ribs, doing its best to freeze the pounding organ within. I didn't dare look anywhere but at my fingers, lest the panic return. Heights were not my friend.

"You know exactly what I want from you. Your confession. My old life back. My innocence. You out of my life." His voice got louder and louder until it formed a crashing crescendo with the last sentence. He beat the wind hands down. The trouble was, I didn't believe him.

"You're a liar, Brandt. That's not all you want." My voice was a little louder and a little braver, but only because I refused to look at the vista below.

"Is that right?" I felt him behind me just moments before his hand gripped my hair and yanked my head back. "Then why don't you open those eyes, Little

Thief, and tell me exactly what I want?" He tugged on my hair for emphasis and my eyes snapped open.

If there was ever a time to keep my mouth shut this was probably it, but when had I ever listened to reason? Don't do it, my subconscious cautioned.

"Come now, Little Thief. You can't say something like that and not follow through." Wrapping my hair around his fist, he tugged again. "Say it, or I'll put my fingers inside you. I'll work you into a frenzy and leave you right on the edge, panting for more. Again."

I glowered at him. "You seem to be very good at that," I bit out, "but don't think I haven't noticed you suffer as much as I do."

"And how do you figure that out?" He crossed his arms over his chest and looked every inch the smug bastard, but I knew better. Prison might have turned him into a very skilled actor, but there were some things he couldn't hide from me.

"The attraction isn't one-sided, Brandt. You might tell yourself that, but your body tells a different story. What do you do when you've finished tormenting me? Go off and meditate? I'm not stupid. I know you want to fuck me." There, I'd said it. Now I was about to pay the price for my stupidity, but at least I'd got that off my chest.

"You know that how? I don't think mindreading is one of your talents, but feel free to advise me otherwise." Brandt sounded furious, as I knew he would be.

"So go ahead and deny it. You're only holding me here until you've scratched that little itch and then you'll wander off into the sunset and marry your rich princess. Why don't you put us both out of our misery and get it over with?" My body had broken out in goose bumps as a result of the frigid air around me, but the bristling anger inside kept me warm.

"I'm not laying a finger on you until you tell me what I want to know." He stood tall, towering over me, and I wrapped my arms around myself as if they would offer some protection from the beast. His face was a stone mask. I recalled the exact same look the day they arrested him when his face had been splashed all over the tabloids. He was not one to wear his emotions on his sleeve.

"Then don't lay a finger on me, but you can't keep me here forever. We both know that."

Brandt's head swung round, full of righteous fury. "You fucking destroyed my life. I would have graduated with good grades and been offered a position in the family firm. Hell, my mother and father would still be speaking to me if it weren't for you. Tell me one good reason why I shouldn't shove you back in that cell and watch you rot."

"Two wrongs never made a right, Brandt. You're not a criminal. You find this situation just as distasteful as I do. When you're not rutting around like a horny beast, that is." Air hissed out of my mouth like a cloud of steam, and I could almost feel the impotent fury bubbling up inside me like a kettle ready to boil.

"Harper, you owe me an explanation. However bad it might be, I deserve at least that much." He gave me a penetrating stare, and I began to feel the chinks in my armour cracking. He did deserve an explanation, and I guessed that was the least I could give him, but every time I'd offered to talk he'd shut me down almost instantly.

"I'll tell you everything you want to know. We need to sit down and talk. That's all I've ever wanted right from the beginning." Although the details of my tale wouldn't exonerate me, after he'd heard me out he might be able to look me in the eye again. Maybe. How would I have felt if someone had put me in prison for something I hadn't done? Would any excuse be enough? Would any reason explain away the lies and deceit? Would he even believe me? Probably not, but I had to take that chance.

He suddenly looked down at his watch. "Shit. I've got to be on a plane in less than three hours, and it'll take me at least two to drive to the airport. We'll have to talk when I get back." He held out his hand, and I took it, because I knew he'd drag me if I refused.

"How long will you be gone for?" If he was getting on a flight it was unlikely he'd be back within a day, and if he intended to keep me locked up on my own, I was in trouble. No one knew I was here and if anything happened to Brandt I was as good as dead.

"Only a day or two. I need to meet someone in London, and then I'll be straight back." He began marching us back towards the house, his strides so long I almost had to run to keep up with him.

"You're not going to leave me here on my own, are you? Who will feed me? What happens if you get stuck in London and can't get back?" The questions tumbled from my mouth so fast I doubted they were even legible, but he must have guessed where my conversation was going for his next words confirmed it.

"I'll leave you plenty of food and if there are any problems I'll send down a babysitter. I might be a monster, but I'm not about to let you die." He didn't look at me as he talked, so his show of support was hardly reassuring. But what choice did I have? Running wasn't an option. I'd already proved that to myself twice. If I was kept locked up, escape wasn't going to be on the cards in any case. The only slight ray of hope on the horizon was that he might get caught out in London. That would mean he'd have to get someone to look after me. If they seemed reasonably sensible, there was always the chance I could appeal to their basic human nature and hope for the best. It was a slim chance, but I would use every opportunity to escape.

"Am I going back to the cell?" I think I already knew the answer to that question, but I just wanted to hear him answer it.

"Yes. I can't trust you anywhere else. You've just proved that." He spun around to face me as we neared the front door. "Goddamnit, you could have killed yourself, Harper. What were you thinking?"

My body jolted back as if stung. Was he going to blame that on me? Oh yeah, why the hell not? "Yeah, I must have been mad to think about jumping. I've been kidnapped by a psychotic ex-con who's kept me locked up in a freezing cold room, naked, and more often than not pinned to the wall by a metal leash. When he does let me out for air, he enjoys sexually torturing me. Why on earth would I think about jumping? My life is like a fairy tale at the moment, Brandt. You keep on doing your thing." I knew that little tirade would rile him, and I was not mistaken. His voice began to roar over me.

"I'm only an ex-con because you lied to get me there, and I don't see why you shouldn't suffer a little for what you did to me, because I suffered a whole fucking lot at your hands. What you've heard is only the tip of the iceberg. There's plenty more where that came from." He spun me around to face him, and I stopped dead in my tracks. When his right hand reached out to grab my neck I didn't try to stop him. I already knew I was outmatched in the strength department, so if he wanted to strangle me he'd best get on with it.

"You will not endanger yourself again on my watch, do you hear me? When I get back I intend to make sure you pay for that little stunt. If I managed to do my five years and come out the other side, then you can damn well toughen up and do yours, Harper Wilkinson. Don't do the crime if you can't take the punishment." His thumb rubbed over the artery in my neck, and my pulse quickened beneath it. "So what were you thinking? What was going through your head when you reached the cliff edge?" He tilted my head, so I'd have no option but to look up at him. I detested him for it.

"I don't think when you're around, Brandt. That's the problem. That's always been the problem." I stared him straight in the eye as the weight of my sentence hit home. As usual I couldn't read the expression on his face, but at least he loosened the grip he had around my throat. Taking my hand, he began to yank me towards the house, and my lacerated feet protested vehemently at his rough treatment, but I kept quiet and wondered how I was going to cope on my own. I hated being on my own. Even after Alex had died, when I should have been grateful for a little solitude, I found myself going crazy in an empty house. I needed to be around people. If left to my own devices I would slowly drive myself insane. I could just about cope with the cell, knowing that Brandt was nearby and would be seeing me daily, but when he was gone, and I was left all alone, well, that was going to drive me nuts. If I wasn't already nuts, and the jury was out on that one.

Before I knew what was happening he had somehow managed to thrust me back in my cell, and the key was in the lock before I barely had time to blink.

"You can't leave me here on my own," I whispered, but the words were wasted on his retreating back because he was already on his way out.

Sitting down on the bed in a horrified daze, I tried to be positive about my situation. He hadn't pinned me to the wall, and he promised he would leave me with food and water. I would have time to sleep, and the duvet from earlier was still here, so at least I would be warm. But they were pretty much all the positives I could think of. On the negative side, I would be alone in a steel cage with no contact to the outside world and no one to turn to should anything happen to me. If I slipped and cracked my head open wide I would bleed to death. If I came down with flu, got food poisoning, a migraine, or some kind of viral infection, I was on my own. He couldn't do this to me, because this, by far, was the worst thing he could impose upon me.

I have no idea how long I sat rocking backwards and forwards on the bed, dreaming about my sudden and catastrophic demise, but it couldn't have been that long. Brandt was back down the stairs, struggling towards me with a square box that trailed an electric plug and a bulging carrier bag that was set on the top. I barely looked at it.

"You can't leave me here," I whimpered again.

He opened the door, set the box down and plugged the socket in. A whirring noise began.

"That's a mini fridge. There are enough meals and drinks to last you for three days in there. Scrap that, about six days considering you eat less than a sparrow. I'll be back in one or I'll send a babysitter, so don't panic. In the bag there are some books; not great ones I'm afraid, but anything is better than nothing. There is also an iPod so you can listen to music and an iPad. Before you get excited, there's no wi-fi, so you can only play about with what's on there, but it might keep you amused for a few minutes or so. Try not to get yourself in any trouble while I'm gone, and I'll be back before you know it. After what's happened earlier today you could probably do with a break. Any questions?"

I grabbed his arm. "You can't leave me here," I pleaded yet again. "Someone else could come and kidnap me. I could fall ill, or I could slip and hurt myself. This is madness." Pulling him towards me, I looked up into his eyes and implored him to take pity on me.

"No one else knows you're here and they'd need a key to kidnap you, so you're safe on that score. You are not going to fall ill, and if you stay in bed as much as possible, that will ensure you don't fall and hurt yourself. It's twenty-four hours, Harper, not five years. Enjoy the break. You might not get another one for a while." With that, he gently removed my hand and slipped back out of the door, while I sat with tears pouring down my cheeks.

"I hate you," I wailed. "I've never hated anyone as much as I hate you right now, Brandt Browning."

He smiled softly. "I believe we might be getting to that point, but you're also still in love with me. The two kind of cancel each other out, don't they?"

"Why you arrogant fucking bastard. Just go," I sobbed, grabbing a book from the carrier bag he'd brought and lobbing it at him. "Get the hell out of here and never come back." He managed to avoid the missile, but he hadn't budged an inch.

"You'd better hope for your sake that I do," he said ominously. "If I die, you die."

"For the next five years I'm already dead, so we may as well speed up the process." Throwing the duvet over my head, I burrowed down into the mattress and shoved my hand into my mouth to stop myself from saying anything more. When there was no response for a few minutes, I peeked out to find that the room was now empty. Straining my ears for the least little sound, I could hear nothing.

A feeling of deep desolation settled in my stomach and curdled my insides. There wasn't an ounce of humanity left in that man if he could do something like this to me. But the worst thing was that I knew I had created the monster. This was all my fault, and it was something I would never be able to put right.

Perhaps I did deserve to die.

Chapter 29 - Brandt

Guilt is a funny thing. It creeps up on you in stages, and before you know what's happening you realise you're the class A asshole you always promised yourself you'd never be. Yeah, well, that was too bad. Once upon a time I was a decent human being with a conscience. Now, I was about as normal as a fucking tap-dancing snail, happily sunbathing in Seattle.

Pressing my foot down on the accelerator, I tried my hardest to think of nothing but the road in front of me, but my head was all over the place. All I could see was Harper's face, tears streaming down her cheeks, while she pleaded with me not to leave her. It appeared there was a small part of me that was alive after all, because that vision began to eat away at me the more miles I put between us. It was a jagged reminder that as much as I liked to think I was impervious to Harper Wilkinson and her charms, the reality was somewhat different.

What the hell was I admitting here? I didn't want to think about it. *Just get on your flight, meet Helena, talk vapid pleasantries for an hour or so, and get the hell out*. It didn't have to be as painful as I'd feared. It could be over and done with before I'd barely even noticed, and as there was a meal at the Ritz involved, it wasn't too dreadful because I could murder a decent steak right now.

Okay, I just needed to get the plan straight. My flight would leave Inverness airport, bound for London and would take one hour and twenty minutes. John Simmons would meet me at the airport, and then we would go out for a meal with Helena. All going well, I could expect to get back to Harper last thing tonight, or first thing in morning, depending on when the last flight left. I'd need to check that. However I looked at it, Harper would survive the night without me. Hell, she was probably now basking delightedly in the knowledge that I was several miles away and for the time being unable to cause her any more grief. But it didn't seem to matter how many times I told myself all of this, because I still knew I was a bastard for leaving her.

It couldn't be helped. I'd received an email from Mr Simmons this morning saying we needed to meet in London urgently, and if I couldn't make it, then my allowance would cut off immediately. My parents played dirtier than most of the criminals I'd spent the last few years with, but seriously, what could I do? I'd play their silly games for the time being until I got my confession, and then I'd disappear. I was done obeying orders. Especially those of the marrying kind.

Thankfully check-in was relatively quiet. The airport wasn't full of tourists at this time of year, so I sped through security with my one small backpack, and before I knew it I was sitting onboard an Airbus being catapulted up into the sky. Usually this would put a smile on my face as I love flying, but not today. All I could do was stare morosely at the thick grey cloud surrounding me, wondering how quickly I could get the damn meeting over with. Simmons was adamant it had to happen as soon as possible, though I couldn't possibly fathom why my parents were in such a rush to send me to the altar. Even though I was the black sheep of the family, surely they didn't hate me that much? What did it matter if I was buried under the carpet next week or a month down the line? They weren't about to set eyes on me or have anything to do with me, so I failed to see what all the fuss was about. There was clearly something afoot, and I couldn't wait to discover what that was - in a sick and twisted kind of way.

My arrival to Gatwick airport was relatively painless bar the excruciatingly long queue I had to wait in to grab a cup of coffee. After my caffeine needs had been adequately dealt with, I went in search of the promised taxi that was supposed to be waiting for me. Sure enough, there was a board that had my name emblazoned all over it, and after the obligatory handshake and introductions had taken place, I found myself in the back of a C class Mercedes, lounging around on black leather seats.

It quickly became apparent that the coffee purchase had been a waste of time. The number of potholes in the road made me glad I'd chosen to wear a black shirt for tonight's festivities rather than white. Mind you, where there's a will there's a way, and I still managed to get the majority of that coffee down my neck long before we reached the M25. In hindsight, it would have made sense to wait. We were stuck in traffic for just over an hour before we made it anywhere near central London. It was doubly annoying because I was dying to get the meeting over and done with, and patience, as you've probably guessed, is not one of my virtues.

When the Ritz finally came into view I nearly stepped out in moving traffic, so great was my desperation to get this ordeal behind me. Somehow I managed to curtail the urge until a doorman came to greet me, but I made short work of locating Mr Simmons in the reception area. He'd been my father's solicitor for years, and though he was short of stature and grey of hair, he was remarkably nimble for his age. He rushed up to greet me and looked almost apologetic at the circumstances that had brought us here. As much as I wanted to be taciturn and curt with the man, I knew it wouldn't solve anything, and he was only doing my father's bidding. There was more to be gained by being polite and amenable, though if that changed, so would my behaviour. Oddly enough, there was no sign of Helena. I guessed she was running late as usual.

"Shall I get us some drinks while we wait?" I enquired politely after the handshaking had ensued.

"No need. Helena's not joining us tonight. That's what I wanted to speak to you about. Let's head on over to our table, and I'll update you on recent events." Rising gracefully from a gilt-edged, red velvet damask chair, he began walking purposefully towards the restaurant, and I had little choice but to follow him. Already annoyed that Helena wouldn't be at the meeting, I knew this meant I would have to arrange another one at some point in the future. My brow furrowed for a moment, but then I realised that might not be as bad as it sounded. The longer the dreaded deed could be put off, the better. This might actually work in my favour.

Sitting down amidst crisp white table linen, sparkling wine glasses, and lots of shiny silver cutlery, I waited for Mr Simmons to begin the conversation. He took his time doing so, which gave me plenty of opportunity to survey the restaurant. It was old world charm, of course. Massive floor to ceiling windows decorated one side of the room, perfectly dressed with heavily brocaded curtains featuring swags and tails. My mother also favoured such things, which was the only reason I could name them. Quaint candelabras were dotted from the ceiling and walls to give adequate 'mood lighting', and Roman-School art, complete with gilded gods and impressive marble columns were placed carefully to impart shock and awe. It wasn't really my thing, but it didn't take a mastermind to figure out that a lot of money had gone into the project. I guessed the Ritz had a long history to uphold, and their establishment was rumoured to be one of the most elegant dining rooms in the world. It wasn't difficult to see why.

Picking up the menu, I perused it with disinterest. I knew I wanted the steak, but if we were going the whole hog, I guessed I'd better pick a starter too. This was probably the last decent meal I was going to have for a while, so I might as well make the best of it. Hmm, what should I choose? I couldn't remember the last time I'd had decent seafood, and Norfolk crab, langoustines, and scallops were staring up at me batting their pretty little Bambi eyes. All of them said 'eat me', but as I fancied getting my fingers dirty this evening, I decided to go with the langoustines.

"So why isn't Helena here? Does she have some pressing engagement that's more important than meeting her future husband?" My mouth twitched at the sarcastic comment, but I couldn't resist voicing it. I failed to see the urgency of the meeting if Helena wasn't even here.

Mr Simmons put his menu down and glanced at me. "Well, as a matter of fact, she does, but I think it's best to wait until the food is..." The last word or so of his sentence trailed off as a waiter came to stand beside us. Grinding my teeth together, I refused to let the interruption annoy me. Relaying my order to the waiter as fast as I could, I waited for Simmons to do the same. Unfortunately, he took his time about the matter, almost as if he were stalling. Well, he could only buy so much time. As soon as the waiter left our side I immediately cornered him.

"We're not waiting for the food," I said. "Why isn't Helena here?"

Simmons made a show of straightening his tie before he said resignedly, "Helena is in New York. You'll need to join her there, shortly."

Looking like a complete idiot for at least the better part of three seconds, I finally managed to close my jaw. "I will do no such thing. If she wants to marry me she can get her ass over here to England." And if Helena didn't want to do the deed, I had no problem with that either.

Simmons sighed, and his fingers began to play with the white linen napkin on his lap. "The situation is delicate. That's another thing we need to discuss."

"I am not going to New York," I reiterated. "I don't care how delicate the situation is."

"I'm afraid you will if you want to keep a hold of your inheritance. Your parents want you married within a week, and it will have to be in America."

Looking much like a fish that had just discovered he's no longer swimming in water, I gave Simmons my most fearsome stare.

"Then the deal is off. They can find some other idiot to marry that little snake, and the best of luck to him." Throwing my napkin down on the table I began to walk away in disgust. Sod the money. I'd find another way.

"If you don't do this they'll fight dirty, Brandt. They'll make you pay back the large sum you just spent on your new house, and then they'll send the police round. I'm not saying that to convince you to get married. I'm just telling you that there will be consequences. They've had you followed ever since you got out. You might think you're clever, but you aren't that clever."

The silence that followed that remark was so painful my chest tightened involuntarily and trying to draw in breath was almost impossible. What exactly did he mean by that remark? How much did they know?

"You're lying." The words lacked conviction because I knew he wasn't. He didn't bother to reply, which told me all I needed to know. Turning around slowly, I made my way back to my chair. I would need to tread carefully now. It was entirely possible that he could be bluffing, but there was a good chance he wasn't. What did I do now?

"Why does Helena need to hide in New York after a bout of shoplifting? The matter has been settled, surely? Is she too embarrassed to come back to the UK? Is that it?" I rubbed my hands over my eyes while Simmons considered his answer to my question. What shit had Helena managed to get into now? What was so bad that she needed to be married off immediately? Let's face facts, I wasn't particularly desirable in the marriage stakes right now. Just about anyone would be a better prospect than me, surely? Something was going on here that I was unaware of, and I intended to find out what.

"No, that's not it." Simmons fidgeted uncomfortably with his tie for a moment, and I had the feeling he was debating whether to tell me something or not.

"Out with it. There's no point hiding anything from me. I'm going to find out sooner rather than later, and we might as well save everyone's time and money by being upfront and straight with each other." The tie and the napkin were looking pretty dishevelled about now. I was making the man decidedly uncomfortable, but I wasn't in the least bit sorry. What was the big secret? If he didn't spit it out in a minute, I was going to beat it out of him. I think he must have read my mind because he closed his eyes tightly and then nodded his head.

"Okay. Okay." His hands came up in the air in front of his chest, as if pleading for me to go easy on him. In actual fact, it made me more angry, but I kept my cool. If I lost my temper now I might never get to the bottom of this. "As I said, it's delicate."

"I heard you the first time. How more delicate can it be?"

He took a great gulp of air and held it until I thought he'd go purple before finally saying, "She's got herself pregnant."

Everything stopped as I tried to digest this new piece of wonderful news. Everything was beginning to make sense now, in an unpleasant and monstrous way.

"So that's what the rush is all about? We need to get married now to suggest that I'm the father?" I smiled grimly. "We're getting married in the US so no one will know the exact date of the birth? Huh. Good luck with that," I added. "Helena has never been able to keep anything off Facebook for very long.

"She will now; her parents have confiscated her phone," Simmons said dryly, and then he looked at me strangely. "I must say you're taking this rather well. I had thought you might start throwing things around by now." He looked somewhat relieved. "Not that I want you to start throwing things around," he added nervously.

I raised my eyes heavenward and counted to ten. "I've had some time to grow up these past five years. You're safe for now." I had to stop myself from laughing when the man visibly relaxed, although this was no laughing matter in any way, shape or form.

"So what are your thoughts on the matter?" Simmons looked everywhere but at me, and I almost felt sorry for the guy, except at the end of the day, he wasn't the one who had to deal with this shit. I was.

"On fathering another man's bastard? Or upon marrying a thieving, cheating whore?" That may have been a little harsh, but I wasn't in a particularly good mood. Simmons winced at my statement and kept quiet for a moment, which was wise. I certainly needed a little time and space to digest this one.

When my langoustines came I was still deep in thought, but I attacked them like a starving man devours a crust of bread. They tasted like manna from heaven, albeit heavily infused with garlic, and there was no way I was going to waste food so good after eating slop for years.

It was only after I'd eaten everything bar the shells that I came up for air. It appeared Simmons had been looking at me for some time because his eyes dipped and he frowned.

"Are you going to do it?" Clearly the question had been playing on his mind. Funnily enough, it had been playing on mine, too.

"I don't know, is the honest answer. I won't know until I meet with Helena. Is that even an option?" I looked at him dully. I didn't know where to go from here, and it felt like the walls were closing in on me. How much did my parents know? Would they go to the police if I didn't follow their instructions? It was a possibility. Could I handle going back to jail? No way.

"I'll talk to them and see if I can get you a little more thinking time, but however you look at it, you'll need to be on a plane to New York tonight if you want to stay in their good graces."

That was funny. "Will I still be able to get a flight at this late notice?" That was the least of my worries. I had a naked girl locked up in a cell, and I was shortly going to be winging my way thousands of miles from her. What the hell was I going to do?

"I already have your ticket in my bag. All you need to do is get a taxi back to the airport when you've finished your meal. Helena will be waiting for you on the other side." Our starter plates were whisked away, while our wine and water glasses were refilled. I immediately knocked back an entire glass of very good Bordeaux, but it did nothing to ease the panic that was beginning to consume me. It felt like a net was closing in around me, getting tighter by the second, and if I didn't do something to stop this awful chain of events it was going to strangle me.

"How long will I be expected to stay in New York?" My brain was working overtime trying to overcome all the rubbish being flung my way, and I could really do with a great big garbage truck right about now.

"Only a day or two, I guess. If you agree to the proposal you'll need to finalise the wedding arrangements with Helena, and once that is done, I'm guessing you won't be needed until the wedding. Depends on how badly Helena wants to get to know you. Will she be happy about the arrangement? How well do you know the lady?"

Not that well. I had no idea if she would be happy about the thought of marrying an ex-con who also happened to be a complete stranger. We'd met on a couple of occasions six or seven years ago, but that was all. We certainly couldn't be described as anything more than acquaintances. She was probably as horrified as me and would be spitting fire when she met me at the airport. Great. I had that to look forward to as well. Taking a great gulp of air, I expelled it through clenched teeth and tried not to think about the splitting headache forming between my eyes.

"When does my flight leave?" I needed to know how much time I would have before I left the country. Somehow I'd have to make arrangements for someone to drop in on Harper. The thought turned my stomach. The only people I knew were men, and a naked Harper was going to be a ridiculously large temptation to most of them. Fuck, fuck, fuckity fuck. This was a problem I would need to sort out and soon.

"You'll have time to finish your meal. We have you on the red eye going out at six-thirty a.m. You're booked in at the airport hotel until then, and you'll find the reservation number with your flight tickets. It's not going to be a great night's sleep, but hopefully you can make some of that up on the plane."

He passed a travel wallet across the table, and I flicked through the contents. It didn't take me long to discover that everything seemed to be in order. I had everything I could possibly need including my passport, plus a seat in business class. My parents were exceptionally keen that I marry Helena, it seemed.

My steak chose that moment to land in front of me; rare and exactly as I like it. Digging in with enthusiasm only my stomach would appreciate, I decided I had no choice but to do as I was told for the time being, while I worked out my contingency plans. All I needed was a couple of extra days with Harper, and then we'd set the record straight, and she could be on her merry way. Seriously, was that too much to ask for? Right at this moment in time I began to fear that it was - but there didn't seem to be any other way forward.

When I'd devoured my meal, I looked up to find Simmons staring at me. I wondered if I had sauce dribbling down my chin, but a quick dab with my napkin confirmed otherwise. We then stared at each other for what seemed like an age, before he cleared his throat and shook his head.

"Will you do it?"

"I took the tickets, didn't I?" Surely that was confirmation enough.

"That doesn't mean a thing. You could take your passport and run."

That idea had crossed my mind, and the thought that he might be bluffing with his earlier threat was still nagging at me, but honestly, it wasn't worth the risk.

"How much do you get paid if I go through with this?" Although the question was extremely rude, I was very curious to the answer.

Simmons smiled ruefully. "A lot."

"Then you'll just have to hope I go through with it, won't you?" Standing up, I flung my napkin on my empty plate and watched as Simmons also got to his feet.

"I'll meet with her. That's as much as I'm prepared to do right now. I won't make a decision on marriage and children within a couple of days. If my parents can't accept that, then the arrangement is off. You can telephone them in a moment to let them know. If they can't accept my terms, then I'll be on my way home. Thank you for your time, Mr Simmons." I didn't hold my hand out to shake his. The whole ordeal had left a particularly unpleasant taste in my mouth, and wisely he didn't push the issue.

"I'll tell them. I think they'll be happy enough with that for the time being."

"Let's hope so." Nodding at him, I quickly took my leave.

Traffic was much better on the drive back to the airport, and I reached my hotel in just over forty-five minutes. Thankfully there was no queue at the front desk, so I wasted no time checking-in. The extremely attractive receptionist looked at my reservation slip, tapped away on her keyboard, and gave me a cheerful smile. It had no effect on me whatsoever. What was wrong with me these days? Harper was all I could think about.

"We have you all booked in, Mr Browning. Handing me a room key and giving me instructions on how to get there, I nodded numbly. Thankfully I'd thought to bring an overnight bag, just in case I had to stay the night, so I at least had a change of clothes and a washbag, but this was the last place I wanted to be right now.

When I got to my room I sat shakily on the bed, which was covered with a standard white-striped duvet ubiquitous to hotels all around the world. Staring silently at the small white kettle in front of me, I decided coffee was the last thing I needed. There was no chance of sleep as it was, and adding caffeine to the mix would not improve my mood. Throwing my hands down on the bed in a fit of temper, I spat out every cuss word I could think of. It did little to relieve my tension, and probably pissed off the people next door, but there was little else I could do.

Pulling my phone out of my pocket, I scrolled through my list of contacts that had become remarkably shorter after my release from prison. Most of my old friends no longer wanted anything to do with me, and those that did had something to prove. None of them could be trusted with the job I had in mind. I would need someone very special.

Hovering over a name, I thought long and hard about pressing the green dial button next to it. I knew that if I did this there would be repercussions, some of which I would not want to pay. The trouble was, if anything happened to Harper while I was gone I would never forgive myself. Yes, I wanted her to pay for her lies, but I did not want her dead. There was a very real chance I could get stuck or delayed in New York, and I'd chanced my luck by doing what I had today. I couldn't leave her on her own for days on end, and not expect her to do something stupid. Shaking my head, I repeated all my favourite expletives. With a groan of frustration I finally hit the dial button, and I wasn't sure if I wanted someone to answer or not. After four rings I wondered if anyone would pick up, but suddenly a voice came on the line.

"Well hello, Brandt. Fancy hearing from you." The guy on the other end sounded mightily pleased with himself, as well he might.

"Are you enjoying your newfound freedom?" I tried to sound equally as cheerful and failed miserably.

"You bet your ass, mate. Getting out on a technicality years before you're supposed to is always fun, and I can't complain. Life is treating me well. Might as well cut the crap, though. What do you want?"

I smiled. This was the guy I knew, loved, and despised all right. "I need you to do me a favour, Gabriel."

"Well, shit. You've just made my day, Brandt. What can I do for you?"

Was I about to make the worst mistake of my life? Probably. But I went and did it anyway.

Thanks for reading!

Please help a starving author by leaving a review

This book was so awesome I forgot to feed my kids. Thankfully they reminded me, over and over again, so I haven't managed to kill them yet. Phew.

This book sucked. It was even worse than a certain president's infamous hairdo, and that is saying something.

Mark and Jennifer are so hot I want a threesome with both of them. As long as I'm allowed a safe word - because Mark is a little bit on the seriously freaky crazy side.

I would rather read War and Peace than this ridiculous smutty drivel and nonsense. Seriously, all Mandara talks about is orgasms, sex, and hot blokes. Who wants to read about that?

Ms Mandara does not write quickly enough. I need her to release a book every month at the very least, and she keeps me waiting for months - and worse - ends everything on a horrendous cliff-hanger. I have a love/hate relationship with this author. She should probably be spanked.

This is not a good book to read on the train. Especially when the hot guy sitting next to me kept trying to read it over my shoulder.

Don't ever read this book to your wife. She will demand sex for days on end and will suddenly become insatiable in bed. Seriously, I have been considering divorce...

Any of these will do (I'm more partial to the nice ones...) and it will give you extra karma points that will be returned to you in due course in the form of cookies, money, hugs, and wine. Honest.

Why not sign up to **Christina's newsletter** to find out what happens to Harper and Brandt in **Beautiful Torture**, book two of the **Beautiful Beasts** series:

Brandt

Harper left me to rot in jail for a crime she committed. I was put away for five years. During that time, there was only one thing that managed to get me through the night - the desire to get even.

It was all too easy to kidnap her, and now she's locked away in my basement I intend to find out by any means necessary why she lied. If that means hurting her, so be it. She's put me through more than any man should have to cope with in a lifetime, so a little payback is only fair.

If she were my only problem, life would be peachy, but my parents are giving me hell. They're currently trying to force me into marriage, and wriggling out of that will be a full time job.

But I'll get what I want eventually. Everyone has a breaking point - and the girl in my basement will be getting close to hers shortly. That's a promise.

Bio

Christina Mandara was born in the UK but has spent most of her life travelling the world. She speaks three languages and has been chiefly employed in the fields of finance and travel. Her favourite city is Sydney, and her favourite holiday destination is the south of France.

She loves keeping fit and enjoys running, cycling, and water sports. Think surfing or sailing. She's a big fan of BDSM in all its glorious forms, and her favourite item in the toy closet (a box simply isn't big enough) is her riding crop.

In her spare time, she's usually cuddled up with a good book, exploring the countryside, or baking in the kitchen. In fact, she loves her kitchen so much she's one of few women who wouldn't mind being tied to it! Her first and foremost love is writing, however, and more often than not you'll find her on a laptop spinning tales of romance, erotica, or dark paranormal fantasies.

facebook.com/cpmandara
twitter.com/cpmandara
christinamandara.com